DANGEROUS INSIGHT

KAROLINE ANDERSON

PUBLISHED BY  FLARE BOOKS

AN IMPRINT OF CATALYST PRESS, EL PASO, TEXAS

For further information, write info@catalystpress.org
In North America, this book is distributed by
Consortium Book Sales & Distribution, a division of Ingram.
Phone: 612/746-2600
cbsdinfo@ingramcontent.com
www.cbsd.com

In South Africa, Namibia, and Botswana,
this book is distributed by Protea Distribution.
For information, email orders@proteadistribution.co.za.

9781963511031 paperback
9781963511185 ebook

Library of Congress Control Number: 2024936185

Original artwork and cover design by Jordan Anderson
http://jordanandersongraphics.com

_____

This is a work of fiction.
Names, characters, businesses, events and incidents
are the products of the author's imagination.
Any resemblance to actual persons, living or dead,
or actual events is purely coincidental.

As always, for my husband and daughters.
You are my sun and moon and stars.

Also, for the many furry family members
who have blessed our lives over the years,
notably our Golden Retriever, Jax,
who passed recently and is dearly missed.

And to the inspiration for Stalker, our current cat,
Smoky, who spent his formative years
idolizing his playmate, Jax,
and is convinced he's also a dog.

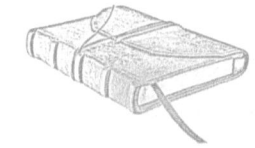

CHAPTER ONE

"Someone called in a dead body."

Joe Riley gestures with his free hand to catch my attention, phone pressed to his ear. He gives me a meaningful look to accompany the grim announcement. After listening for a moment, he hangs up and stares at his phone. He says nothing, and I don't break the silence, knowing he'll speak when he's ready. Joe and I have worked side-by-side as homicide detectives for almost six years now. I've never seen him so shaken by a call to a crime scene.

I put down the paperwork I was examining. "You okay?"

"Kaitlyn..." His voice is raw. "The victim is a young girl. Chloe's age."

Chloe is his daughter. College-aged. "God, Joe, I'm sorry." I know him well enough to understand the toll this particular crime scene will take on him. "Is it bad?"

"A car dragged her down a city block. There isn't going to be much left for us to look at."

"Damn," I say softly.

Joe sighs and visibly gathers himself, turning his attention to his phone. Probably using a location app to find his daughter and ensure she's safe.

He stands and grabs his signature trench coat from the back of his chair. His shoelaces are yellow today. A sunny, cheerful color. He has different color laces in all his shoes and selects them according to his mood. Today isn't going to match his optimistic color choice.

I grab my suit jacket and follow Joe. The hallway is crowded. We dodge officers carrying steaming cardboard cups of coffee. The break-room-coffee tastes terrible. Joe and I get our coffee elsewhere whenever possible. But there's no time for coffee today.

The presence of so many officers reflects the importance of the day for our precinct of the Seattle Police Department. Officers gather in clusters, animated as they chat with one another. Our boss, Captain Elizabeth Garcia, was promoted to Deputy Chief of Police and our new captain is due to arrive later this morning. In anticipation, the officers' shoes are brightly polished, and their attire freshly pressed. Everyone wants to make a good impression on the new boss. I tamp down a pang of disappointment that we might not be here when he makes his first appearance.

As we enter the lobby, Bob, a junior officer we've worked with in the past, greets us with enthusiasm. His hair is carefully combed, uniform immaculate. He reminds me of a tail-wagging puppy. I suppress a smile at his obvious eagerness to make a good first impression, instead giving him a nod of acknowledgement and approval.

As we pass a group of officers by the front door, Ethan Carter reaches out to stop me. "Hey Kruse, where are you off to? Not waiting to meet the captain? Or are you just too good for the rest of us since you made detective?" Ethan was my first partner after I completed training and before my promotion to detective. I learned a lot under his mentorship. He's a good officer and I respect his work, but we never really clicked. At least, not like Joe and I have. Ethan's age is starting to show with some softening of his previously trim figure. With the importance he puts on his physical appearance, this probably grates on him.

"Of course not," I shoot back, giving him a reproachful look. "We got called out to a crime scene. Sounds like a bad one."

He raises his hands as if I'm over-reacting. "Hey, I'm only teasing. Don't get bent out of shape."

"Gotcha." I force a smile and give a wink and a little finger-gun shot in his direction to show I'm in on the joke. *You're lucky it's not loaded,* I think.

"Ethan, let the woman get to her crime scene." Ravi Singh, Ethan's current partner, is one of the officers standing with him. As usual he's running interference, maintaining the relationships Ethan strains.

"Off you go then, Kaitlyn, don't let me hold you up." Ethan dismisses me, going back to talking with the officer next to him.

Joe looks back for me, already holding open the exit door.

It's a relief to leave the undercurrent of restless anticipation flowing through the precinct. I take a deep breath of the cool fall air, readying myself for the task ahead. We find our unmarked cruiser in the police lot. Its worn leather seats are a familiar comfort as we slide in next to one another.

Neither of us is in the mood to make small talk on the drive to the crime scene. It hasn't been long since we wrapped up our last big case involving a burial site with multiple victims. That crime scene was shocking. Now, somehow, it seems we're likely to find something worse.

I roll down my window, letting the slight breeze in.

Our route takes us past trees decked out in vibrant autumn hues of yellow, orange, and red, brilliant against the backdrop of the emerald evergreens. The sidewalks are strewn with the huge foot-wide maple leaves found only in this corner of the world.

The transition of summer into fall brings fair weather to the Pacific Northwest, my favorite time of year to live in Seattle. This fall we've had so many clear days, one could even forget the ever-present rain of the rest of the year. We've been blessed with crisp cool mornings and pleasantly warm afternoons.

These past few days have been the exception to the fine weather, with some fog and misty drizzle setting in. Last night's rain is just starting to dry as the morning sun warms the streets.

We're nearing the crime scene as we turn into a modest Seattle suburb. The houses in the neighborhood are tightly packed single-story homes with small front yards and overgrown vegetation.

A cruiser is positioned at an intersection, lights flashing. Joe pulls up to the yellow crime scene tape blocking off the street, our attention immediately drawn to the lifeless form laying in the street almost a block away.

Clint Lydiate sits in the driver's seat of the patrol car, guarding the street. His cruiser door is propped open, and he stares at the street with a glazed look in his eyes. There's a splatter of vomit on his shirt.

"Lydiate!" Joe addresses him. "Why'd you put the crime scene tape so far from the body?"

Clint gets out of the cruiser, straightening his uniform and trying to hide his distress. He's a seasoned officer. We've witnessed many crime scenes together. I'm surprised to see him so affected.

Trepidation. That's what I feel when I see the slight tremble of his finger as he points to the road.

Joe and I look in the direction of his gesture, seeing what we initially overlooked when our attention was captured by the obvious sight of the body. There's a swath of blood in the road accompanying a path of debris leading to the lifeless form. Human debris.

Even after several years in this line of work, I'm still surprised by the sheer brutality that accompanies some deaths. A murder is not just a murder. There's a stunning difference in the intentionality that's evident at crime scenes. At one extreme, you have an accidental death with a reverent burial, and at the other, a spectacle like this where a human has been literally erased.

A slow burn of anger starts in my chest. How could someone do this to another person?

Joe and I reluctantly duck under the crime scene tape and start our trek down the street. I don't want to look at what's in the path of blood. But it's my job.

As we walk, we scan for identifiable remains. Mostly the scene reveals bits of clothing and tissue torn off the body as it was dragged down the street. A green umbrella looks like a crushed insect. A piece of scalp, clump of dark hair still attached, makes me wince. Over there is a shoe. A foot still inside.

The fractured remains of a phone. More bits of tissue. Now a battered arm, severed from the body, left discarded in the road. Like a glove that fell out of someone's pocket. A watch is still attached, a blue plastic ring on the pinky finger. A person used to own this arm. The contents of my stomach lurch up my esophagus, but I quell the nausea, narrowly avoiding vomiting on the crime scene.

When we reach the end of the blood trail, I steel myself in preparation for viewing what remains of the body.

The face is a wreck. Nose eroded away, as is most of the skin on the cheeks. An eyelid missing. Some hair and the globes of the eyes remain. The body is a bloody mass, some fabric still randomly clinging to it. I take some deep breaths, grateful the press hasn't gotten wind of this. Yet.

After the gut-wrenching trip down the road, it's almost impossible to force my brain to start thinking like a detective. What can I learn about the killer from this excruciating task? *Think, Kaitlyn.*

The first thing that strikes me is that the act was intentional. There are no skid marks on the street. No signs the driver attempted to stop or avoid the victim. Someone wanted her eliminated. No chance of survival. It's a brutal and brazen act. The killer took a lot of risk. Someone may have witnessed the collision or seen the vehicle driving away.

Dr. Beth Mitchell, the medical examiner, approaches from the side of the road. Her wavy brown hair, recently cut short, suits her. She still has the same thick black glasses. A man I don't recognize accompanies her. He's tall with blond hair, greying almost imperceptibly at the temples. As he squints at us, his brown eyes crinkle at the corners. He's built like a runner, slim and fit.

Dr. Mitchell introduces us. "Captain, these are detectives Joe Riley and Kaitlyn Kruse. Detectives, this is Captain Mark Bennett."

The new captain. I automatically straighten my posture and surreptitiously check my attire. I notice Joe doing the same.

"Detectives." Captain Bennett shakes our hands with a firm grip and a direct gaze that comes across as confident and friendly. "Sorry we had to meet under such circumstances, but I wanted to be present for the first homicide case I'll oversee."

A hands-on approach. I like him already.

Dr. Mitchell leads us to the body and squats down beside it, taking an uncharacteristic deep breath before starting. "The victim is a female in her early twenties, approximately five-foot-three-inches tall with dark brown hair and green eyes. Based on body temperature, I estimate the time of death to be between midnight and 2:00 a.m. It appears she was struck by a vehicle at the start of the blood trail and dragged up the street until the vehicle drove over her. There is an impression from the right front and rear tires—here." She points to indentations on the lower legs. "The tires on the left side missed driving over her head by inches."

"Usually, we see victims of car accidents thrown up onto the hood, or even the windshield. How do you think she ended up being dragged?" I ask.

"I suspect the driver slowed long enough for the body to fall back into the road and then accelerated up the road with the victim pinned against the bumper or spoiler, something low profile. There are no skid marks so the stop would not have been abrupt. More like an intentional slowing to position the body back in front of the vehicle," Dr. Mitchell responds.

This killing is so deliberate and so callous. My earlier anger deepens in intensity. The murderer must be made to account for what they did to this young woman. I'll do everything in my power to make that happen.

I tamp down my emotions and force my attention back to the ongoing conversation.

"Any ID on the victim?" the captain asks.

"We didn't find any, but we may still find something in the street." The ME looks at the path of debris.

"Who reported the murder?" I ask.

"A call was made to 911 at 5:30 a.m." Dr. Mitchell checks some notes on her phone. "A neighbor, Mr. Keegan, noticed the body when he was headed out to work." I look at the mutilated body poor Mr. Keegan would've encountered on what he thought would be an ordinary workday. My gaze travels back down the street to the trail of debris. Crime scene workers are placing small yellow markers to indicate pieces of tissue, clothing or other evidence. The sheer number of markers is visually shocking.

Overwhelmed, I turn my attention away from the gruesome scene and to the surrounding neighborhood. It's midmorning, the sun burning off the remaining clouds from the overnight rain. A small crowd of neighbors gather at the barrier of the yellow crime scene tape, talking quietly with each other.

The houses lining the street are small. Some properties are well-kept, some are in disrepair. There are no garages; cars are parked on drives beside the houses. Most of the back yards are fenced. Beside one house, a Doberman growls and bounces off a high chain-link fence.

There are eight houses on one side of the street, a neighborhood park on the opposite side. The park has a few pieces of worn playground equipment and some scattered trees. The park looks lonely without children present.

"I'm going to go talk to these neighbors," I tell Joe, indicating the cluster of observers. He nods and turns back to the medical examiner with further questions. I glance at my jacket lapel to ensure my body cam is active before starting the interviews.

Typically, I'd greet the observers with a "good morning," but I just can't say that in light of the horrific crime scene.

"Hello," I say instead. "I'm Detective Kruse of the Seattle PD. Is there a Mr. Keegan here?"

A middle-aged man in a business suit raises his hand. "That's me." He's short and thin, his second-hand suit hanging loosely on him.

"Did you call 911 this morning?"

"Yes."

I lead Mr. Keegan a short distance away to take his statement. "Can you tell me in detail what happened before you placed the call?"

"I came out of my house to go to work." He indicates a blue house directly in line with the body. A beaten-up Buick is parked in the driveway. "Before I got in my car, I noticed something in the street. I was worried I would back right into it, so I went to check it out. When I got closer, I saw what it was..." His voice breaks. He shakes his head as if he can shake the image away. "I called right away..."

"I'm glad you did." Thank goodness he found this before one of the neighborhood children headed off to school.

I glance down the street to ensure no children are present and I notice a curtain in a window a few houses down drop closed. Perhaps a child told to stay inside but too curious not to risk a peek?

"Wasn't it dark out at 5:30 in the morning?" I return to the interview.

"It was, but the streetlight was still on."

"Do you usually get such an early start, Mr. Keegan?"

"Yes, I work early hours at an insurance company down-town. Seven to three. Lets me beat the downtown traffic."

"Has anything changed since you discovered the body this morning? Did you move it or touch it in any way?"

"No, I waited out here until Officer Lydiate arrived. No one was out yet. It only took about fifteen minutes."

"Did you hear the incident when it occurred?"

"No, I didn't know it happened until I saw the body."

Thanking Mr. Keegan, I head back to the group of neighbors. "Did anyone hear or see the incident last night?"

The neighbors look at each other. No one responds. It was raining the night before. This might have made it more difficult to hear. Still.

"No one?" I ask.

An elderly lady speaks up. "I was woken up just after midnight by a thump. Then I heard a car engine revving, but I didn't hear any squealing tires like you would with an accident, so I just went back to sleep."

Again, there's general nodding, and a few people comment they also heard a car around the same time.

"Can I have your name, ma'am? And can you tell me what house you live in?" I pull out a notepad from my back pocket and draw a grid with the eight houses on the block represented. Old school. I put Mr. Keegan's name in the house opposite the body.

"Latesha Washington. I live right there in that yellow house." She points to a house near the start of the blood trail. I identify her home on my notepad. Asking the other neighbors for their names, I fill in a few more squares, noting details about their families and asking the current location of other family members and neighbors. After I fill in all the details, all the houses are accounted for except one.

"Josie isn't here." Latesha pulls anxiously at her tight salt and pepper curls. "It's not her in the street, is it?"

"Why do you ask?"

"Josie lives right next to me. She works late most nights at a suicide call line a few blocks away. She walks home through the park. I told her not to do that. Anyone could be lurking that late at night. She shouldn't have the same times for comin' and goin'. Not a pretty girl like that. And so late at night." She shakes her head, her voice fading off.

"Does she wear any rings?" I ask.

"Yeah, an ugly blue plastic thing. She said it was some reminder of her past."

It sounds like this could be our victim.

"Which house does Josie live in?" I ask.

Latesha points to the house beside hers, a white house with peeling paint. No car in the drive. One of the green shutters hangs loose. The grass is barely alive.

"I guess we better find out if she's home."

As I head toward the house, the neighbors trail behind me, trying unsuccessfully to be inconspicuous.

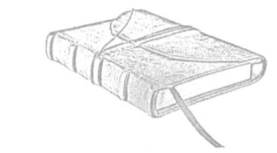

CHAPTER TWO

There's no response to my knock at Josie's front door, so I ring the bell. Then knock again. Still nothing.

Shielding my eyes, I peer through the large front window. The room is dark. No sign of anyone home.

Backing away from the window, I run straight into Latesha, standing right on my heels, looking over my shoulder. Grabbing her arm, I manage to prevent her from toppling over.

"Does Josie live alone?" I ask once she's steady on her feet again.

"Yeah." She pauses. "But I have a key in case of emergencies. Josie 'n I look out for one another." She squints in concern, looking back into the dark house. "She sleeps late 'cause she gets home after midnight, but she's usually up by now."

"How old is she?"

"Twenty-two. Just had her birthday in June. I got her two big candles and two little ones to put on the chocolate cake I made her. From scratch, mind you. I make a fine cake and chocolate's her favorite..."

"Can you give me Josie's full name?"

"Jocelyn Miller."

"Would you get the key for me, Ms. Washington? I'm going to get my partner. We'll want to make sure Josie's okay."

Latesha heads off toward her home.

Joe, Dr. Mitchell, and the new captain are still deep in conversation over the body.

"I have a possible ID on the victim," I say, approaching. "A twenty-two-year-old lives in the white house down the block and there's no answer at my knock. The neighbor says she walks home from work late at night, around the time a few neighbors heard noises in the street."

"Could be her." Joe nods.

"She also wears a blue plastic ring. I saw one on the hand back there."

"The severed one?" Dr. Mitchell asks.

I nod, the thought of the detached arm making my stomach contract. The image of the body is unlikely to ever leave my mind.

"I'm impressed, Detective," Captain Bennett says. "Nice catch on the blue ring."

Giving a head tip in acknowledgement, I try not to let on how pleased I am at the praise. "The neighbor has a key so we should be able to get in," I say to deflect the attention.

"We need to be careful," Joe comments as we walk toward Josie's home. "We don't know what we're dealing with yet. The killer could be in the house if the victim had something they wanted."

"Agreed," says the captain. "I'm happy to take the lead on this." He's the most senior officer, and, let's face it, he probably wants to show off a little on his first day. And now we get to see what kind of leader is joining our police force.

The last thing we want to do is startle Josie out of a sound sleep with three armed officers entering her home. That could get someone killed. I'm hoping the captain will err on the side of caution.

We stop on the street in front of the house to discuss strategy.

"I plan to give a lot of warning when we enter. We may lose the advantage of surprise, but it will be safer." The captain looks at us. "Do either of you have any input?"

Now I'm the one who is impressed. Not only is Captain Bennett cautious but he asked our opinion. He has the confidence to involve his team, and not just blindly take the lead.

Joe glances at me and I see the respect in his eyes. He gives me a barely perceptible nod.

"Agreed," Joe tells the captain. "We'll follow your lead."

Latesha hands the captain the house key.

As we approach the house my heart rate rises in anticipation, muscles tensing in readiness—ready to face whatever dangers lurk behind Josie's door.

The captain knocks on the door and announces, "Seattle Police Department, please open the door."

We wait, listening.

No response.

He inserts the key and opens the door, pushing it inward with his foot.

The door creaks, and my heart rate spikes.

Again, he announces our presence and again, we're greeted with silence.

"We're now entering the premises," he warns.

We go through the door, guns drawn, fanning out into the house.

The living room is empty.

I cross to an open door at the back of the home. With a quick glance from where I stand behind the doorframe, I check the bedroom, then enter with my gun trained on the space in front of me.

It's a small house. There's one main room and an open kitchen. A bathroom and bedroom to the side. The search doesn't take long.

"Clear," I yell and hear echoing "clear" responses from Joe and the captain. The residence has been secured. I holster my gun. The tension in my muscles loosens.

We gather in the bedroom. The bed is still made and empty.

"It looks like Josie didn't make it home last night." Joe sighs and holsters his gun.

Pulling on our crime scene gloves, we begin searching the house.

I pick up a framed photo from the bedside table, showing a young girl in a graduation cap flanked by what appears to be her parents. She has shoulder-length dark brown hair and green eyes the color of new leaves. Just like the remains in the street. And yet...not like the remains at all. For how can I reconcile those smeared parts with this vibrant smiling girl in the picture?

Taking out my phone, I snap a photo of her.

Joe takes hair from her hairbrush and places it into an evidence bag. Likely it'll be a DNA match to the remains.

The captain and Joe head off to check the other rooms while I finish with the bedroom. I remember seeing parts of a phone in the street, so we won't find a cell phone. What else might help us identify her?

This is what I'm thinking as I open the drawer of the bedside table, and a sudden blur of movement catches my eye.

Something hurtles toward me.

I raise my arms to ward off the blow, but it catches me full in the chest and knocks me back onto the bed.

My foot hits the bedside table, and the photo frame topples to the floor and shatters.

I cry out as something sharp penetrates my chest.

Looking down, I see blood blooming on my white shirt.

Joe whirls around, hand on his gun.

The captain's running footsteps approach from the other room.

He appears in the doorway, gun drawn.

"A cat," I manage to croak as I catch my breath. "It was just a cat."

The captain lowers his gun.

Joe makes a strangled noise.

We look over at him.

He's trying valiantly to suppress his amusement. His red face makes me laugh in relief. Then we're all laughing. Joe doubles over. The captain leans on the doorframe, chuckling.

I get up off the bed and straighten my clothing. Spots of blood dot my blouse where the fiend of a cat sank its claws into me. Who would have predicted Josie had a guard-cat?

We look under the bed and in the closet, but that cat is nowhere to be found. It's taken the opportunity to flee after launching itself at me.

When my heart rate returns to normal, I resume my investigation of the bedroom.

There's a small closet jammed with inexpensive clothing and shoes. A mirror hangs on one wall and a travel poster of a tropical beach is taped behind the twin bed. A thin comforter covers the bed, pillow leaning toward a small bedside table.

I carefully pick up the broken photo frame and the glass pieces and place them in an evidence bag.

In the single drawer of the nightstand lays a bound journal that appears to be a diary. A handwritten journal is pretty unusual for a girl this age. I thumb through it and notice entries on recent dates. I'll check this out later. It also goes into an evidence bag.

I inspect the rest of the bedroom and the closet but don't find anything else of interest.

Re-entering the main room, I note the large window facing the park across the street. Mount Rainier is visible far off in the distance, glaciers shining in the sunlight.

The kitchen cabinets and appliances show their age, the wood cracking and the hinges sagging, but they have a fresh coat of navy paint. Two stools sit under a bar overhang of chipped laminate. A couch and chair are placed carefully around a throw rug, a television situated opposite.

The captain is at a small desk in the corner. "There's a laptop here," he says. "I can't get it to boot up. Maybe the battery is dead." He shrugs sheepishly. "I'm not that tech-savvy. If Josie turns out to be the victim we'll bring it in for IT to have a look."

Joe exits the small bathroom. "I didn't find anything worth collecting in there. It doesn't look like she had any prescription medications."

Satisfied with our initial search, we leave the house together to find the neighbors still gathered outside.

"Is it her?" Latesha asks, worry creasing her brow.

"I'm sorry but we won't know for certain until we have DNA confirmation."

Latesha looks tearful and I wish I could share more with her.

Joe secures the door and we place crime scene tape in an x across it.

I bring the journal with me as we head back to the station. We need to find out more about Josie so we can discover what put her in the path of such a ruthless killer.

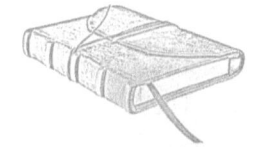

CHAPTER THREE

"That was the worst crime scene I've ever seen," I tell Joe as we get back in the cruiser.

"I wish I could say it was the worst one I've seen," Joe says with a heavy sigh.

"What's the worst?" I ask before thinking better of it. "Never mind, I don't want to know."

"You doing okay?" Typical Joe, looking out for his more junior partner.

"I think so. I may have some crazy dreams for a few nights." If only he knew how strange my dreams really are.

We drive back to the department with the windows down, taking in the rare Seattle sunshine. Seagulls whirl and call as we near the harbor. Their cries remind me of days spent at the beach. When I was a kid, I used to love searching under rocks for tiny shore crabs. My dad taught me how to pick them up just behind the claws, so I didn't get pinched.

Nothing like a brutal death to make you value the little things in life.

When we get back to the precinct, I quickly change into a spare shirt. Then, from my desk I hear Captain Garcia announcing her replacement, Captain Bennett, in the conference room.

"It's my distinct pleasure to introduce you to your new captain, Mark Bennett." There's a round of applause. "You couldn't find a more dedicated and trustworthy person to run this department. I'm happy to leave it in his capable hands."

As we enter the crowded conference room, Bennett gets up to say a few words. "Thank you, Captain Garcia. You leave me with big shoes to fill. I'll do my best to live up to the high standards you've set here. I've had the pleasure of meeting some of you out in the field this morning and I can already see you are a talented group of officers. I hope to get to know the rest of you over the next few weeks. I like to get out there on the streets with you whenever I can. You know, get my hands dirty. Or my shirt," he says, swiping at a smudge on his shirt that he likely got this morning, causing the assembled officers to laugh, and dispelling the tension in the room.

"Thanks for the warm welcome. I look forward to working together." The captain smiles and looks around, taking everyone in.

"Now let's get back to work!" he says with a wink, producing a chuckle from the crowd.

The conference room is slow to empty out as officers mill about discussing the new captain. He stops to talk to Ethan and Clint Lydiate. A few other officers wait to meet him.

"Was it you two the captain was talking about?" Ravi stops to ask. "Did you already meet him?"

"Yeah, he came out to see the crime scene," I volunteer.

"What do you think of him?"

"I like him. He seems willing to put in the time to actually get to know us, and he's confident but careful."

Ravi nods approval. He's one to hold back his support until someone proves themselves, but he's already won over.

Seeing Bob heading our way, I smile and wave him over. I have a soft spot where Bob is concerned.

"I heard you got a new case." His expression is like a golden retriever waiting for its owner to throw a tennis ball.

"Yep. A messy one," Joe says.

"Literally," I say under my breath, wincing as the memory of the crime scene comes flooding back.

"Can I help?"

"You sure can. Follow me." I lead him back to our desk space. "We need to find out everything we can about Jocelyn Miller. She's likely the victim." I send her address and the photo I took of her graduation picture to his phone.

"After you log this into evidence, I need copies of the pages of her journal so I can look through them." I hand him the journal.

"I'm on it," he says and heads off in the direction of his desk at an energetic pace. Partway across the room, he catches himself and with some obvious effort slows to a walk.

Bob returns while Joe and I are still wading through crime scene reports. He puts a stack of papers on my desk. "Here's a start. I'll keep looking tomorrow."

"Thanks, Bob." I grab the papers, thinking I'll read through them tonight. Joe and I walk out together.

My phone buzzes, a text from my dad. I'm due at my parents' place for dinner tonight.

"Ready for salmon? We have plenty so why don't you invite

Joe and his wife? Haven't seen them in a while. Need proof of life." That's just like my dad, always including everyone.

Although I'm exhausted from the events of the day, I know I ought to go. Depending on how this case develops, we might be working long hours in the days or even weeks to come.

Joe and my parents were instant friends when I introduced them a few years ago. I don't *always* want to see Joe in my free time, after all, it's nice to leave the job behind sometimes. But we both could use a little distraction tonight.

"My parents are cooking out tonight," I tell him. "Grilled salmon. Why don't you and Sandra stop by?"

"Hmmm. That does sound good. It's the perfect night for barbequing..."

"You know I'll never hear the end of it if you don't come," I push.

"Well, in that case, since I'll be saving you, I'll pick up Sandra and meet you there." Joe smiles and claps me on the back solidly enough that I almost drop the stack of papers.

"Sounds good. Bring a sweater—we eat outside unless it's raining or snowing," I say, punching him on the shoulder enthusiastically, in retribution.

He pretends to wince and rubs his arm. "Hey! I just got my flu shot yesterday. Be gentle with me."

I lift my fist like I might punch his shoulder again. He sidesteps me and, waving, he heads off to his car. I get in my Prius and head to my parents' place.

The house where I grew up is in an older neighborhood, nestled among soaring fir and cedar trees. It's updated and well maintained, the gardens a testament to my dad's talent as a landscape architect. But my favorite part of my parent's home is the large back deck with a view out over the harbor.

I'm certain that view has inspired some of the settings in my mom's novels.

I enter without knocking, heading out the large sliding door in the dining room, knowing they'll be out back. The sun is starting toward the horizon, but the air is still mild, with just a hint of winter chill.

My dad looks up from a smoking grill when I step out onto the deck. "Well, hello!" He gives me a nod and a smile as he tends the food. "Hope you're hungry. I picked up a whole salmon fresh from Pike's today." Dad enjoys the trip to Pike Place Market, loving the bustling commercial atmosphere, even though he could get the fish for less elsewhere. I've gone with him many times. Just thinking about it, I can almost smell the briny scent of the fish shops, and see the giant crabs with the huge claws, the spiny sea urchins and whole fish displayed in rows on ice. I always loved to smell all the flowers for sale in huge colorful bunches and placed just at the right height for a child's nose. And, of course, the fish throwing. It was a magical place for a child.

"You bet! It smells amazing. Did you make that dill sauce I love?"

"Sure did," comes my mom's voice from behind me. "Are Joe and Sandra coming too?" She hands me a sweater.

"Yep, they'll be along shortly. We got a new case today and it was pretty disturbing. I thought cooking out would be the perfect thing to get our minds off the case, even if just for a moment."

The reds and golds of sunset start to reflect off the water of the harbor. We turn on the patio lights and heat lamps and set the outdoor table. A pretty row of string lights is draped over the patio rail.

I follow my mom inside to help with food prep. We fall into an easy routine borne of many nights, just like this one, spent fixing a meal together.

Returning inside after taking a side dish out to the table, I spot Joe and Sandra arriving and open the front door to welcome them.

Sandra pulls me into a big hug. "Kaitlyn! So nice to see you." She hands me a fruit salad. "Here, put this out for dessert, will you, dear?"

The silent subtext: Joe is watching his saturated fats. He had some chest pain chasing a suspect and it turned out he has arterial blockage in his heart. A myocardial infarction waiting to happen. No pie or butter-laden desserts for him.

"Ah, Rachel and Jerry!" Sandra spots my parents and she and Joe greet them warmly. The women exchanging hugs and the men, handshakes. I'm thankful they enjoy each other's company since they're the most important people in my life.

We gather round a large wooden table on the deck for the meal and pass platters of food. Some white wine makes the rounds.

"Kaitlyn tells us you have a new case," my mom says to Joe, pouring him some wine.

"Yeah. It was a pretty grim crime scene." Joe nods, taking the offered glass. Taking a sip, he murmurs in appreciation. "Sauvignon Blanc? I don't know this winery."

"It's a place we like in Napa," Dad volunteers.

Please, don't get him started, I silently signal Joe.

"So, this might be your last good meal for a while if I know you two. Always staying late once you have a lead on a case," my mom prompts.

"Could be, although it might take a bit of time to develop

24

a list of suspects. We don't know anything about the victim yet." Joe takes some salmon from the platter. "Jerry, this looks mouthwatering." My dad nods, looking pleased.

I chime in. "Case work is starting already. I have some paperwork to go through yet tonight."

"Thanksgiving might be your next good meal." Sandra winks at me. The holiday is almost two weeks away.

I glance at my parents as it occurs to me that I'm going to have to cancel my plans with them to travel to Nebraska. "I'm just realizing that I won't be able to join you at Gran and Grandad's."

Dad fills in Joe and Sandra. "We visit Rachel's parents and siblings in Nebraska each Thanksgiving. This year Rachel's mom isn't well enough to prepare the meal, so we plan to go early to help her out. It's too bad you'll miss it this year, Kaitlyn..."

"Right, I'll need to stay here." I'm disappointed, having always enjoyed the time with my mom's side of the family in Omaha. I have fond memories of traditional turkey dinners spent around a huge family table at my grandparents' home. All the holiday lights were always strung when we arrived, and we would help with the rest of the decorating and tree trimming once the whole family was together. My mom's two brothers and two sisters all try to make it home for the holidays. I make a mental note to cancel my flight. The case has to take priority.

"Well, Kaitlyn, you'll be joining us then. I wouldn't hear of anything else so don't even try to protest." Sandra smiles warmly at me.

Sandra's a force to be reckoned with. None of us even consider arguing with her. I return her smile. "I'd love to, Sandra.

Thanks for the invitation." Honestly, spending Thanksgiving with Sandra and Joe sounds nice. Second best to being with my own family.

"Oh, I'm so relieved!" my mom says. "If I know you'll be with Sandra and Joe, I won't feel so conflicted going to Nebraska without you."

Sitting here with people I care about, all of them looking out for my wellbeing, makes me wonder who might be missing Josie tonight. Is someone trying to reach her? I'm anxious to find out more about her and the means to do so awaits me in the stack of papers from Bob.

We clean up the meal and then, fortified in both body and mind by the good food and company, I head home. The lights of the city burn brightly against the dark night as I make the drive.

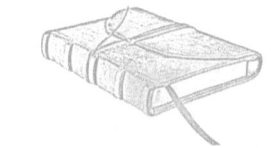

CHAPTER FOUR

Tired from the long day, I trudge up the stairs to my third-floor apartment. Elevators make me feel claustrophobic so I take the stairs whenever I can.

There's a small piece of napkin stuck between my doorframe and the door. It's so small that you have to know it's there to see it. I still have a habit of sticking a napkin in my door like this to see if anyone entered my apartment while I was away. Even though I don't feel like I'm being followed like I did on our last case, I can't seem to stop doing it. So much has happened since I placed this napkin shred in the door this morning, it feels like a lifetime ago.

"Hello, empty apartment," I say, entering. It doesn't answer. I sigh and sit down at my small kitchen table to sort through the pages Bob gave me.

Josie's basic demographics are at the top of the stack, a copy of her driver's license and a graduation certificate. Her high school is located near her current address, so she hadn't moved far in her short life. Her credit reports are next—

credit scores are poor with all three reporting agencies.

Bob included her home rental documents. I can't believe how much she was paying for that small, run-down space. Likely she was forced to accept the rate offered by any landlord willing to take a risk on someone with her poor credit.

An employment agreement shows that she worked five nights a week, 4:00 p.m. to midnight, at a suicide hotline. Looks like she started about six months after high school graduation, over four years ago.

Bob found death certificates and a will belonging to her parents killed in a car crash just after she graduated. Their will reveals they had little in the way of assets to leave her. A small amount of cash and a fully mortgaged house. There's a guardian listed, Mable Frank, her aunt. Josie's financial information is dismal. She has two maxed out credit cards and a bank account with a balance of $34.17.

Her health records are sparse. Regular visits to the pediatrician until she went to kindergarten, then the visits drop off. She received basic vaccinations at a county health department after that. This makes me suspect her parents couldn't afford further health care. I've seen situations like this before where families make too much to qualify for Medicaid but can't afford health care copays and deductibles. They're forced to stop going for routine doctor visits. Josie had one visit to an Emergency Room when she was six and fell out of a tree, breaking her left arm.

The documents paint a bleak picture. The next pages are copies of Josie's journal. I'm curious what they might reveal about her. Maybe I can get a sense of who she was and what her activities were. If we're lucky, it might even give us a clue who'd be angry enough to run her down.

The cover of the journal is worn brown leather, beat up a bit. I remember what it looked like when I took it from her nightstand but now it's in an evidence bag at the precinct. The first copied page is the inside of the front cover with an inscription: "To Josie: Happy Birthday! Love, Mom and Dad."

Josie's entries start on the first page. I go to the last printed page to find the most recent entries. It looks like Bob didn't get a chance to copy the entire journal. I'll just start at the beginning so I can get a sense of who Josie is.

Her writing is exuberant, her letters cherubic, reflecting her youth. The journal starts five years ago in 2018.

JUNE 20, 2018

It's my 17th birthday. Happy birthday to me! So, my parents gave me this journal as a gift. Apparently, my mom had one when she was my age and she says it's cool to look back and see what she was thinking about when her whole life was still ahead of her.

To be honest, it feels kinda weird writing stuff down with, like, an actual pen instead of just posting something on my Insta story. But it's also kind of nice that this is just for me. No likes, no comments, no pressure.

Anyway, life is pretty great right now! My parents can be annoying sometimes, but they're mostly pretty chill as long as I get my chores done.

My friends are seriously the best!!! There are four of us that are super tight. Lana, Lorraine, Alison, and me. We all plan to go to the same college and join the same sorority. Fingers crossed we actually pull it off.

JULY 8, 2018

This summer is amazing!!! I've been spending a ton of time with my friends and working as a hostess at The Freshest Catch. It's low-key boring, but the money's decent. My boss says he might let me start waiting tables if I "keep up the good work." That would be *way* better! I'm saving up for these super cute jeans I saw online, but ugh, it's taking FOREVER!!!

Most weekends, I go to bonfire parties on the beach with a whole bunch of my friends. Some of them like to smoke weed but I'm not really into it—it just makes me feel weird. Last weekend, Jake brought beer, and I tried some. Let's just say: never again.

So far, the only crime I'm finding is the overuse of exclamation points. I skip a bit of these typical teenage concerns—friends, boys, clothing...

AUGUST 25, 2018

OMG, I finally saved up enough to get those jeans I've been obsessing over. I'm 100% wearing them on the first day of senior year!!!

Okay, so I'd *never* tell my friends this, but I'm actually kinda excited about going back to school. Not for the classes, *obviously*, but to hang out with my friends more. It's our last year together, and that's kinda crazy to think about.

Maybe I'll have some cute guys in my classes this year FOR ONCE.

I skip a bit more...

SEPTEMBER 25, 2018

Ugh, school sucks right now. Senior year isn't nearly as much fun as I thought it would be. It's so much pressure. I seriously wish my grades were better. Math? Forget it. It might as well be some alien language because I'm never going to figure it out.

Okay, but my history teacher? He's this young guy and he's soooo dreamy!!! Like actual movie star vibes. He makes us leave our phones in our backpacks, so yesterday we were all passing around a little note saying to write your name if you think he's dreamy. Then, OF COURSE, he catches us passing it. He looked right at Lana and asked her to give him the note. She was so freaked out that she stuffed it right in her mouth and literally swallowed it. I swear, I thought I would die from laughing and you could tell he was trying not to laugh too.

This cute boy Keith keeps looking over at me in homeroom. I followed him on Insta yesterday. Maybe he'll follow me back.

OCTOBER 12, 2018

Keith and Joy are dating. I'm so sad. I really thought he liked *me*. Guess not. My mom took me to a movie to cheer me up, which was sweet. She says there are "plenty of other fish in the sea."

Not very enlightening. Maybe the journal will be a dead end. Regardless, right now, I'm exhausted. The rest will have to wait.

I facetime my best friend Isabella as I get ready for bed. She's a night owl; she'll be up. She appears on my phone, a yoga video paused on the screen behind her, her dark hair secured loosely in a clip. How can the woman look so good exercising?

"Hey, girl!" she greets me.

"Sorry, you're busy turning yourself into a human pretzel. Want me to call back?"

"Nah, I was almost finished anyway. What's up?"

"We got a new case today. A bad one," I say, washing my face, the phone propped on my mirror.

"Oh no! Bad crime scene?"

"Yep. Worst yet. Makes me want to get the SOB who did this."

"I bet. Go get 'em, girl!" She pumps her fist in the air.

"I'm on it."

"I know combing through every fact is probably drudgery for *you* but *I* would love it! Going through the details of someone's life to find out what put them in danger? All that true crime stuff is *so* intriguing."

"You find everything intriguing," I chuckle.

"Hey, speaking of *intriguing*—have you heard from the cute doctor?"

She's referring to the hunky Blake Shaw. I met Dr. Shaw in the ER last spring when I injured my wrist. Then he called me under the guise of a follow-up medical call and asked me out. Our date seemed to be going well until, well, okay—I pulled a gun on him. But in my defense, I had my reasons. Unfortunately, they turned out to be unfounded. To say it was horrifyingly awkward is a gross understatement. I didn't expect to hear from him again afterward.

But then...

"He called me once after the disaster of a date we had," I remind Isabella.

"Ooooh! That's right! So don't keep me in suspense. Are you going to see him again?" Her face lights up with expectation.

I pause in the middle of changing into my usual sleepwear, loose yoga pants and a tank top. "We never had a chance. The serial killer trial kept me busy for a bit and now Blake's off saving lives with Doctors Without Borders."

"When's he back?" She's not going to let this go.

"Not sure. I bet he's back and just forgotten about me."

"Might be hard to forget the woman who pulled a gun on him."

"I don't know what you're talking about." I feign innocence. "You must be thinking of some other hopelessly vigilant best friend."

"Hmmm. Right. Well, don't give up on the hunky doctor."

Wanting out of the conversation about Blake, I beg off. "Gotta go. I need to get some sleep. Big day tomorrow."

CHAPTER FIVE

My thoughts keep drifting aimlessly, I'm so exhausted after spending the past couple of days at the hospital. I managed to lie down on a cot for an hour here and there, just long enough to torment my depleted mind with promised rest before I was wrenched awake again. Now I crave sleep like an addict craves a drug. My relief at turning my patients' care over to another physician for a few hours feels like the weight of the world has been lifted from my shoulders. I'll finally be able to give in to my need for rest without the demands of the hospital constantly seeking me out.

It's late. The sun has already set on another day. As I exit the hospital, I hesitate, realizing it's raining hard.

"Dr. Abrams!" It's Dr. Goodman, one of my supervising doctors. My spine stiffens. Is he about to ask me to come back to check on something? "You forgot your umbrella. I saw it in the stand beside mine." Handing me the umbrella, he hurries past. I suspect he's anxious to get home to his wife and children; he talks of them often.

"Thank you, have a good night," I call after him, relieved both to have the umbrella and that he didn't call me back to attend to yet another endless task. Stepping outside, I open the umbrella against the rain and start down the hospital steps, careful not to trip in my state of near-sleep.

Suddenly, a terrible screeching of brakes jolts my senses back to awareness. A heavily loaded Model T slides as it attempts to stop in front of the hospital. Time seems to stand still, my heartbeat pounding in my ears. I tear down the remaining stairs, but it's too late. The bumper hits Dr. Goodman in the legs and throws him up onto the hood of the car. His head makes an awful thudding sound as it hits the hood. He slides back onto the street, limp as a rag doll.

The driver gets out, clutching his Fedora in distress, and we both run toward the motionless form slumped in the road.

"I couldn't stop!" The driver is beside himself. "He ran right out! Did you see it?"

Ignoring the panicking driver, I force my beleaguered brain to focus as I kneel and grope for a carotid pulse. It's strong and steady. Thank God. "Dr. Goodman!" I call out desperately. "Stay with me."

He opens his eyes slowly, confused. "What happened?" he croaks, attempting to get up.

"You were hit by a car." I press his shoulders down. "Please stay still."

The driver moans, pacing and clutching his sides in torment. "Are you hurt?" I ask the driver.

He looks down at himself, taking stock. He dabs at some blood on his lip. "No. Not seriously anyway."

"Okay. Then run inside the hospital, get that lip looked at, and send someone out to help me."

He runs off, disappearing inside the hospital.

Dr. Goodman tries to get up again. "Lie still," I tell him. I suspect both his legs are broken, and maybe a few ribs. The rain soaks through my clothing, but I barely notice.

Help arrives shortly, a motley crew of tired nurses and doctors, suddenly realizing they have a second wind when faced with the injury of one of their own. Together, we lift Dr. Goodman onto a gurney and carry him up the stairs into the hospital.

Once inside the building, we work quickly to assess his condition. Nurses use scissors to strip his clothes away so his injuries can be evaluated. There are bruises already forming on his shins. His lower legs are bent at odd angles, but there are no bones sticking through the skin, thank goodness. One of the senior doctors indicates I should hold Dr. Goodman's left foot. We take advantage of his state of shock to draw his displaced bones back into alignment. Despite his semi-conscious state, he still shrieks when we align each tibia and fibula.

"Sorry," I mutter under my breath. "Had to be done." Splints are placed on each leg to hold the new position.

Further examination confirms two rib fractures, so we wind a bedsheet around his torso to reduce the expansion of the rib cage and stabilize it. This will mitigate the pain, and, with luck, prevent a rib edge from puncturing a lung.

There's a nasty bruise and a laceration on Dr. Goodman's forehead, but the skull underneath feels intact when palpated. I use a light to check his pupils and am relieved to find they're equal and responsive. No brain hemorrhage. We'll have to keep checking on him for the next twelve hours though, he's not out of the woods yet.

Medication is administered for pain, and Dr. Goodman eases back on the gurney, the adrenaline produced at the time *of the accident ebbing from his blood stream. The critical injuries attended to, I take my time to clean and suture the laceration on his forehead. By the time I finish, my clothes are almost dry.*

After the focused work of tending to Dr. Goodman's injuries is over, I stop to tidy up and find my own adrenaline is also waning. A twinge of nausea hits and I hurry into the hallway, grabbing the nearest trash bin and vomiting into it. Leaning back against the wall, sweaty and shaky, I wipe my mouth and put my hands on my knees, loosening my tie and taking large breaths to steady myself. It's not the medical situation that has me nauseated, it's the dawning realization that if Dr. Goodman hadn't hailed me on the way out the door, it would be me lying on that gurney. He's lucky to have survived and wouldn't have if the driver hadn't slowed down.

I take a moment, then wipe the cold sweat from my forehead and straighten my clothing—steady again.

When I reenter the ward, a senior doctor stops me. "Any of that blood yours, Abrams?"

Looking down, I'm surprised at the amount of blood on my shirt. "No sir. It's from Dr. Goodman's head wound."

"Okay, well, if you're not hurt, you better go home and get some rest. I expect you back here first thing in the morning."

Waking, I have a sense of disaster narrowly averted. Uh oh, and nausea, it seems. I stagger to the bathroom and splash water on my face. Slowly the feeling eases and I crawl back under the covers.

As usual, my dream has the all-too-real feeling of a memory re-experienced. Only, the memory being replayed isn't *my* memory, it's that of one of my past realities, in this case

Dr. Abrams. He completed his medical training in the early 1920s in Iowa. When I started experiencing his life-memories, I looked him up in the Iowa licensing records.

These dream-memories leave me with lingering emotions and newly acquired knowledge after I wake. My subconscious seems to bring up memories related to my current life and often I'm left pondering their meaning. In this case, through Dr. Abram's memory, I saw firsthand the head, rib, and leg injuries resulting from an automobile accident and how they were inflicted. I consider the car accident I just re-witnessed through my memories of Dr. Abram's life, and how it differed from the one we're investigating. The most obvious difference: the driver attempted to stop, and the victim survived. It highlights that in our current case, the driver made no attempt to avoid the collision, even accelerating after the crash and deliberately dragging the victim. The murderer had no intention of letting the victim live to talk about it.

Needing to clear my head of the grim dream, I reluctantly crawl out of my warm bed into the cool air of my apartment. The sun is rising as I put on my running clothes and secure my gun in an ankle holster. Heading out into the neighborhood, I take deep breaths of the fall air and start to relax.

The leaves are in full fall color. The fallen ones crunch pleasantly underfoot. Taking my time, I extend my run to a few extra streets and enjoy the morning. Slowly, I feel ready to take on the day.

After taking a quick shower, I head to work, skipping breakfast because we plan on a trip to the morgue. Visiting the morgue with a full stomach has previously resulted in the spectacular evacuation of my stomach contents into the morgue sink. Best to avoid that.

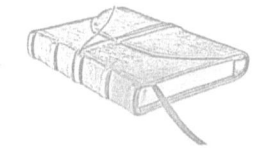

CHAPTER SIX

Dr. Mitchell is on the phone when we arrive, speaking with her usual top-volume phone voice. Somehow, she feels the need to raise her voice when on the phone, as if to emphasize her message. I picture the person on the other end holding the phone away from their ear in defense of the loud exchange. Wearing her typical serious expression, she gestures for us to enter as she continues her conversation.

One of the autopsy tables is covered with a sheet. My mind flashes back to the bloody crime scene. I'm already dreading seeing the condition of this body again.

We wait as Dr. Mitchell finishes her call. I wish she'd hurry up, I'm starting to sweat in anticipation. Taking some large breaths, I turn away from the autopsy table.

"Okay, Kruse?" Joe asks, raising an eyebrow.

"Yeah, fine. I just want to get this over with."

Dr. Mitchell finally gets off the phone and joins us. "That was the molecular lab. Yesterday I sent them the hair from the brush in Jocelyn's house and a swab from the victim's remains. They put a rush on it for me, and it just came back." She doesn't say right away if the DNA samples are a match. She likes to build up to the big reveal.

"What did they find?" I nudge her. She gives us a drum roll. *Ugh, just tell us already*, I think. "They're a match," she confirms.

Turning to the autopsy table, she asks, "Ready to look at the autopsy findings?" Joe and I nod silently, still digesting the news that Jocelyn is the young girl who was robbed of her life.

"As we'll ever be," Joe manages.

"Okay. Here we go." She pulls back the sheet covering the body. I brace for an eroded body but all that remains is the skeleton, laid out in anatomic order. I let out my breath in relief.

"I had to remove the bits of flesh and clothing to sort out what was left of the skeleton."

The damage is shocking. Every bone seems to be fractured in some way.

"The skull has a fracture on the right temple here..." Dr. Mitchell points to the right side of the forehead, "...likely from striking the hood of the car. She would have lost consciousness from a blow like this." Thank goodness.

"And here." She points to the shin bones. "The tibia and fibula of both legs are fractured at the same point, indicating she was struck by the car bumper when upright. There is more fracturing, lower on the legs where the vehicle drove over the victim." Most of these injuries are analogous to those experienced by Dr. Goodman in my dream, but that's where the similarities end.

"The remainder of the injuries are from being dragged

down the street. Most of the bones are fractured." She moves us to a set of X-rays taken when the tissue was still in place. Bones are lying at odd angles. "All the ribs are broken. The right arm was traumatically amputated. I left that arm with the flesh intact." She points to the X-ray of the left arm. "This is the only remodeled fracture. The injury occurred when she was five or six."

"She was six," I say. "I have her medical records. She broke her arm falling out of a tree." The innocent image of a six-year-old girl climbing a tree in conjunction with the brutality of her later death is almost too much. I grip the edge of a near-by counter, struggling to maintain the professional veneer that threatens to slip away. The muscles in Joe's jaw flex as he clenches it. He's feeling the emotions too. Probably thinking of his daughter Chloe. We carefully avoid each other's eyes so neither of us succumbs to the weight of the moment.

Oblivious to our discomfort, Dr. Mitchell leads us to some glass jars on the countertop. The first contains a brain in formaldehyde. "There was injury to the brain anteriorly in the right frontal lobe and posteriorly in the left occipital lobe." She points to the areas located directly under the right side of the forehead and the back of the skull on the left. "We call this a coup-contrecoup injury. It happens when a head hits a hard object and bounces back. You get the 'coup' injury where the brain hits the front of the skull during impact, and then the 'contrecoup' injury when the brain rebounds back against the other side of the skull. This confirms her head was moving when it hit a solid object with some force. Likely the vehicle hood or windshield."

"So, if she was flung onto the front of the vehicle during impact, the murderer must have stopped to let her fall back into the road before accelerating up the street, just like you said at the crime scene," Joe remarks.

"This confirms it," she says.

"I'm no profiler, but it seems like the work of a psychopath. Who else would have such disregard for another life?" I say in disgust, looking at the mangled skeleton.

"I'm with you, Kruse," Joe says. "This is a particularly disturbing murder. This person also seems to have no fear at all about getting caught. They did this right in the middle of a neighborhood."

Dr. Mitchell leads us over to another metal morgue slab. "What we collected from the road were mostly scraps of tissue and clothing. Here are the items that were notable."

The first item is Josie's right arm, a smartwatch still eerily strapped to the wrist and a blue plastic ring on the pinky finger. The presence of the personal items makes the arm seem like it might suddenly reanimate and start moving. "The right arm was torn away from the body at the shoulder," Dr. Mitchell comments. "We'll send the watch to the IT department to see if it has any information on it."

Next is the slaughtered umbrella. All the spokes are fractured, and the fabric is shredded. It still looks like a crushed insect, but now its pieces are secured in a plastic evidence bag.

"There's some white paint on the umbrella handle." Dr. Mitchell points to a white smudge. "The hand with the umbrella might have struck the hood of the car as she fell, transferring paint to the umbrella handle. Forensics will sample the paint to analyze it."

This could be the key to finding our killer. Each vehicle manufacturer has their own paint compositions so we may be able to identify the make and model from the sample. Unfortunately, white is the most common vehicle color in the country. Almost a quarter of all vehicles are that color.

Dr. Mitchell turns to an evidence bag full of tiny electronic pieces and glass. "This is her phone. It's not recoverable," she says, unnecessarily. "Even the SIM card was in pieces." We'll have to get what we can from phone records.

"No wallet, ID, or purse?" I ask.

"We didn't find one, even after searching the surrounding area for anything flung off by impact."

It's disappointing that the autopsy is so unrevealing, but we expected this. The crime scene was pretty explicit, no secrets withheld. The paint on the umbrella is at least a possible way of identifying the vehicle that killed Josie. Now we need to find a vehicle to compare the paint to.

We're glad to exit the windowless morgue.

"Whew, that was a rough one," Joe says. His laces are blood red today.

Now that we made it through the stress of the autopsy results, my appetite is returning. "Let's grab some lunch and brainstorm. We need to come up with some ideas regarding next moves."

We head to Barrett's Café, across the street from the precinct, grabbing our order and settling into the relative privacy of a booth. After the draining morning, we need to refuel. Joe sips on some soul-warming chicken noodle soup. The value of comfort food during stressful assignments can't be overemphasized.

I dig into my mac 'n cheese. "We should go back to Josie's house and do a more thorough search. We need to get the computer so IT can look at it."

"Yep. We also need to canvas all the neighbors and maybe go a block up the street to find out if anyone saw anything," Joe says. "And I want to make sure no one in the neighborhood has a damaged car. A neighbor would be able to observe Josie's schedule and know the right timing to run her down."

"Sounds like a good start." I pause, mulling over the information we have. "So, we're thinking the murder stems from passion or rage. They *chose* her. *Targeted her.* Maybe even *stalked* her. We should also see if the neighbors noticed anyone watching her."

"Any other leads you think we should be following?"

I sip on my water, thinking. "I was looking through her records last night and she has an aunt that was her guardian after her parents died. We should try to find her."

"Sounds like we need some more officers to help us with the busy work."

"Yeah. Let's get Bob. And maybe Lydiate if he'll come back. He seemed pretty shaken up at the crime scene." I can still picture his pale face when we pulled up. "What's Bob's last name, by the way? I don't think I know it."

"Maybe it's just 'Bob,' one word, like Beyoncé." Joe grins at his own wit.

"He's not cool enough to pull that off." I laugh.

"Agreed. And I think we'll need a couple more officers besides 'just Bob.'"

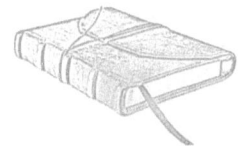

CHAPTER SEVEN

There's significant improvement in the state of Josie's neighborhood when we return. The street has been cleaned after all the evidence was collected, so there's no sign the horrifying blood streak was ever there. Just thinking about it makes me shudder.

We arrive with a posse. Bob, of course, and Clint Lydiate and his partner, Ray Kirkland, who was on sick leave yesterday. Ray is a hulking, middle-aged, dark-haired man, the picture of health today. Also with us are partners Sean Lin and Sally Finnegan. Sean's the tallest officer on the force and Sally's the shortest, so they are quite a mismatched pair. What she doesn't have in height though, Sally more than makes up for in feistiness.

I pull our car in behind the squad cars parked in front of Josie's house. I'm sure the neighbors have noticed the not-so-subtle gathering of police officers. We congregate in front of the house to discuss assignments.

"The captain appointed Clint, Ray, and Bob to the house.

I'll take you in." Joe starts forming plans. "Sean and Sally, you'll head up to the block just west of Josie's, where we suspect the vehicle that hit her originated. We'll have you canvass the homeowners to find out if they saw or heard anything. Look for any damaged vehicles, especially ones with white paint. There aren't many garages on the street, so vehicles should be visible. We also want to know if anyone noticed someone following Josie or if she was afraid of anyone."

Sean and Sally nod and head off toward the houses on the next block.

Joe leads the three officers through a quick tour of Josie's house and discusses what items we might be interested in removing for further evaluation.

Joe and I will interview the neighbors on Josie's block. Some homeowners were present when we were here yesterday, but now that we're certain the victim is Josie, we'll need to dig a little deeper. I pull out my old-school notepad where I took down names and details.

We start at the far end of the block. Where Josie's body came to rest.

"Arthur and Betty Wimple," I read off my notepad. "They're an elderly couple who were present yesterday."

Arthur and Betty own a tidy white house with an undamaged black sedan on the drive. We knock on the front door and wait. Just as I raise my hand to knock again, Mr. Wimple opens the door.

"Mr. Wimple, we met yesterday. I'm Detective Kruse and this is Detective Riley. Can we ask you some questions about your neighbor, Jocelyn Miller? You probably knew her as Josie."

"Eh?" Mr. Wimple adjusts the volume on his hearing aid.

I repeat the question.

"Oh. Oh, sure." He turns and yells into the house, "Betty, the police are here!" His hearing aid screeches, and he removes it for a second, gives it a reproving look, and then replaces it. "Darn thing," he says under his breath.

His wife shuffles her way to the door dressed in a housecoat, wig askew. She squints at her husband. "Arthur, what did you say?"

"These nice officers have come to ask us about Josie."

"What?" she yells, tugging her wig into place.

He points to his ear. "Turn on your hearing aid!" he yells. She fiddles with a receiver on the belt of her housecoat.

Arthur turns back to us. "So, it was Josie who was killed yesterday?"

"Yes, the remains in the street were those of your neighbor Josie. Did you know her well?"

"No, ma'am, we did not. She lived all the way down the block. We rarely talked to her."

Betty interrupts, "Why did you only check the brains?"

"Sorry?" I don't know what she's getting at.

"She thinks you said brains instead of remains." Arthur takes hold of his wife's shoulders and yells at her, "She said 'remains in the street.'"

"Oh! Well, of course she remains in the street! Where would she be going after all her arms and legs were ripped off?" She peers at me as if I'd better step up my game.

I'm momentarily speechless, trying to remember my next question.

"Did either of you hear anything on the night Josie died?" Joe bails me out.

"No, sir," Arthur responds. "We didn't hear a peep. We always keep watch over the neighborhood in the daytime. But we're old, in case you hadn't noticed. We go to bed early. We were asleep when it happened."

"Do you take out your hearing aids at night?" The answer dawns on me.

"Yep. Both of us. Every night."

Okay. We aren't going to learn anything more here. We thank the Wimples and move on.

"Liam Keegan," I read off my notepad as we walk up to the front door of the next house on the block. He's the one who made the 911 call.

There's no answer at our knock.

"He works in the city during the day," I tell Joe with a shrug.

We move on to the next home. A white house with a little picket fence. There are children's riding toys in the drive but no car. The Patels. The couple was present yesterday and gave their names as Ari and Jaya. They have three children instructed to stay inside the morning of the accident, watched by the oldest, who's eight.

Jaya answers our knock holding the youngest child, an infant, in her arms. We ask if she'll answer some questions about the night of the accident.

"Sure," she says, bouncing the baby in her arms.

"Could you expand on what you heard after midnight when the incident occurred?" Joe starts in.

"I heard something." She pauses to think while she rocks the baby. She has dark circles under her eyes. "It sounded like a car accelerating. Maybe a thud first. I'm not sure."

"Did you get up to check on it?"

"No. I told my husband to go see what it was and then I fell back to sleep."

"Did he get up?"

"No. I don't think he even heard me. The baby's teething, and he's keeping us up all night. We aren't getting any sleep. I can't think straight."

The baby chooses this moment to smile innocently and coo.

"Do you own a vehicle?" Joe resumes questioning.

"My husband has it. He dropped off the older children at school and then went to work."

"What color is your vehicle?"

"Blue."

"Did you know Josie at all?"

"I've seen her around. She's outside sometimes when I'm at the park with my kids. We never really talked."

We leave Jaya and move on to the next house where there's no answer to our knock except from a Doberman, which greets us with a flurry of barking and flings itself against the chain-link fence, same as yesterday. There's a car in the drive, an old beat-up orange Dodge.

As we're leaving the house with the foaming-at-the-mouth Doberman, a man with a little girl who appears to be about ten exits the front door of the next house on the block. He's dressed in a suit and tie, and she has a school backpack with her. They're direct next-door neighbors to Josie. I recognize the man from yesterday. According to my notebook, he gave his name as Xavier Robinson. This is the house that I noted a curtain drop when I looked toward it yesterday. Xavier must've told his daughter to stay inside.

"Hello!" I call out.

They turn at my voice, startled to see us hurrying toward them.

"Sorry to surprise you, Xavier. We met yesterday. I'm Detective Kruse and this is my partner, Detective Riley. Could we ask you some more questions?"

"Sure, I'm just taking Destiny to school. She had a stomach-ache this morning but she's feeling better now."

"Do you know the man who lives in the house we were just at? The one with the dog. Yesterday someone told us his name is James White."

"Yep, that's Jimmy. I'm guessing he won't answer if he sees you're the police. He has an attitude about authority."

"And he's mean," adds Destiny. "Just like his dog."

"Destiny," Xavier reprimands her.

"Well, he is," she says, feigning teenage bravado. "You always say to tell the truth."

Xavier rolls his eyes. "Kids. They never forget to remind you of every last thing you ever said."

"We have reason to believe your neighbor Josie was the victim of the incident yesterday. Did you know her very well?"

I can see Destiny's bravado fade and she looks much more like a little girl now than the teenager she wants to emulate. Tears shine in her eyes and she hastily blinks them away. Xavier puts his arm around her.

"We knew her some. She would talk to Destiny sometimes in the yard. She didn't seem to have any friends, or anyone who visited regularly. Seemed kinda lonely if you ask me."

"She used to bring us cookies," says Destiny. "She liked to bake but couldn't eat them all herself."

"Did it seem like she was worried about being followed?" Joe asks.

"I don't think so. She never mentioned anything to me," Xavier says.

"She bought pepper spray last week," Destiny volunteers. "She said it would keep her safe from stalkers."

"She did?" Xavier seems surprised.

"Yeah, she had it on her keychain. It was in this real pretty and sparkly bottle so I asked her what it was."

Xavier looks apologetic as he says, "Well, I'm sorry, detectives, but I need to get to work and get Destiny to school." They leave in an undamaged white Mazda.

The next house is Josie's. Before going on to the last two properties on the block, we stop to see how Bob, Ray, and Clint are doing with the home investigation.

"Knock, knock," I say as I open Josie's front door.

The three men look up from their work. Ray is packing up the laptop.

"Did you manage to get the laptop to boot up?" I ask. "The captain didn't have any luck with it yesterday."

"Nope. I charged it up to see if that would help, but I couldn't get it to open either. It turns on but has no information on the main screen. I'll take it back to IT to see if they can work some magic on it."

"Sounds good."

Clint is looking through some books on a shelf, turning them upside down and shaking them out to see if any notes are stuck inside.

"Anyone find anything interesting?" Joe asks.

Bob looks up from rooting through the trash can. "I found some packaging from some pepper spray and a few notes in the trash. I saved the notes." He points to some crumpled papers on the counter in an evidence bag. "They seem to be addresses and a grocery list."

"What's that?" I ask Bob, pointing to the large container

covered by a blanket beside him.

"Josie's cat," he says. "I found the transport case in the closet. We're taking it to the humane society. I'm not sure who'll adopt it, though. It has a mean streak." He shows me a scratch on his arm.

"I've been on the receiving end of that mean streak," I say, my hand unconsciously drifting to my chest where the scratches are healing. "Sorry, I didn't warn you about it."

"I saw it run under the bed and tried to coax it out, but it just tried to dig its claws into me. I found its food and lured it out. Poor thing hadn't been fed in a couple of days."

I regret I didn't think to feed it in the chaos yesterday.

"The next-door neighbor, Ms. Washington, was out front," he continues. "I asked her if one of the neighbors might want the cat. She said no one would want 'that mean thing'—her words. Says Josie was the only one it liked."

With caution, I lift the blanket. The cat peers back at me with green eyes. It's a black shorthaired cat with no markings. I reach my hand toward the kennel and the cat responds with a hiss and a swipe of its claws. I yank back my hand. It has a nasty temper. And yet...I can't quite bring myself to let it go to some undetermined fate at the humane society.

"Just leave it with me, will you, Bob?"

He looks at me in surprise. "Sure thing."

I'll just bring it home and feed it for a few days. Make up for leaving it to starve.

I walk to the door leading to the back yard. There's a small pet door placed so the cat can come and go, and a window in the top half. The yard is mostly dead grass. Two plastic lawn chairs and a table sit on a concrete pad. A bird house in the tree.

Joe and I head next door to talk with Latesha. I like the nosy neighbor. It seems she was one of the few people on the block who looked out for Josie. She's sitting on a porch swing on her front stoop.

"Nice day to sit outside," I say in greeting, although I'm suspicious Latesha isn't outside because of the weather. She wants to make sure she's present for anything going on at Josie's house.

"Sure is!" she says. "I heard you found that stalker."

"What? Did Josie have a stalker?"

"Well, she may have. But I'm talking about that mean cat of hers."

"Oh. It's named 'Stalker?'" I ask.

"Yep. It was a stray that followed Josie around for so long, she finally had to choose between adopting it or calling the humane society to come get it. Had its name long before she adopted it. She used to tell it, 'Stop following me, you stalker.' The name just stuck. If you ask me, she should've just let the pound pick it up, but Josie had a soft spot for those in need. Animal or human. That cat is always leaving things for me on my front porch. Mostly mice and birds, but today, this." She holds up a set of keys with a sparkly pepper spray container attached.

"Josie's keys," Joe says, pulling out an evidence bag and indicating for her to drop them in. "I bet they were thrown out of Josie's hand as she was hit by the car."

Sometimes items are thrown a good distance from an accident site. It's not a good look that the crime scene investigators missed this. But maybe it was farther afield than they would've been expected to search.

"Latesha, why would Josie have the pepper spray? Was

she worried about being followed?"

"She never mentioned anything to me, but maybe she finally started listening to what I said. She was a young girl out alone late at night. She couldn't afford a car, so she walked alone a lot. I told her that wasn't a good idea. But would she listen? No ma'am." She shakes her head.

"Is it possible any of the neighbors were bothering Josie? Anyone she might have been concerned about?"

"Well, Jimmy would be on my list. He lives two doors up from Josie's, and he's a mean one. Everyone avoids him. A couple of months ago, I heard him yelling at Josie. His dog chased her cat, and she told him he better put that dog on a leash. He didn't take too kindly to that." She pauses, pushing the swing. "I didn't like it one bit how Xavier looked at her, neither. He lives on the other side of Josie's house, and his daughter Destiny talked with Josie here and there. Josie babysat sometimes, too. Josie told me he asked her out once and she said no. Said he was too old. He's got to be ten years older than her. What's he doin' asking out such a young girl?"

She thinks for a moment. "Also, her landlord seemed to have a *lot* of things he had to come and check on. I saw him at her house quite a bit, and one time he was looking in her windows when she was home. Creeped me out." She shudders, making a face.

"Thanks for the help, Latesha."

She nods in acknowledgement, looking pleased.

"We're going to pop next door and talk to the last neighbor on the street. Yesterday, you said Aiko Kobiashi is her name, is that right?"

"Yep. But she won't answer," Latesha says.

"Why not?" I ask.

"Aiko pretty much keeps to herself. Gardens in that fancy backyard of hers, but never goes off her property. Even has her groceries delivered."

We knock on Aiko's door, but as promised, she doesn't materialize. There's no car in her drive. Her house is on the corner, so we walk down the sidewalk beside the four-foot fence surrounding the yard. I peer over. There's a lush garden of neatly clipped hedges and pruned trees. I can see a small pond in the middle and a stone lantern with a bench beside it. The garden is quite remarkable, reminding me of a miniature version of the Japanese Gardens in Washington Park.

A slight figure hurries out of our line of view.

"Aiko?" I call.

"No, not home. Please come again later," a quiet, accented voice comes from the center of the garden.

"Aiko, we are with the Seattle PD. Could we ask you some questions about your neighbor Josie?" I try again.

"Don't know no Josie. Please, you leave now," is the response.

Joe and I exchange amused looks. I knock on the back gate. Nothing.

"Aiko, we're not going to leave until we talk to you."

The gate slowly creeps open to reveal a tiny woman with shiny dark hair wearing a kimono. She's holding hedge clippers in a slightly menacing way.

"A pedestrian was hit by a car on your street two nights ago. Did you hear anything that night?" I'm trying to be as non-threatening as possible so I don't scare her off.

"Aiko no hear anything, no see anything. You leave now, okay?"

"Are you sure? It's very important."

"Yes. Sure." She gives a decisive head nod, then starts closing the gate on us. "Bye-bye now."

I stand for a second staring at the closed gate, contemplating further interaction. Obviously, we've been dismissed. I glance at Joe who raises an eyebrow, the ghost of a grin on his face. I shrug and we walk back around the front of the house.

"If only just one person had a security camera or a doorbell with a camera, we might have caught the accident on video," I comment.

"I know. I've been looking for them too. No such luck."

Joe waves at Sean and Sally as they walk back toward us from the next block. "Any luck?"

"Not much," Sally responds. "A couple of people on that block heard a revving car engine in the middle of the night, but no one heard a crash."

"Thought that would probably be the case," I say, but I'm still disappointed they didn't find more.

"We had a look out for damaged vehicles. Didn't find anything, but there's a house up the street where no one answered. It has a vehicle in the drive with a tarp over it. Thought it might be worth a look but wanted to check with you."

Together we walk back up the block to the house with the covered car. Knocking on the door one more time, we're surprised when it's jerked open by a man in a tank top, boxers, and a cap. He stands in the doorway looking rumpled and sleepy and distinctly surprised to see four police officers at his front door. He's accompanied by an overwhelming smell of alcohol.

"Sir, we are with the Seattle PD. We have a few questions for you about an incident that occurred two nights ago," Sally starts. "Do you mind if these detectives have a look at the car in your front yard while we speak with you?"

"Yeah, I gesh," he responds with a slur, swaying unsteadily in the doorway.

Joe and I remove the tarp from the car. It turns out to be a rusted old black Ford pickup that looks like it hasn't been driven in many years.

Sally and Sean join us after they finish their questioning.

"We didn't get anything," Sally reports. "He's pretty drunk."

Joe goes to pull the tarp back over the car but stops, looking in the side window. "What's that?" he asks and moves to open the side door.

Suddenly, we hear a rifle cock behind us and all of us freeze.

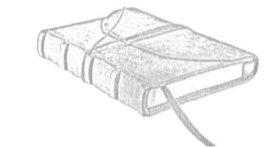

CHAPTER EIGHT

"Officersss, you need t' kindly leave my property now," comes the slurred voice from behind us. Icy fear snakes down my spine.

With slow, deliberate movements, we all raise our hands and turn to face the imminent threat. The gun sways in the hands of the drunk homeowner.

"Sir, you need to put the gun down immediately," Joe says, taking charge.

The man squints at him.

Joe inches forward, hands out, attempting to engage him. "Sir, I'm afraid you might hurt yourself with that. Time to put the gun down."

Joe gestures for the rest of us to back away. "Fall back."

Sally and Sean start backing up, following his directions. There's no way I'm leaving him here with this lunatic. I stay where I am.

"Sssstay away." The man refocuses, aiming the rifle at us.

Everyone freezes.

Joe backs off a couple of steps.

"Sir, what's your name?" I ask.

"My name? *My* name?" He looks confused, but then his face brightens. "Chuck! Charles. I'm Prince Charles of course! I'm king now, eh? Very nice!" he declares, the gun swinging wildly.

Shit! This guy's going to get someone killed.

"Charles, you need to give me the gun," I try.

He laughs maniacally. "Never!" What's this guy on? There's more than alcohol at play here. In his inebriated state, his eyelids drift shut, and I consider rushing him. As if in slow motion, he stumbles forward. My mind, in its heightened state of alert, registers the tiny details: his left foot catching the ground, the lurch of the rifle and then the sudden pop of a round discharging. We all look frantically at each other, making sure the bullet didn't hit anyone. No blood. No one clutching a chest or a limb. My knees go liquid with relief.

For his part, the homeowner looks just as shocked as we are. He lets the rifle drop. Sean takes the opportunity to tackle the man, bringing him to the ground. Swiftly, he secures his hands behind his back and handcuffs him. *Nice work, Sean.*

I look at Joe and shake my head. You never know which direction trouble will come from in this job. It's amazing how quickly a routine bit of detective work can suddenly become a dangerous situation.

Joe puts on crime scene gloves. He opens the door of the pickup and pulls out a bulging burlap bag. He lifts out multiple small plastic packets of marijuana. He raises an eyebrow at the large amount.

Sean hauls the man to his feet and Sally starts reading him his rights. "We'll come back and search the house. I suspect he has more than just weed stashed, based on his behavior," Sally says.

Still dazed, Joe and I head back to Josie's house.

"Well, that was scary," I remark.

"Agreed. He was hard to predict. The worst kind. I noticed you didn't start backing off when I told you to."

"No way I was leaving you alone with that guy."

"I appreciate that but there's no need for both of us to get hurt."

"So, you chose to be the one taking the risk?" My fear comes out as anger. I can't get the image of him walking toward the shooter out of my mind.

He knows it. "Take some time to think about it. Then we'll talk." I nod, not trusting myself to speak. We walk the rest of the way in silence.

At Josie's home, we help the others finish looking through the items in the house and pack up the laptop to bring to IT. I pick up the crate containing the cat.

"You sure you want to take that cat?" Joe asks skeptically.

"I can't let it go to the humane society. I'll take it home and feed it for a few days. My apartment building allows small pets. We had a cat when I was a kid, so I know the basics. Hopefully I can find it a home."

Joe nods, but the look on his face says he's remaining quiet about a questionable decision on my part.

"Hey, do you think we should put surveillance on this street?" I ask. "Latesha mentioned a couple of the neighbors and the landlord might be possible suspects. One of them may try to look in the house."

"Sounds good. I'll set that up," Joe responds.

When we get back in the cruiser, Joe hesitates before he

starts it up. "Can we talk about earlier?"

"Yes," I sigh. "I know, you're right, I blew it."

"There has to be a chain of command. We're partners but I'm the senior officer, you need to follow my orders."

Joe always treats me as an equal but in reality, one of us has to be in charge, and it's him. There's a reason for the hierarchy. I screwed up.

"You're right. I let my emotions get in the way. I apologize. It won't happen again." I look him in the eye, so he knows I mean it.

He nods and gives me a soft punch on the shoulder, taking some of the sting out of the reprimand.

On the way home, I stop at a grocery store for cat food, bowls, and litter, throwing a few cat toys in with the other items. Then I lug the cat and supplies up the three stories to my apartment.

Putting the crate on the floor of the living room, I slowly take off the blanket. The cat hisses at me.

"Right back at ya," I say to it.

Now I'm talking to cats. Great.

I set up the litter box and put out some water and food. This was an outdoor cat, so I'm not confident he'll know how to use a litter box.

My hand drifts to the scratches from the last time the cat and I interacted. I'm not sure what's going to happen when I let him out. Confirming my concerns, he hisses again when I get near the crate.

"Okay, Stalker, let's see if you're ready to be friends." Slowly I release the catch and open the carrier door. The cat watches me warily, then eases out of the crate. He's not in a rush, just taking his own sweet feline time, stretching his legs—a study in nonchalance. Then, in spite of himself, he smells the food and makes a quick beeline for it. With a twinge of guilt, I note that he's clearly hungry, wolfing the food down greedily.

To my relief, he then uses the litter box. He looks at me with those green eyes as if to say, "Got it. Frankly, I'm kind of embarrassed for you that you thought I wouldn't know how to use this." It's a look of disdain that's never more perfectly executed than by a cat. He takes up residence in one of my cozy chairs, keeping a wary eye on me.

I remove the cat toys from their packaging, but he isn't interested. "Okay, Stalker, I'll let you be, if you let me be."

I take a photo of him and text it to Isabella.

"Look, I have a Stalker," I text her.

"???" she texts back.

"Victim's cat. Keeping him until he gets a home. Name's Stalker."

"OMG! Can't wait to meet him!" she responds.

"He's mean. So, beware!"

"Got it. Drinks soon?"

"Sure. Friday?"

"Sounds good. OK if Darius tags along?" Darius is her boyfriend. I love him like a brother.

"NP."

I spot Josie's journal pages sitting on my end table and pick them up, flipping past where I ended last night and skimming a few months of entries, searching for something helpful.

APRIL 20, 2019

I've decided not to go to college. Lana, Lorraine,

and Alison are all going to different schools and I just couldn't pick one. I think I might be an artist instead. I love my art teacher. He's pretty awesome and he says I'm good at painting. I'm super into painting ocean scenes right now—it's kinda my thing. I've been having this dream where I'm on this amazing island with a sandy beach and I'm walking into these wild, crashing waves. I've talked about it so much that Dad's like, "If you want I'll bring you one of those beach travel posters from work," so I can put it up in my room.

MAY 15, 2019

I actually graduated! It's official—finally! I seriously thought this day would never come!

Now I'm so ready to find a job and make some real money. Dad says I can work at the travel agency answering phones until I find something else.

As for my painting...turns out I'm just okay at it, not amazing or anything. My teacher says I just need to practice more, but art supplies are super expensive, and I'm just not vibing with it right now.

JULY 10, 2019

Same old summer crowd hanging out at the beach at night. I've decided beer is okay. Jake keeps giving me some. I've started to think he's kinda cute, not gonna lie.

JULY 18, 2019

I had my first kiss last night!

Jake and I were sitting on a log at the beach—just

talking. He brought more beer, and we were sharing one so I was feeling a little tipsy. Then out of nowhere he leaned right in and gave me a little kiss on the lips. The second I got home, I texted *everyone*!

AUGUST 20, 2019

Yesterday was the worst day of my life. Mom and Dad were killed in a car crash and I had no idea until police officers came to the house and told me I need-ed to come with them to the police station. It was scary riding in the back of the car like a criminal, and I didn't know why I had to go with them. I thought maybe someone told them about the beer I've been sipping at the beach.

For some crazy reason, I was really worried the dinner I made would get cold sitting in foil on the counter. Dad always picks Mom up from work and they come home at exactly 6:30. They were late, and I was trying to call them, but they wouldn't answer. Sometimes they forget to tell me they have to run an errand on the way home so I wasn't too freaked out. Until the police car pulled up.

When we got to the station the police got me a Coke from the machine and they were being all nice. I didn't know what to think. Did my parents get called down here too? Were the police going to ask me about the beer? Did they know Jake was drinking too? Should I lie to protect him?

A woman took me to a conference room and sat me down. She told me there'd been a terrible car accident, and both my parents died. A part of me was so afraid it was true, and I felt this incredible jolt of fear go through me as if I was struck by lightning. The other part of me was sure it couldn't be true. I told her my parents were on their way home for dinner so she couldn't be right. She told me they found ID with both of my parents, and she was sure.

I don't remember a lot after that. They called my aunt Mable to come get me. She took me back to her house to stay until things get sorted. I kept telling her dinner was getting cold. I don't know why I was so worried about the damn dinner. I think a small, hopeful part of me thought the police were wrong and my parents would still come home, and we would eat together. I know that's wrong now. They will never come home again.

Poor Josie. This is heartbreaking. She must have felt so alone in the world after her parents died.

AUGUST 23, 2019

We buried my parents today. I don't know how I'll live without them.

SEPTEMBER 10, 2019

I told Jake I don't want to see him anymore. I'm still so sad. I just don't want to even try to be someone's girlfriend. It's too much work.

SEPTEMBER 18, 2019

I've been having that tropical island dream again, but something seems wrong. In the dream, I feel

like someone else. I'm so sad, that it's like the surg-
ing waves are pulling me under. Like I might drown.
I don't like it when I walk into the waves anymore.
Something isn't right.

OCTOBER 10, 2019

I've been having the ocean dream a lot lately. I just
walk out into the waves and allow them to take me
with them. Then the pain finally goes away.

Uh oh. I don't like where this is going. Dreams can be
pretty powerful. I certainly know about that.

OCTOBER 18, 2019

I called a suicide hotline today. The girl that answered the phone saved my life. She seemed to understand me, when I felt like no one would. Just being
able to talk to someone about what I've been feeling
was a huge relief. I cried and we must've talked for
like an hour. She was so nice. I didn't feel so alone
when I was talking to her. She found me a therapist
and made me an appointment. I feel better than I
have since my parents died.

NOVEMBER 25, 2019

My life has changed a lot in the past month since
I found my therapist. I'm working through the grief
in my sessions with her. She helped me to see that
keeping busy is important, so I don't get too deep in
my sadness.

I got a job at the suicide hotline. The same one

that saved my life. I'm only routing calls but I still love it. Each call that helps someone through what I went through, it's like it saves me all over again. Over and over. With each life I help save, I dig myself a little further out of my grief.

I found the girl who saved *my* life, and I gave her the biggest hug. She thought it was so cool that I came to work for the hotline. She cried a little and that made me cry too.

I found a little house to rent near the hotline. I think it'll be good to get out of my aunt's house. It's too small for the two of us.

DECEMBER 10, 2019

I love my rental house. It's MINE! It's so nice to have my own space. I can think again. I can't wait to decorate it.

My aunt helped me move a few things in from our old house. When I packed my stuff up, I found the little blue ring my mom got me when I was six, after I broke my arm. She said if I was brave while they put my cast on, I could have a prize from the toy vending machine at the hospital. When I opened the little capsule, this blue ring was inside. I decided to wear it again as a reminder that I AM BRAVE. I feel brave getting my own place and a real job. I think I'm "adulting" pretty well. Slaying it, in fact.

I put the poster I got from Dad right above my bed. It reminds me of the dreams and helps me to remember how far I've come. I rarely ever have that dream anymore. Now the poster just makes me think of a dream vacation. I've come a long way since those dark days after my parents died.

DECEMBER 28, 2019

A black cat has been trailing after me for about a month. I've named him Stalker since he keeps following me so much. I think he's cold and hungry, and he doesn't seem to have anyone to take care of him. Maybe he's lonely like me. Today I watched him sitting out in the rain in front of the house. He was trying to stay dry but water kept dripping off the gutters and getting him wet. Every time a drop hit him, he would do this pathetic little shudder. It was pretty extra. But still, I couldn't help myself, I had to let him inside. I gave him some of my tuna sandwich and now it seems we're great friends.

I look up at Stalker asleep on the chair across the room. He's had a tough life, just like Josie. I can see why they bonded. Reading about Josie losing her parents so young and about her thoughts of suicide has left me feeling sad and pensive. Josie put so much effort into pulling herself through her grief and all for what? So, she could be murdered in such a brutal way? It doesn't seem fair.

The cat follows when I head to my room to get ready for bed. "Not so fast," I tell it, wary of closing my eyes to sleep with this attack cat in the same room. Shutting my bedroom door puts a barrier between us. Stalker slumps against the closed door with a soft thump. I have a moment's regret leaving him alone, but then I remember the scratches on my chest.

CHAPTER NINE

Trying not to spook the young colt, I slip as quietly as possible through the paddock gate. He raises his head and eyes me warily, still a little jumpy. We'll have to get to know each other before he can trust me. He tosses his mane and paws the ground, a sure sign of agitation. His ears flatten against his head, warning me to stay away.

Holding my hands out and standing absolutely still, I speak in a soft voice, soothing, attempting to calm him. "See, Champ, I mean you no harm." He eyes me warily but doesn't move, a subtle turn of one ear the only sign he's listening.

Keeping my hands low and visible, I slowly advance toward him, hoping he'll let me get nearer. He lifts his head high and shows me the whites of his eyes, but he doesn't move away.

A few yards away from him, I stop and reach into my pocket for a handful of oats. His interest piqued, he watches my hand inch toward him.

"Come on, Champ," I murmur. Champion is his formal name but it's too much name for such a young horse. He's a

sturdy bay gelding. Handsome, but solid. He'll make a fine pack horse if I can just get him gentled.

He lowers his head slightly and his nostrils flare as he gets a whiff of the enticing scent of the oats. His ears flick forward for a moment, and I'm tempted to move toward him, but I remain patient and wait. He watches me. I watch him. Ever so slowly, he takes a step toward me, then another. The muscles in my arm are starting to spasm but I hold it steady. Now he's very close.

Extending his head and neck, Champ attempts to reach the oats without moving closer, but he can't reach. His lips flap at the empty air.

Snorting in irritation, he gives in and takes one more step. His lips now extend, reaching for the oats.

I want to laugh at the colt as he does the horse equivalent of a human standing on tip toes—straining for something that can't quite be reached. I manage to keep quiet though, knowing the sound of a laugh will likely cause him to go galloping off.

He gets a few oats and crunches them between his teeth, then takes a step closer, approving of the taste. Forgetting himself, he snatches the oats from my flat hand, overlooking for a second that I'm there. A fleeting moment of trust.

With slow movements, I reach back in my pocket and bring out more oats. His ears flicker in unease, but then he gives in to his enjoyment of the treat, his lips lifting oats directly from my hand.

Slowly, I move my other hand to touch the soft end of his nose. He withdraws for a second, unsure, but then resumes munching the oats, and allows the gentle touch. The price paid for the treat.

When the oats are gone, he retreats again to the other side of the paddock, but he moves slowly, less guarded. A small bond is forming. Progress has been made.

I'm sure my strained interactions with the cat have prompted this dream. I love George's dream-memories. He's so good with animals. It seems to come naturally to him. George lived in the early 1800s but the knowledge is timeless. It gives me an idea.

I go to the kitchen and pull out a tin of tuna. Josie said in her journal that Stalker liked tuna.

When I puncture the tin with a can opener, Stalker moseys into the kitchen with an attitude of indifference, as if he doesn't notice what I'm doing. As the tin opens, the scent of tuna fills the kitchen. Stalker's ears are now pricked straight up, and his nose twitches.

I drain the liquid from the tuna and then sit on the floor with the tin in my lap.

The cat sits and watches me. Clearly, he isn't planning to get any closer. I take a few flakes of tuna and put them in a little line leading toward me, with the last piece in my hand.

The cat does an imitation of what the horse did in the dream—extending his head to get the closest morsel and staying back as far as possible from scary ol' me.

He can't help himself, though. Once each tidbit is gone, he's compelled to get the next one. He keeps an eye on me, wary of any sudden moves, getting closer until he encounters the piece in my hand. He grabs it and moves his head back, but he doesn't back away. I put the tuna tin in my lap. He grabs a chunk of tuna out of the tin and runs off with it in his mouth.

Alright, you win. Some headway was made. We'll try again later.

I put the remainder of the tuna in the fridge and get ready for a run.

The sun is just clearing the horizon, and I'm grateful to be here to see another sunrise. Victims like Josie didn't get so lucky. Relishing the feeling of air filling my lungs and the heat generated by my body, I go a little further today, taking a few extra turns. Varying my route provides safety, especially after our last case when I was being followed. Thank goodness, that seems to be behind me.

I head back, shower and throw on my suit, holster and gun. Ready for the day.

Stalker is sleeping on the same chair as the previous night. I set some fresh food and water out for him. He doesn't stir. "No, no, don't get up," I tell him sarcastically.

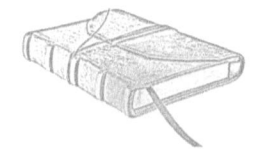

CHAPTER TEN

Before heading into the station, I pick up bagels and coffee from Barrett's Café. I only drink police department coffee if it's absolutely necessary. Joe and I take turns bringing in the good stuff.

When I enter the station, I run straight into Ethan Carter in the hall. Great.

"Hey Kruse, you got one of those for me?" he asks.

"Of course." I always buy extra for just such an occasion. He takes his time selecting a bagel out of the bag.

"You going to interview those bagels, Ethan?" I ask him wryly.

"Ha, ha." Ethan finally pulls out his selected bagel. "So, what do you think of the new captain?"

"I like him," I say. "I like that he's hands-on and he wants to get to know us individually."

"Yeah, sure." He shrugs.

"You don't like him?"

"I don't really have an opinion. At the end of the day, he's just another boss to please."

"Right."

"Thanks for the bagel, Kruse." Ethan claps me on the shoulder and ambles off.

I unload the bagels and coffee on Joe's desk. He looks up, distracted.

"Anything new?" I ask.

"Yep. IT downloaded the information from the smartwatch. It's kind of interesting."

He pulls up a PDF on his phone. "They sent over a file this morning. It's an old smartwatch, probably second hand, so it doesn't have all the typical bells and whistles. However, it would've connected to her phone's activity app." He pulls up the file and "Outdoor Walk" is listed. "She started recording a walk on her watch when she left work. Here you can see the route she walked on the map as she heads back home. As she crosses the road and gets hit by the car, it shows the change in direction and the trip up the road. Well ... at least, until the arm is left in the road." He gives me an apologetic look for the gruesome detail.

"You can see her relative pace represented in color," he continues. "The walking pace is slower, so it's in red. Then when she's hit, it turns yellow and then green as she travels up the street at a faster pace. She was walking fifteen minutes per mile, so a good pace, and then the pace is forty miles per hour up the street at its fastest. Acceleration. This is proof of the intention to kill. It also shows Josie's heart rate go from eighty-five beats per minute when she's walking quickly to one hundred sixty beats per minute when she realizes she's in danger."

This is the same information my smartwatch shows when

I run. It's amazing to have such a visual on what happened that night. "This will be very persuasive with a jury," I comment. "It will put them in her shoes: walking home late at night, the sudden, unexpected impact of the car. And the change in her pulse will make them *feel* her fear. Did IT say if they found anything on the laptop?"

"They said it was wiped. Couldn't recover anything."

"Maybe Josie was suspicious someone was looking for something and she wiped it to prevent them from finding it on the laptop?"

"Could be, but it's so final. She would lose everything she had. Seems easier to just take off the important part and hide it." Joe shakes his head, perplexed.

"That's what I'd think too. Was there anything in her phone records?"

"Bob's going through them now, but at a quick glance, it doesn't seem she made any unusual calls recently."

"Do we have any information on her social media accounts?" I ask.

"She really didn't have much. She had an Instagram account where she kept in touch with a few high school friends. She mostly posted funny cat videos. You know, like the cat falling off the fence while trying to catch a bird, stuff like that. She hadn't posted in a week."

Captain Bennett pokes his head out of his office, sees us talking, and heads over to join us. "How's our case going, detectives?"

"We haven't gotten too far yet. The house was pretty clean. We found a few papers with some addresses on them in the trash. There are no witnesses. No one in the neighborhood seems to have noticed anything other than some noises at the time of the collision. Most people didn't know Josie very well," Joe reports. "Here's the information downloaded from the smartwatch..." Joe goes over what we just discussed. As he finishes explaining the data, another officer enters the room and catches the captain's eye.

"Okay. Well, keep me in the loop," the captain says and heads off to speak with the officer. I guess that's the job of a captain, always urgently needing to tend to something.

"Hey, have we heard anything about the guy who pulled a gun on us?" I ask Joe.

"Yeah. He's in lockup, sobering up. Name's Charles Thornton. Goes by Chuck. They found a large amount of hash in the house under a floorboard. With intent to distribute and possession of over forty grams he'll be looking at spending some time in jail." He pauses. "There was something interesting though. In a kitchen drawer, they found a phone number scrawled on a napkin with the name 'Jimmy.' Wasn't that the nickname of the neighbor two down from Josie, James White?"

"Yeah. You're right."

"We'll have to look into that, but today I was thinking we should talk to Josie's aunt, Mable Frank."

"Agreed. Did Bob find the address?"

"Yep, he sent it to me. She lives south of Bellingham now. I called her earlier to make sure she would be home," he says, grabbing his jacket. "It's over an hour drive. We should head out."

The drive north is scenic. Tall evergreens flank the road as we tunnel through on I-5. There's a distinctive smell near Possession Sound. We'll generously call it seaweed but it really borders on sewage. Thereafter, only the smell of evergreen trees and here and there the tang of salt air is detect-able. Beautiful blue stretches of lakes and rivers dip in and out of view.

It's a long drive. We drift to discussing Joe's family.

"Is Sandra going to make the usual huge Thanksgiving spread again this year?" I ask. Her Thanksgiving dinners are legendary, and this year I'll be a part of it. Thanksgiving is a nice time of year for Joe, his entire family usually comes home. He misses his sons, and the holiday gives them the chance to reconnect and for him to see his grandkids. Chloe, his daughter, lives in Seattle with her girlfriend, Liz, so he sees her more often.

"Yep. She's making me some fat-free version of her po-tatoes." He shakes his head. It's those saturated fats again. Sandra follows his dietary restrictions carefully. If he has a few dietary slips while we are on the job, I choose to look the other way. He gets enough monitoring at home.

"Sounds healthy," I say.

"Right."

"That woman loves the heck out of you, you know. Not ev-eryone would get their own special side dishes." I'm teasing him gently. He loves his wife, even if he grumbles about the unwanted fussing.

"She wants me to invite the captain over for Thanksgiving dinner. Says he doesn't have any family nearby."

"Sounds like her. Including everyone." I've never known her to have a Thanksgiving dinner with any less than fifteen people. It's typical for her to have Joe invite any officers that don't have family in town.

"Are Bryce and Connor coming home?"

"Yeah. Bryce and Trisha just had baby number two.

I'm looking forward to having a baby in the house again. Unfortunately, Connor and Sara are still doing IVF so having a baby around is bound to bring up some feelings about their difficulty conceiving. I hope we don't get into any drama this year. At least Chloe and Liz seem to be in a good place after they got back together." Chloe moved home for a few months in the spring when she and Liz had an argument, but things seem to be back on solid ground.

"What's the new baby's name?"

"Ella. She's cute as a button." Joe looks smitten.

"What does her older brother think of her?"

"Greg's a little jealous, I think. Bryce says he's been building seesaw-like contraptions and plotting to 'launch' Ella."

"Sounds like he'd like to return her."

"Sounds that way," Joe chuckles.

"What's Sandra making this year?"

"A huge turkey, all the usual sides, and five pies."

"Five pies? Wow. Now I'm getting hungry."

"Yep. Two different pumpkin pies, then some with fruit. It takes her a week to get everything ready."

"I bet. What can I bring?"

"Why don't you bring some wine?"

"I think I can handle that. You know me well enough not to ask me to cook something."

Joe smiles.

As we near Bellingham we glimpse the water of Bellingham Bay, the San Juan Islands visible in the distance. Lost in the views and our thoughts of Thanksgiving feasts, we miss the turnoff for Mable Frank's place. We circle back around and find ourselves in a nice neighborhood with towering old trees and large yards.

Mable's home is in an apartment building at the edge of the neighborhood. We press her buzzer and her voice comes through the scratchy intercom. "Yes?"

"Ms. Frank? This is Detective Riley. I talked to you on the phone earlier. I'm here with my partner, Detective Kruse. May we come up?"

The buzzer sounds without an answer and Joe grabs the door. We walk up one flight to her apartment and knock. She opens the door with the chain still in place. "Hold up your badges, will you?"

We hold them up for her inspection. She opens the door, allowing the scent of freshly baked cookies to waft into the hallway. "You can't be too careful these days," she says, stepping back for us to enter.

Mable Frank is less than five feet tall and adorably plump. She's dressed in what resembles a red, seasonal tablecloth covered in green trees and cinched at the waist. Her cheeks are flushed and her grey hair hangs in a large braid down her back. Flour seems to hover in a cloud around her.

Mable greets us effusively. She's so pleasant, I immediately wonder why Josie wanted to move out of her aunt's home.

Joe makes introductions.

"Sit, sit." Mable ushers us in and indicates we should take a seat on the overstuffed couch. I look at it for a long second. It's covered in papers and photographs. A profusion of such clutter covers nearly every surface.

"Oh!" Mable laughs. "So sorry! I'm writing a cookbook, and it seems to be taking over." She bustles about removing papers, so we have some space to sit. The apartment is tiny, and the papers make it feel claustrophobic. I'm beginning to see why Josie might've felt suffocated living with her aunt.

We take a seat on the newly unearthed couch.

"Would you like some cookies? I just made some fresh. They're a test run for my cookbook." She looks at us hopefully.

Last year, Captain Garcia was forced to issue a policy on taking homemade gifts after an officer got high on brownies brought to the station by a thankful citizen. She was a sweet elderly lady and likely meant no harm, but unfortunately, we can't accept the delicious-smelling cookies.

"Detective Riley's on a strict no-sweets diet, I'm afraid. His wife would never let me live it down if I let him have one." I give Joe a look that says *just go with it*.

"Oh," she says, visibly deflating. "How about you?" she asks, brightening.

"Can't do it. I have to support my partner. We appreciate the offer though. They sure smell good." As if on cue, my stomach growls in protest. All that talk about food during our drive and now the scent of fresh baked cookies. Can't say I blame my stomach one bit.

Joe chuckles in spite of the gravity of the situation.

"Ms. Frank..." he starts.

"Call me Mable," she interjects.

"Mable. Could I ask you to sit for a moment?"

Mable's bright smile slips off her face. She sinks slowly into the chair she cleared opposite us and chews her bottom lip.

"I'm afraid I have some bad news. Your niece, Jocelyn Miller, was killed three nights ago."

Mable buries her head in her hands, tears flowing freely. "No, no, no," she says softly as tears pool in her palms and leak down her arms. "Not that poor girl. She's had such a tough life. I thought we had so much more time..."

We give her a moment to gather herself.

After some time, she looks up, tears and flour streaking her face and asks, "How did she die?"

"She was hit by a car while she was walking home from work."

"How awful," she murmurs. I'm glad she won't know how awful it really was. This is one kindness we can give her. But we can't avoid the issue of murder entirely. We need to find out what she might know about her niece's life.

"Mable, I know this is hard to hear, but we have reason to believe Josie was hit intentionally."

The color drains from Mable's face. "What? You mean someone wanted to hurt her? But everyone loved that girl."

"True, it seems people generally liked her," I'm quick to reassure her. "That's why we're hoping you might know if anyone would benefit from her death or if anyone was threatening her."

She thinks for a few minutes. "I really can't think of anyone. She didn't have much money so it can't be that. She had a few high school friends she kept in touch with, but no one she really saw much of."

"Did she have any boyfriends in the past few years?"

"No one serious. Online dating made her nervous, so she stayed clear of that. She went on one, maybe two, dates that friends set up, but they didn't turn into anything serious."

Mable looks thoughtful and then seems to have a sudden idea. "Now that I think of it, she did mention someone. A boy who was pestering her at work."

"Do you know his name?" I prompt.

"Hmmmm. Let me think...Oh, I remember now. It was Eli. She said he always offered to walk her home, but she didn't want him to."

That's interesting. Was she afraid to walk home in the dark with him? Didn't she trust him?

"Do you know why she didn't want him to walk her home?"

"I'm not sure. I didn't ask. I just assumed it was because she wasn't interested in him romantically and didn't want to give him the wrong impression."

"Was she concerned about any of her neighbors?"

"She never mentioned anything. I always worried about her living alone though. I wanted her to get a security system."

"When did you see her last?"

"A couple of months ago I drove to Seattle, and I took her out for brunch. It seemed like things were going well for her. She loved working at the suicide hotline. Felt she was helping people, you know? That was Josie. She was a giving soul. How could I have missed that someone wanted to hurt her?"

Mable dissolves into tears again. We try to comfort her but all we can offer are the typical platitudes, the words intended to comfort her, but unable to find purchase in the fresh onslaught of grief.

When she gathers herself, Mable asks that the remains be sent to her for burial in a plot beside Josie's parents. We leave our information in case she thinks of something else.

We're quiet as we head back to Seattle, each of us feeling the weight of the interaction with Mable. Notifying family members of a death is a very intimate and profound moment and it leaves its mark on us every time.

I arrive home after dark, in a somber mood. Distracted, I turn on my apartment lights, still lost in thought. A blur of black movement streaks across the room and dives under the end table like a bolt of lightning. The unexpected movement sends a thrill of fear skittering down my spine. I momentarily forgot about Stalker. Clutching my chest, I wait for my heart rate to return to normal.

On the floor is the piece of napkin I placed in the door this morning. The cat rushes out and grabs the napkin fragment in his mouth, mistaking it for a morsel of food. Diving under the end table, he chews on the napkin for a minute, and then, finding it lacking, spits it out. He looks out from under the end table at me and hisses.

"My feelings exactly," I tell him, rolling my eyes.

I refresh his food and water bowl and grab a carton of cookies from the cupboard. I've been craving them since we were at Mable's. I sit down on the couch and feed my feelings.

My phone rings. Unusual. I look at the ID, expecting to see a spam call. It's...Blake? What? Oh no! I can't believe he's calling right now. I haven't talked to him in a while. I'm not sure if I'm ready. Ahhhhh. I have to pick up or he'll think I'm ignoring him. Crap.

"Hello...?"

"I didn't think you were going to answer."

"I almost didn't."

"Should I be worried?" he jokes.

"I wouldn't read too much into it," I quip.

"Ever the air of mystery. I guess that's what makes me keep calling," he chuckles.

"Truly." I sigh. "I was just distracted. We have a new case, and I was mulling it over. The phone surprised me." Admittedly, I was wallowing in gloomy thoughts after the emotional visit with Mable, but Isabella is the only person I'd actually admit that to.

"Sounds interesting."

"Maybe." I try for a change of subject. "You must be taking a break from saving the world."

"Why yes, I hung up my superhero cape and have turned back into a mere mortal."

I laugh in spite of myself. "I didn't mean to make light of it. What you do for those kids is truly amazing."

"Well, thank you for saying so. I feel like someone trying to stop the flow of water out of a fire hydrant with my bare hands. It never feels like enough." Ah, so we are both a little emotionally wrecked tonight.

"I know you make a difference. You touch those lives one at a time. It's all anyone can do. I'll tell you what. If it makes you feel better, I'll make you a promise."

"Oh?"

"Yes, if you agree to a second date, I promise to listen to all your travel stories and, added bonus, I won't pull a gun on you."

"Are you sure you can refrain? Because I'm not sure my heart can withstand another scare like that. Should I bring an AED along just in case?"

I laugh at his teasing. I'm feeling better in spite of myself. "It'll be tough, but I think I can refrain. But I must warn you, I have a new roommate. It's him you should be worried about."

"You do?"

"Yep, Stalker."

"What? You have a stalker? Are you safe?" He sounds worried.

"No, no! Stalker's a cat. He belonged to the victim in our case. I'm feeding him for a while."

Now it's Blake's turn to laugh. "I think I can take on the cat."

Uh oh, never underestimate a cat, I think.

"How about Saturday? I have an idea I think will be fun," he says mysteriously.

"I'd like that. No chance you're going to tell me what we'll be doing?"

"Nope. But dress warmly."

After we hang up, I sit there for a moment until I realize I'm grinning like a fool.

The cat in question has been getting closer while I was on the phone. I'm avoiding eye contact with him, hoping he might come nearer if he doesn't feel threatened. He has the toy mouse in his mouth, which he places beside me on the couch.

I'm not sure what he wants. "A gift?" I ask and pick up the mouse, oddly touched. Stalker looks at me with clear expectations. I toss the mouse to him. He picks it up and brings it back. I try throwing it a couple of feet away. Sure enough, the cat runs and gets it and brings it back. A cat that fetches? What the heck?

After several dozen more throws and returns, I'm tired of the fetch game and I ignore the mouse he places by my leg. Stalker curls up on a throw at the other side of my couch. A truce seems to have been reached, and thankfully, without any more bloodshed.

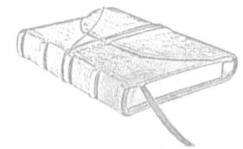

CHAPTER ELEVEN

Devin's back on my therapy couch with another workplace drama. He's draped over the couch, reclining languidly, comfortable in his own skin. Too comfortable, perhaps. When I first met Devin, I found him charming, but over time I've started to find his callousness grating. It's getting harder and harder to hide my growing dislike for him.

It didn't take many sessions before I recognized Devin as a classic narcissist. Trying to advise him to change his actions is like trying to stop a lion from killing, the behavior is innate. My sessions with him are tiresome. I can do little to improve his insight, so instead I try my best to help him through his interpersonal struggles one at a time.

"Doctor Steel, are you listening?" Devin needs a constant audience to feed his narcissistic ego.

"Yes, of course. You were saying?"

"Jill still isn't talking to me. I don't really care, but she's my boss, I don't want her to fire me."

"Why isn't she talking to you?"

"She's sooooo sensitive. Who knows what it is this time."

"Is she unhappy with your work?"

He scoffs. "Of course not. I'm her best employee."

"Can you think of something else it could be?"

He ponders this for a minute, then has a thought, "It could be because I didn't eat her lunch."

"Because you didn't eat her lunch?"

"She makes these really nice lunches to impress me. It's kind of our secret love-language. But sometimes I have to eat someone else's lunch. I can't play favorites."

"She wants you to eat her lunch?"

"Yes, of course." He looks genuinely dumbfounded I would ask that.

"Why would she want that?"

"She wants me to like her– you know, romantically. Now, I don't actually like her. She's a sad, lonely little person, but she thinks I do."

"So, she's making these lunches for you, and you eat them every day?"

"Yes, mostly. But you see, I have to eat other people's lunches as well. It's only fair. And I wouldn't want her to get too comfortable thinking I like her lunch the best."

"So, you eat your other coworkers' lunches as well?"

"I do. It's a sacrifice though. Hers is usually the best."

"Do your coworkers tell you that you can eat their lunches?"

"No, but they don't have to. They know I work harder than them. I deserve it. There's a secret competition, but of course, I've figured it out. They all try to make the best lunch so I'll pick theirs."

I'm speechless. My own lunch is sometimes eaten before I get to it, and I'm always baffled that someone would take it.

Now it's making more sense. In Devin's case, he feels entitled to it, as if his coworkers know they ought to provide him lunch because he's deserving of it. Maybe the person who took mine felt the same way and didn't even feel guilty about taking it. Somehow this makes the offense even worse.

I tamp down my rising annoyance and force myself to concentrate on the issue at hand. "Right. So, can you remember exactly when this became a problem for Jill?"

He considers the question. "Well, now that I think about it, it might have been when I ate her birthday cake."

"She brought leftover cake from her birthday, and you ate it?"

"Yes. It was right on the shelf everyone knows I choose my lunch from."

"What did you do when she asked about it?"

"Well, I laughed, of course, so she would know she was being too sensitive. I told her it wasn't any good anyway."

Typical narcissist. Convinced the world exists for his enjoyment. No regard for others. Devin's displaying a shocking lack of insight. Pointing out the flaw in his interpretation of the situation hasn't worked in the past. What has worked is for me to explain the appropriate behavior to him in his terms, so he can adjust his actions and keep his job.

"I wonder what would happen if you started bringing your own lunch to work. Then you could show your coworkers the best way to do it. You know, set an example for them."

He looks surprised at the idea. "Interesting. I can show them how it should be done. Then I wouldn't have to eat their terrible lunches. That might just work."

He has no understanding of social boundaries. It's like talking to a third grader. I'd recommend he apologize, but narcis-

sists are notorious for refusing to express regret. It's impossible for him to see his own actions from his coworkers' perspective. How they might have been wronged by him.

"Okay, next time you can let me know how that works out."

"Okay. I'll start working on that right away. It's a great idea. I'm glad I thought of it."

I wake up chuckling about the man from Sam Steel's memory. I could *feel* her inner eye roll when dealing with his misperceptions.

Samantha Steel was a psychologist practicing in the late 1970s and '80s. Her memories often give me insights into the personality traits of murderers. They address the question of what kind of person willingly ends the life of another. A personality disorder such as narcissism, and some psychopathic tendencies, might explain how someone could kill in the cruel manner in which Josie was murdered.

It's early still, but I know I won't be able to fall back asleep with my mind working through these thoughts. Time for a run.

I pull on sweats against the fall chill. It's still dark. I open my bedroom door and my foot hits an object on the floor. I reach down. It's the stuffed mouse. The cat's still bringing me gifts. This must be a good sign. Maybe we're getting to be friends after all.

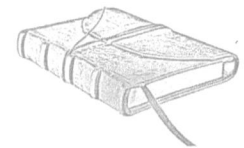

CHAPTER TWELVE

"Whatcha got there?" I grab a coffee and asiago bagel off Joe's desk, looking over his shoulder at the papers littering the surface.

"The phone records from Bob." He lifts up some paperwork. He likes to print out the reports instead of reviewing them on the computer. He's not saving any trees, but I understand. That's how he's always done it.

"Anything interesting?"

"Not really. Josie didn't do much calling or texting. When she did text, it was mostly to her Aunt Mable. I didn't find anything we could follow up on."

"We should go to the call line and speak with her boss."

"I was thinking the same thing. We could walk the route she took that night too."

We gather up our things, taking our coffee and bagels to go.

The Suicide Hotline is located in a non-descript brick building set back from a main road a few blocks from Josie's home. When we enter the tiny reception area, we're greeted by an efficient-looking young woman with a headset answering and directing incoming calls. She looks a little startled when we ask to see the person in charge.

"If you'll wait right here for a moment." She bustles off, flustered, and reappears a few minutes later followed by a huge bear of a man. He must be over six-and-a-half feet tall, and his shoulders are enormous. He fills the doorway and I hold my breath, wondering if he'll make it through, but he manages to push past the doorframe and extend his hand to us.

"Good morning. Brad Dunford." His voice booms in the small space.

When he shakes my hand, it's swallowed up in his meaty grip. His face is lit with a huge, engaging smile. He exudes enthusiasm, very life-affirming. Just the right fit for a suicide hotline.

"I oversee the crisis center. What can I do for you?"

Joe shows his badge, and immediately clouds form in Brad's previously sunny expression.

"We're here to talk to you about Jocelyn Miller," Joe says.

"Oh, Josie. Yeah." The sunny countenance is back. Unfortunately, we're going to cause the clouds to reappear.

"She was employed here?" Joe asks.

"Is something wrong? She didn't come in for her shift last night. I've been trying to contact her." Brad looks worried. Storm clouds ahead.

"Can we go somewhere private to talk?"

"Of course, come with me."

He leads us past brightly lit cubicles, each outfitted with computer screens and bulletin boards of crisis-related information. Fall decorations are sprinkled throughout the space.

The decor is cheerful, almost luridly so. It's obvious an attempt has been made to keep the decor uplifting as a fortification against the gloomy incoming calls.

The employees sit at the cubicles with headsets on. Some are on calls, and others are chatting while they wait for a new call. Silence accompanies us as we pass. My heart aches with the thought of bringing unhappy news to these people who work so hard to push back the sadness for others.

We reach a small office in the back with windows overlooking a small green space. Brad closes the door behind us and folds himself into a chair behind the desk. It's a tight fit. The desk is covered with stacks of fliers and account books. We move paperwork off the chairs and sit opposite him. Clearly, he doesn't have many visitors.

Joe breaks the news quickly so Brad doesn't have to agonize any longer over why we're here. "I'm sorry to have to tell you Jocelyn Miller died a few nights ago."

Brad just looks at us for a moment, taking it in, like someone hit by a bullet that notices the wound, but the pain has yet to materialize.

"How? How did she die?" he asks softly.

"She was hit by a car."

"Oh, poor Josie." He shakes his head sadly, tears filling his eyes. He grabs a tissue and dabs at his eyes. We give him a moment.

When Brad appears ready to continue, Joe eases into more bad news. "We have reason to believe she may have been targeted."

"Josie? Who would want to hurt that sweet girl?"

"We're hoping you might be able to help us with that. Could you tell us how she got along with the other employees at the hotline?"

"Everyone loved working with her."

"How long did she work here?"

Getting up, Brad pulls an employee file out of a filing cabinet. Squeezing himself back into the tight chair, he flips the file open on his desk.

"Let's see, she started here in 2019." He scans the pages. "I remember she came to us, saying we'd saved her life. She'd called the hotline when she had thoughts of suicide. As I remember it, she was having a repeating dream about drowning just after her parents died. Beth took the call and helped her through it. Put her in touch with a therapist and Josie turned her life around." Brad rubs his face, thinking back. "She came here, wanting work. But she didn't have any training and no degree. She was so anxious to help, I decided to hire her to work up front and direct calls."

"Is that where she worked then? Up front?"

"At first. Eventually, she took our training course and did some volunteer hours. We helped her apply for online courses too. She started on the warm lines—where the calls are more general and about mental health. We supervised her through some crisis calls and she did a great job. She was willing to take the night calls, so we started giving her shifts while she completed her training."

"Was there anyone here she didn't get along with?" I ask.

"I can't think of anyone. Those that work the late hours are very busy, so they don't socialize a lot. We get lots of calls at night and there are fewer employees to handle them."

"Was there anyone who took an interest in seeing her outside of work?" I'm thinking of Eli, the boy Mable mentioned.

"One of the other nighttime employees, Eli, was a little

extra-friendly with her, but from what I heard, she always turned him down. I got the impression it didn't go anywhere."

"Could we talk with him?"

"Of course. I can give you his contact information, but he won't be here for his shift for a few hours yet."

He pulls out another employee file and writes out Eli's address and phone number and passes the scrap of paper to me. Eli Rodriguez.

"Did Eli work on Monday night, the night she died?" I ask.

Brad looks at a schedule on his computer. "It looks like he did."

"Do you know if she was worried about anyone following her home at night? Or did anyone come here to harass her?"

"Not that I know of."

"Did you know she walked home alone late at night?"

"No. I work eight to four, so I was never here when she finished work. Most late-night employees drive home. The lot is well lit, and we have security cameras."

"Could we see the security footage from that night?"

"Yep. Let me pull it up."

Brad accesses the security footage on his computer. "I'll start it at midnight so we can see Josie leaving." He turns the monitor around so we can all view the recording. The camera takes in the parking lot and the adjacent street. A time stamp advances from midnight.

At 12:06 a.m., we see Josie leaving the building and putting up her green umbrella. She walks out to the street and takes a look both ways. Turning left, she begins her walk home. No cars are visible on the street. We watch for a few minutes to be sure she wasn't followed. Another female employee leaves, getting in her car and turning the opposite direction out of the lot. No one else is seen on the video by 12:32 a.m.

"There's one more thing which may be relevant." Brad steeples his hands and looks pensive. "We had an employee leave a few months ago. She was well qualified, but we didn't feel she was handling the calls appropriately. The advice she gave was questionable, and sometimes even dangerous. She once told a suicidal caller that drug overdose was a better method of suicide than his plans to use a gun, because it was painless. We tried to redirect her to more appropriate methods, but ultimately, when she refused to make changes, we had to let her go."

Brad pauses and repositions himself in his chair. "After all the disciplinary action we took, I thought she would've seen the writing on the wall, but apparently this wasn't the case. Not only was she surprised when we let her go, but the anger she showed was disturbing. She threatened to plant a bomb in the hotline building, and she harassed the other employees. She would call pretending to be a suicidal caller and then start swearing at the hotline worker handling the call, telling them she was better at counseling and should be the one answering calls. We got the police involved but there was little they could do since she never followed through on any threats. A few times, I saw her sitting in her car in the parking lot and asked her to leave."

"Wow. She sounds like a real loose cannon. Must've had you worried," I comment.

"I was at first, but as time passed, the behavior was trailing off. I heard she'd gotten a new job." He sits back in his chair and runs his hands through his hair. "But then in the last couple of weeks, things picked back up again. I was worried maybe she'd lost her new position and was taking it out on us."

"Have you seen her in the parking lot recently?"

"A few days ago. It must have been a couple of days before Josie was killed."

"Did you ask her to leave again?"

"I went out to ask her, but she saw me coming and left before I got to her car."

"What color car does she drive?"

"A red Kia."

This disgruntled employee fits the narcissist profile. She has a sense of entitlement and an inflated sense of her own importance. There are sociopathic tendencies mixed in there too. We'll need to investigate her. Brad gives us her name, Jennifer Klein, and her contact information.

As we leave the crisis office, we stop for a moment on the street, out of camera range.

"Did you see on the footage where Josie looked up and down the street?" I ask Joe.

"Yeah. It looked like she was making sure no one was following her."

"Maybe she was looking for this Jennifer Klein. She sounds volatile enough to hit someone with her car."

"Agreed. She sounds downright scary."

Joe pulls up Josie's smartwatch information on his phone so we can follow her route on foot. We exit the lot, mirroring the left turn Josie took on the camera. She lived only four blocks from the hotline.

Her path takes us through residential streets. The neighborhood is low income, but reasonably well kept. As we walk, we put ourselves in her footsteps. There are streetlights and sidewalks for the entire journey. It seems relatively safe.

When we get closer to Josie's house, we see why she would've cut through the park and then crossed the street over to her house. This is the only time she would've crossed mid-street.

I imagine what she was thinking that night, trying to put myself in her place. Perhaps she was alert to every noise, making sure she was alone and safe. Or maybe she was thinking of her last call and not paying attention. Hard to know what her last thoughts were before she saw the car hurtling toward her. No one heard her scream, so it's likely she didn't notice the threat until it was too late. We know her heart rate kicked up when she anticipated the impact since her smartwatch recorded that.

There's a white van with "Tim's Painting" stenciled on it sitting around the corner from the park. The surveillance we requested. We acknowledge them with a low two finger wave, careful not to alert anyone to their presence. Today it's Sally and Sean sitting in the van, keeping an eye on the house.

Dawning gloves, we return to the house for a final look around. There's a layer of dust starting to form. We take a quick survey. Nothing seems out of order.

I want to take one last look in the typical hiding places to ensure we haven't missed anything Josie was concealing. We check Josie's desk for hidden data storage devices camouflaged as toys or key fobs. All that's in her desk is a few pens, a stapler, and some sticky notes. I open the stapler just in case. It's just a stapler. There are no handwritten notes in the desk. Pulling out the drawer, I look behind it. Then check under the desk. Nothing.

Clint checked the books on the shelves for hidden notes, but I check them again. Joe looks through the kitchen drawers and cabinets, then heads to the small bathroom to look under the sink, in the toilet tank and behind the drawers.

I search under Josie's mattress and move her dresser to check behind it. Either Josie didn't leave us any clues, or the other officers were just as thorough because we aren't discovering anything new. *Josie, didn't you have any secrets?*

Suddenly, our search is interrupted by shouts and cursing coming from the front of the house.

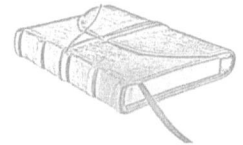

CHAPTER THIRTEEN

Joe and I rush through the front door to investigate the ruckus and we find Sally and Sean detaining a man. They were instructed to apprehend anyone creeping around the house.

The suspect is handcuffed and feisty. Sean's struggling to hold him even though he's at least a foot taller than the suspect, a scrawny, scruffy man with long blond hair tied back in a ponytail.

Sally pats him down, removing his wallet from his back pocket. She takes a look at his ID then hands the wallet to me. James White, AKA Jimmy, the neighbor from two houses away.

"Jimmy, perfect, we've been wanting to talk to you." I stay well back from the thrashing trespasser.

"I have nothin' to say to you," he spits.

"Why are you snooping around Josie's house?" I try a different angle.

"I ain't snooping. I just wanted to know if ya found her. That's all. I ain't doin' nothin' wrong."

"You were worried about her?"

"Maybe."

"You didn't know she was killed?"

His face transforms with a comical mix of emotions. I'm not certain if he was unaware she was killed and he's trying to cover up his surprise, or if he'd suspected she'd died and is trying to hide his distress.

"No, o' course not," he splutters.

"I understand you two had words in the past."

"I'm not saying nothin' more."

"Do you know Charles Thornton from up the street?" Joe tries.

"Nope."

"Chuck Thornton? Prince Charles?" Joe chuckles. Jimmy glances up when Joe says "Prince Charles."

"Did you recognize that name? Prince Charles? Is that his street name?"

Jimmy glances away and refuses to answer.

We try a few more questions, but Jimmy ignores us. He's not talking.

Joe tries scaring him into revealing something. "Jimmy, we found you trespassing. If we find any reason to believe you're lying, or you had any involvement in Josie's death, we'll be coming to talk to you again. It will go easier on you if you tell us what you know now."

"I don't know nothin'."

"If that's the way you want to play it." To Sean he says, "You can let him go."

Latesha reported that Jimmy and Josie had a heated exchange recently, a fight over his dog chasing her cat. This doesn't seem a probable motive to kill someone, but perhaps there's more to it. However, his car is orange, not white.

Jimmy glares and rubs his wrists when Sean opens the handcuffs. He grabs his wallet and all but runs back to his house and slams the door. We'll definitely be keeping an eye on him.

My thoughts go to the conversation I had with Latesha a couple of days ago where she suggested that Jimmy, Xavier, and the landlord were suspicious.

"Latesha said Josie's next-door neighbor, Xavier, was suspicious too. She didn't like that he'd asked Josie out. Maybe we should see if he's home. His car's there."

We walk down Xavier's driveway and take a closer look at his white Mazda. It's undamaged and has no evidence of recent repair.

He answers the door when we knock, looking slightly apprehensive. "Hello again, officers. I can spare a few minutes but I'm working from home today, so I can't be long."

"Just a few more questions. We won't take too much of your time," I reassure him. "May we come in?"

He stands aside and ushers us into a small front room. He has a used but comfortable black leather sectional. The room is decorated with football posters and models of fast cars. Blinds on the front window but no curtains. Very masculine, tidy and clean.

"Did you ever play?" Joe asks, nodding at the posters.

"Yeah, in college. Wide receiver. I was pretty good back in the day. Until I tore my ACL."

"I was a tight end," Joe comments. "Played in high school but didn't try out in college."

Xavier acknowledges this with a nod and we all find places on the sectional.

"What can I do for you?" Xavier asks.

"Could you tell us more about your relationship with Josie?" Joe starts in.

"Not much to tell. She was kind to Destiny, and she baby-sat sometimes."

"Is Destiny's mom not around?"

"Nah, she left when Destiny was two. Found some other guy and they just skipped town. Never heard from her again."

"She never talks to Destiny?"

"Nope. She got hooked on oxy and it just changed her. Never was right in the head after that. I don't think we'll see her again." His look is faraway and sad.

"Destiny mentioned Josie brought over cookies some-times." I try for a change of subject. After the loss of her mother, Josie's kindness would've provided a little of the maternal attention Destiny was missing.

"Yeah, always said she couldn't eat them all. She would try out her aunt's recipes and then bring us the leftovers."

"Would she come in? Did you spend some time together?"

"I guess a bit. I thought she seemed lonely. I tried to be friendly. She would stay and talk to Destiny sometimes."

"Did you have any interest in her romantically?"

"I thought she was attractive. I asked once if she'd want to go out for a drink with me."

"How did that go?"

"Not well. I could tell right away I'd made a mistake. She got all flustered, said she had other plans. I got the hint and didn't ask her again." He looks sheepish.

"She didn't think of you that way?"

"Nope. I can see why, I'm older than her. But she just seemed so lonely…" He looks wistful. I suspect he's lonely too.

"It was a momentary lapse in judgement. Later, I wished I'd kept my mouth shut."

"Did her turning you down make you mad?"

"Lord, no. Like I said, I just wished I'd never opened my mouth."

"Did you ever monitor her coming and going from her house?"

"No. I don't have time for stuff like that. I have a daughter and a job. Who has time to watch what some neighbor is doing?"

"Understood. Did she ever do anything that pissed you off? Maybe say something mean to Destiny? Set her sprinkler so it hit the side of your house? Stuff like that."

"Well, sure. What are neighbors for if not to get under your skin?" He laughs. "She used to text me all the time when Destiny was playing music in her room. It was a bit loud, but she's young. I thought she should be able to have a little fun, ya know? I bought Destiny some headphones and that solved the issue."

"Anything else?"

"Well, a few weeks ago, she asked to borrow my car, didn't say what for. I thought it was okay. I was working from home that day, so I let her take it. She brought it back all muddy and no gas left in it. Kind of pissed me off. Felt like she should've cleaned it and filled it up since I was nice enough to lend it to her."

"I see what you mean. Did you tell her?"

"Nah. Didn't seem worth making a fuss about. I just wanted to keep the peace."

When Joe and I leave, we discuss Xavier as a suspect. He doesn't seem like the type that would harbor a grudge and act on it so violently. However, he may just be good at covering. He seems just a little too polished. Maybe another incident that he's not telling us about caused him to hurt Josie. His car looks undamaged, so maybe he used someone else's car? We'll keep him in mind.

We call Bob and have him forward us the information about Josie's landlord. We need to look into him as well.

As we start our walk back to our cruiser, we take a detour and head up the street where Josie's killer would've come from. We figure the car would've had to sit a few houses up the street, putting us at the location of Chuck Thornton's house. The man with the gun and the drugs. If the killer sat in just the right spot, the tarped truck would hide the vehicle from view of the house. A few bushes would also hide it from the house on the other side of the road. This is the likely spot the murderer sat in wait, watching for Josie to emerge from the park and enter the street. Waiting to kill her.

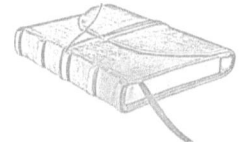

CHAPTER FOURTEEN

By the time we walk back to the lot beside the suicide hotline to pick up our cruiser, Bob has texted me Josie's landlord's address. It turns out his house is only a few blocks away.

We sit in the cruiser for a moment, researching him on our phones.

Bill Crawley is fifty-eight. He owns a few properties that he inherited from his late wife, who died a couple years ago from poor health. The properties are older and not very well-maintained, judging from the website photos. A silver Ford truck is registered in his name. He doesn't have much of a presence on social media, but there's a profile on a dating app. In his dating app video, he describes himself as loving to hunt and fish, "financially secure," and looking for a "pretty little woman" to share his life with. The video is shot with him crouching beside a lake, rifle in hand.

When we pull up, we can see his own house is as dilapidated as his rental properties. The paint is peeling, and there's almost no living vegetation. His silver truck is parked in the drive with the back liftgate open, tools and materials haphazardly strewn in the truck bed.

As we head up his driveway, he exits the side door of his house and enters the garage. He's tall and lanky with greasy hair, and he's wearing a dirty work coverall. He looks startled when he notices us coming up the drive. For a moment, it looks like he might decide to run. I can see the fleeting thought and his body start to turn away from us. I tense, hand on my gun, ready to take chase. But then he seems to think better of it and tries to play it cool. "You're trespassing," he drawls at us.

"We're with the Seattle PD," Joe explains. We introduce ourselves, flash the badges.

Crawley is on edge. His eyes flit around as if he's afraid he left something incriminating lying in view and needs to hide it. His demeanor makes me uneasy. I find myself looking in the garage and his pockets for possible weapons. I don't trust this guy.

"We have a few questions for you about Jocelyn Miller." With a casual movement, Joe shifts his hand closer to his gun holster. He doesn't like this guy either.

"Yeah? What about her?"

"She was a tenant of yours. Recently deceased."

"I know. I'm not too excited about having my property covered in crime scene tape."

"We'll take it down shortly."

"Yeah, right. I'll believe that when I see it."

"Was Josie a good tenant? Didn't cause you any trouble?"

"She was fine."

"We saw what you charged her for rent. Seemed pretty steep to us."

"She had bad credit. I was taking a risk. If anything, *she* owed *me* 'cause I took her on as a tenant." He wipes his nose with his hand.

"So, you felt she owed you?"

"Yeah."

"In what way?"

"Just that she better be a good tenant because she wasn't gonna find another place to rent."

"Did you ever threaten to kick her out?"

"Didn't have to. She behaved."

"How often were you at the property?"

"Just here and there. Had to keep the maintenance up."

"What kind of maintenance?" I say, trying to hide my incredulity. Josie's place was falling apart.

"Fixing the roof, painting the siding, maintaining the grass. That sort of thing."

"To be honest, Mr. Crawley, it didn't look to us like you did any of those things recently," Joe needles him.

"Well, of course I did." His voice is sharp with false indignation. "Had to go over there quite a bit."

"A neighbor said you were over there peeping in the windows."

"That's a lie! I'm just doing my job. I'm entitled to be there."

"Did you ever warn Josie when you would be coming over for 'maintenance'?" I struggle to say the word "maintenance" with a straight face.

"I didn't have to, it's my property." Not true, legally he had to inform her, but that's not why we're here.

"Did she ever question your presence on her property?" Joe asks.

"Yeah. She was real snarky. Got all up in my face about it."

He turns and spits. Gross.

"Bet that pissed you off," Joe prods him.

"Well, yeah, it did. I was just trying to do my job."

"Did you ever ask her out?" I ask.

"No." He crosses his arms.

"Were you attracted to her?"

"No." He glares at me.

"Sure, about that?" I'm not letting him off the hook.

"Yes, I'm sure!" He juts his chin defensively.

"What were you doing last Monday night?"

He thinks for a split second. "I was home."

"Can anyone confirm this?"

"No."

"Mind if we take a look at what's under that tarp over there?" I point to the corner.

He looks distinctly alarmed at the change in subject, glancing nervously over at the tarped vehicle. "Why? You got a warrant?"

"Well, no, we don't, but here's the thing, if you make me go get a warrant just to check on your vehicle then I might just need to extend that to your house since I'm already making the effort. Is that what you want?" I raise an eyebrow.

"No," Crawley says sullenly.

Joe pulls the tarp off the vehicle revealing an older white Kia. It's in poor condition. The front bumper and fenders are missing.

"What happened here?" Joe asks.

"Rusted out. Just waiting for parts." Crawley spits again.

"Is this vehicle registered?"

"No. It was my wife's. I don't use it very much."

"You need to get this registered."

"Right. I'll be sure and do that," he says sarcastically.

I notice tracks behind the Kia on the garage floor with dried mud. It looks like it was driven recently.

"Mr. Crawley, we're going to have to have someone come out to get a paint sample from your vehicle."

"Well, now, I guess you're going to need a warrant for that," he says belligerently.

When we leave, I have to fight my instincts to turn and make sure Creepy Crawley isn't aiming a gun at our backs. But I know he wouldn't dare. He's really a coward who targets vulnerable women when it comes right down to it.

Later that night, I meet up with Darius and Isabella for drinks at Bar None. Some months ago, it looked like Darius was going to propose, but he's holding out for the perfect moment and there's no ring on Isabella's finger yet. I know she's getting antsy about it, but she's wise enough to keep it to herself. I happen to be in on Darius's plan, and she's going to love it. If only we can keep it a secret long enough.

I'm the first to arrive, so I grab a table. It's Friday night and the bar is filling up.

"Hey, girl!" I look up from my phone to Isabella's happy smile.

"Bella!" I get up to give her a big hug. "Wow, you look great." She has her long dark hair done up in an artfully messy bun, and she's wearing a new cropped sherpa jacket, a white shirt, and high-waisted black faux-leather pants. She always looks so put together. I make a mental note to get her to take me shopping sometime soon. Real soon. It's officially a fashion emergency. I'm down to a black blazer and jeans. They've been in my wardrobe long enough to be considered "classics." Not a fashion statement I want to make at my age.

"You look great too, Darius." I suspect Isabella picked out his dark jeans and hooded leather jacket. I pull him in for a hug.

"It's great to see you." Darius returns my hug with a crushing bear hug. The man doesn't know his own strength.

"What's up with you, Kait?" Isabella settles into her chair and grabs a drink menu.

"The usual. Chasing down murderers."

"Well look out, murderers. Kait's got you in her sights."

"Right." I laugh. Then, coyly: "But I do have some news."

"Do tell," Darius and Isabella say in unison.

"You two are *so* cute," I tease them, and they laugh good-naturedly.

"So, the news…" Isabella raises her eyebrows.

"Well, it seems I didn't scare Dr. McHunky off after all."

"No way! He called?" Isabella's interested now.

The waitress picks this moment to stop and take our drink order. I get my usual Dark and Stormy. Isabella wants to try something new. She discusses the menu with the waitress, and they come up with a Smoked Old Fashioned for her. Darius orders a local IPA.

"Okay. Back to Dr. McHunky. What happened?" Isabella won't be side-tracked by the interruption.

"He called last night and agreed to a do-over date."

"Yes!" She pumps her fist in triumph. "What are you going to do for your 'do-over?'"

"That's a great question."

"Oooh, so mysterious. Any idea what it might be?"

"He said dress warmly."

"Maybe an ice bar?" Darius muses.

"That would be fun." Isabella smiles dreamily. "There's that one downtown where the whole bar is made of ice, and they give you warm blankets and handwarmers. They run the drinks down an ice shoot to chill them."

"That does sound fun, but I don't think that's it."

"Maybe a hockey game?" Darius loves his sports.

"Or star gazing?" Isabella guesses. "Maybe he owns a telescope. That always seemed romantic to me."

"All good guesses, but we're going in the daylight. Don't worry. I'll tell you what we end up doing. I kind of like the mystery of not knowing."

The drinks arrive. Isabella's still has a haze of smoke in the glass. She takes a sip. "Wow, I feel like I'm in a speakeasy." She coughs and laughs, waving the residual smoke away.

I take a sip of mine. "Wow, I feel like I'm on a stormy sea..."

"Shush," she says in a husky voice.

"So is the raspy voice free with your drink?" I ask.

"I kinda like it." Darius winks at her.

"Oh, you do?" She takes another sip and rasps, "How about now?"

"Do that again and I may just whisk you home right now," Darius growls.

"Okay, you two frisky kids, remember I'm still here." I pretend to pull the pin out of an imaginary fire extinguisher and spray them down. "Any cute third grader stories, Bella?" She's an elementary school teacher and always has an adorable story about "her kids."

Isabella thinks for a moment. "Oh, I have a good one. A little girl, Zuri, asked me yesterday about the story of the princess kissing the frog and turning it into a prince. So, I retold her the story, and she gets these tears in her eyes. It's such a cute story and I can't imagine why she's sad so I ask her what's wrong. She says the family was all sitting down at dinner the night before and her mom says to her dad, 'You sound like a frog.' His voice is hoarse because he's sick. I saw him at pick up the other day."

"Is she worried about her dad?" I can't help but ask.

"Well, yes. But not in the way you would think."

"What's she worried about?"

"I had to call her mom because, after the frog story, Zuri was pretty distraught, and I couldn't figure out what she was worried about. Her mom tells me she always calls Zuri's dad her 'prince' and now Zuri's worried her dad is turning back into a frog."

I laugh and almost choke on the alcohol I was swallowing.

Darius snorts. "Yeah, after all, I've always been your frog-to-prince project. Hope no frog is showing." He ribbits like a frog and gives her a wide-eyed look, covering his mouth. "Oops!"

Isabella thumps him on the arm.

As we leave the bar that night, Isabella gives me a hug and then holds me at shoulder length. "Do NOT, under any circumstances, bring your gun on your date tomorrow."

"Yes, Mom," I laugh.

"I'm not kidding, Kait. No gun."

"Got it."

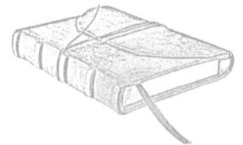

CHAPTER FIFTEEN

A knock at the door. It'll be Will, here to pick me up. Last week he finally got up the courage to ask if he could accompany me to the church picnic. And now here it is, picnic day already! Giving my petticoats a final fluffing, I hurry toward the stairs, trying to make it before my father scares Will off.

"Hello." My father's gruff voice drifts up from the main floor as he opens the door. Oh, no! I'm too late. I pick up my skirts and hurry down the hallway toward the stairs.

"Hello, Mr. Moore. How are you this fine day?" Will is as po-lite as ever.

"I'm as good as a man can be when he is trusting someone else to escort his only daughter safely. How good is that, do you think, Will? Hmmmm?"

"Uh, good, sir?" Will gulps audibly.

"Is that a question, Will? Or are you trying unsuccessfully to convince me of your ability to take care of Abigail?" I slow to a walk, smooth my skirts and slow my breath, so I don't give away my headlong rush to the front door.

"You should feel good, sir." Will's voice has an uncharacteristic quaver. Bloody hell, never underestimate a father's ability to put the fear of God into your perfectly respectable suitor.

Plastering on a bright smile, I take this opportunity to present myself at the front door.

"Why, Will, don't you look dapper this afternoon," I chirp, taking in his tailored suit.

"Miss Abigail. You look right fine yourself."

Before my father can provoke the poor man further, I sashay out the door and down to the waiting phaeton carriage, inviting Will to follow me. I swing my hips a bit to swirl my skirts, hoping he notices the new dress I had made for the occasion. It's an emerald-green silk which shows off my slim waist to great effect, if I do say so myself.

"What a beautiful gown, Miss Abigail." He noticed alright.

"Will, there's no one in earshot. You can call me Abby."

"Miss Abby." Better, but not what I meant.

Will gives me a hand up to the open phaeton and we wait a bit for my family. His perky grey horse gives a snort and stamps a foreleg, impatient to be off. I know how it feels.

Once my family is settled in their carriage, we head to the church, leading the way. Will is excited to show off the small, trendy phaeton. On the way, he sneaks side-glances at me, making sure I'm suitably impressed, no doubt.

"What a fine carriage you have. I've never ridden in a phaeton before," I make an attempt at flattery. It doesn't seem to come naturally to me as it does to the other girls. My mother is always getting after me. "You need to make sure the man knows you respect and admire him, Abigail. The way to win a man's attention is to praise him and appreciate him. You must try harder," she tells me every chance she gets.

Will straightens noticeably at the compliment and proceeds to supply me with the fine details of the carriage's virtues. I attempt to appear interested.

Admittedly, I'm a little giddy at the tiny bit of freedom of riding alone with Will and it's made all the better by the extremely fine weather. I continue to pretend to be enthralled with Will's monologue. My family follows at a respectful distance. Even though Will and I are in a separate carriage, we are far from being alone. Everything we do together requires chaperoning. It's tedious at best.

There's a large group already assembled at the picnic site when we arrive. Women in fashionable dresses of many bright colors twirl parasols and chatter with gentlemen in tailored suits.

In the shade of a huge oak tree, a long wooden banquet table sits, looking incongruous with its outdoor location. It's covered with a fancy tablecloth and laden with extravagant food brought by parishioners.

My mother hands me two of her famous blackberry pies to place on the table. As I set them down, I look at what others have brought. Everyone has contributed their very best items. There's cold roast chicken, biscuits, bread and butter, meat pies, hard boiled eggs, cheese, fruit pies, cake and fresh berries. My mouth waters.

Cold pitchers of cider, mead, and claret sit at the end of the table, rivulets forming in the condensation. Uh oh, this could be trouble. My father and some of his companions do not approve of the consumption of alcohol. He's a member of the temperance movement and he doesn't miss a moment to lecture us about the perils of alcohol in all its forms. His rigid position on the matter is brought on by his brother's condition. The drinking of spirits has consumed my uncle, nearly taking his life. His attempts to stop have left him weak and shaking, only resolved by returning to the bottle. We're afraid we will lose him to either the effects of attempting to abstain or to the delirium caused by excessive drinking itself. I'm uncertain which is worse.

I shake off the thoughts of my uncle and return my attention to the picturesque scene before me. I recognize several of the staff from the hospital where I work as a nurse. Clara, a friend of mine, talks with another nurse. As I pass, hand-in-hand with Will, she gives me a conspiratorial smile, knowing how excited I am to be accompanied by him. Edith, the head nurse, makes a beeline toward Clara and I cringe. Edith's mean as a rattlesnake. Poor Clara.

The ladies are all decked out in bonnets and gloves, and they use their colorful parasols to shield their pale skin from the bright sunshine. I twirl mine to make sure everyone notices me passing with my handsome escort. Doctor Elliot, one of the doctors from the hospital, alights from a carriage with his wife and gives an approving nod in our direction.

Will lays out a blanket for us to sit on. "May I?" He holds out his hand and I take it as I sit, allowing my skirts to fan out prettily. I watch admiringly as he assembles us a plate of food and chats with others by the table. The man does cut a fine figure.

Will returns with two plates heaped with tasty morsels.

"Why Miss Abig...I mean, Abby, what a fine day we have for our picnic." He settles on the blanket beside me and passes me a plate.

"What a fine day indeed. I find I am exceedingly happy." I give him my best smile and bat my eyelashes like a dim-witted coquette. I sigh inwardly, it's just not my style to flirt so brain-

lessly like the other girls. I can see by the surprise in his eyes and the tepid smile, he knows I'm not being sincere. Alright, I'll try being myself, consequences be damned.

"I've been wanting to tell you about a surgery I saw this past week."

He glances sharply at me, a true smile returning to his face. Now I have his attention. "How did you come to see it?"

"I snuck into the back of the operating theater. No one pays much attention. They're too interested in the operation going on down below."

"What were they doing?"

"An amputation." I tell him about the details of the surgery, the miracle of chloroform, the sterilized instruments, the surgery itself. He listens with rapt attention.

"Miss Abby, you are, without a doubt, the most interesting woman I've ever met." Now the smile reaches his eyes.

After the feasting, some take a leisurely nap in the shade. Others socialize, taking walks and playing lawn games. Will and I take a nice walk through the grounds, ensuring we're seen and commented on. We nod at the noticers.

There's a sudden loud commotion by the croquet game. Dr. Elliot stumbles and grabs onto another man's coat, righting himself at the last moment. His companion laughs it off. "Steady, old fellow," he says agreeably.

Another man confronts the doctor. "Elliot, you rascal! You put money in. Now you have to pay up."

Dr. Elliot looks as if he's about to reply to the challenge, but before he can say anything, he turns a noticeable shade of green, stumbles off into the bushes, and throws up. His friends turn away from his disgrace. The doctor's wife gathers him and steers him to their carriage.

The picnic resumes in the wake of the disruption, everyone pretending not to have noticed the incident, but I know tongues will be wagging behind closed doors. The man is becoming a danger to himself and to his patients. The nurses and other doctors have to watch him closely.

As the afternoon wanes, the picnic comes to an end. I put my gloved hand in Will's, and climb back into the phaeton. We head for home, followed closely by my family. Will and I seem to have confirmed a mutual attraction today. He helps me out of the carriage and up to the house. As he heads back to his carriage, my father gives him a tip of his hat. Large praise from a man such as him.

I awaken from the dream and lie for a moment looking up at the ceiling. Courting as my past life, Abby, sure was a different endeavor than my plans with Blake for today. I suppose the take-home message is to be myself. Or maybe it's "Don't drink too much."

Blake has instructed me to dress warmly, but I don't know exactly what we're doing today. It's a surprise. I'm a bit too much of a control freak to truly like a surprise, but I do love the mystery of it. He's pushing me out of my comfort zone. It has a certain appeal.

Pick up time is 10:00 a.m., so I have some time before he arrives. I shower and dress warmly as instructed.

The cat brings me his stuffed mouse and I throw it a few times for him.

"You're actually a dog, aren't you?" I ask him.

He gives me a look that shows his disdain for dogs. Okay, it might just be his usual look of disdain.

"Well, you fetch, you attack intruders, you meet me at the

door when I come home. See...dog."

Stalker turns his back on me, flicks his tail, and walks away.

"Fine. Keep up the cat pretense," I tell his backside.

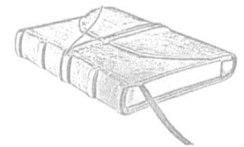

CHAPTER SIXTEEN

When Blake pulls up in front of my apartment, I head down to meet him in my parka, gloves, and scarf. Wrapping the scarf around my face and putting out my gloved hands, I give him a playful, "Ta-da!" I think I'm overdressed, but it turns out I'm on the right track after all.

"Perfect," he approves of my outfit. "You should be warm in that."

We hit the road, leaving Seattle behind, and heading off in a direction known only to Blake.

"Where are we going?" I ask.

"Patience. Soon all will be revealed." He winks at me.

"You're talking to a detective you know. We aren't known for our 'sit back and don't look for clues' attitude."

He chuckles. "So, enjoy this rare moment when you don't need to know the answer. You can just enjoy the mystery."

I really do try to follow this advice, but soon I find myself looking for more clues. *Stop it*, I think.

Determined to be present in this moment, one with all the

anticipation of an enjoyable day ahead, I tap into my curiosity about Blake's recent travels with Doctors Without Borders. "So, tell me about your trip to Somalia. What was it like to be there?"

He thinks for a moment. "Well, it's hard to describe. Our stay there always had this overriding feeling of danger because of the instability of the area, but I really felt pretty safe. We had a security detail, but they mostly spent their days playing cards." He laughs softly. "I was located in a small fishing village on the coast. The people that lived there were amazing, so resilient and self-sufficient. They just didn't have all the resources they needed."

"What was the area like?" Somalia seems a world away from the brisk fall weather here.

"It was beautiful. One of the best parts of the day was getting up early, when it was still dark. I would sit on the patio of the clinic with this strong Somali coffee called Qaxwo." He pronounces it "kah-wo." A distant smile forms on Blake's face. "No one else was up, so it was this perfect quiet moment when I could watch the sun come up and think about the day ahead. Sunrises there were the most amazing bright colors. Oranges and reds, all reflected in the water. Each day was different. It was a great way to start off a long day, before the heat really set in."

"I bet you put in long hours."

"Yes, they were long, but the time went by so fast. Before I knew it, the day would be over. I was so tired sometimes that I could barely get something to eat before I fell asleep. The work was exhausting. Not just the physical part, but also from the feeling of trying to help every patient but often falling short because we just didn't have what we needed to help everyone." Blake glances my way. "We worked with some local doctors and some of my favorite times were when I got a chance to sit with them in the evening, sharing a meal and exchanging stories. Hearing about their struggles and the ways they found to overcome them was eye-opening."

"It sounds hard, but rewarding," I say, and he nods with a faraway look, his thoughts momentarily in Somalia. "Did you have a favorite patient?" I ask to bring him back.

Blake ponders the question. "Well, one of the most satisfying was a one-month-old baby boy called Ahmed. He was brought in by his very frightened and very young mother. She was beside herself, sobbing and jostling him up and down. He was limp, just lying in her arms, dehydrated and lethargic. Then Ahmed vomited and out came this projectile gush of milk. It was impressive, hitting the wall a few feet away with a splash. Gives me chills, even now, just thinking about it."

"Yikes. That sounds scary." I take in Blake's grave expression. "What made him so sick?"

"Well, I wasn't sure until I examined him, but when I pressed on his stomach, I could feel this round mass under the right side of his rib cage. The muscle that regulates the flow of stomach contents into the small intestine was thickened and stopping the passage of food. It's called pyloric stenosis. No food can leave the stomach, so it all comes back up. The poor infants that have it vomit forcefully, over and over. They lose weight and can have life-threatening dehydration and electrolyte imbalances. Ahmed was so low on fluids that his mouth was dry, and his skin would tent up when I pulled on it."

My stomach drops with thoughts of the tiny sick infant.

"How did it turn out?"

"He survived, thank goodness. We managed to get an IV in him and transferred him to a larger center where he had imaging and then surgery, a pyloromyotomy. It cuts the tight muscle and cures the condition. His mother brought him back to see me a few weeks later when he had gained some weight, and he was smiling and cooing." A smile transforms Blake's face. "It was gratifying to see how well he was doing. I didn't always get to see the difference I was making firsthand like that."

I'm so engrossed in the story that I'm surprised when Blake brakes suddenly as an SUV cuts in front of him. My mind takes a moment to leave the warm coast of Somalia and return to the winding road we're traveling. I glance around and notice we're a distance from Seattle.

We start to climb in elevation, and now the hillsides are topped with new-fallen snow, as if icing sugar was dusted over them. A distinct line shows where it was cold enough that the rain became snow.

"I can see now why you said to dress warmly."

"Can't shake off the detective role, huh? Still looking for clues?"

"Guilty."

We pull into a resort town, tires crunching on the snow. A light snow drifts down, and the storefronts are cheerful and bright. It's like we're inside a snow globe. Very romantic. Taking in the scenery, and contemplating the mysterious plans for the day, I find I'm enjoying myself immensely.

Blake takes a few turns and then stops the car in front of a ski rental store.

I raise one eyebrow at him. "Skiing?"

"Good job, detective. What deductive skills did you use?"

"My 'we're parked in front of the ski rental store' observation."

Blake grins. "I'm never going to be able to put one over on you, am I?"

"Not likely."

"One thing you might not be expecting though, we're going to try Nordic skiing—cross country, not downhill."

"Okay. I've tried that once, but it's been years. It's pretty good exercise from what I remember."

"Yep, but less skill required."

"I'm not sure how to take that."

"Just that I didn't know if you'd skied before, and this is easier to do on a first try."

After Blake enquires about ski rentals, we're asked to provide our body measurements. Height, weight, shoe size. It's a little personal somehow.

"You just wanted to know my weight, didn't you? There are easier ways to find out, you know," I tease Blake.

He just scoffs in response, not dignifying this with an answer.

The rental staff loads us up with equipment. I buckle into the ski boots and throw the skis and poles over my shoulder. The air's cool and fresh as we exit the rental store. Blake follows me out.

"You're going to be really good at this, aren't you?" I ask.

"Well, I've skied downhill a lot, but I've only Nordic skied a couple of times. I thought it would be fun for us both to try something we haven't done much. Something new."

"Annoying."

He laughs. "What?"

"Oh, I just figured you for one of those naturally athletic people that makes the rest of us look like we never got a body user manual."

"Hardly."

Blake takes a backpack out of the trunk of the car and puts it on.

"What are you bringing? Flares in case I need a helicopter rescue when I get too tired?"

"Wouldn't you like to know?"

"So mysterious. I don't remember telling you that tall, dark, and mysterious was my type."

He laughs. "Well, I hope it is."

Blake leads the way to the start of a trail, and we clip into our skis. We start out at an easy pace on the level terrain, the skis sliding into a steady rhythm. We head uphill for a while. My hip flexors are complaining, but the exercise gets my blood flowing, and it feels good in the crisp air.

I'm looking for wildlife but all I've seen is a few bunny tracks. The animals probably know better than to come too close to the ski trail.

Suddenly Blake slows down and points off to the side of the trail. My heart rate picks up, wondering what he's looking at, but when I pull up beside him, he points to a doe and fawn heading for some trees. The snow is deep enough, the fawn has to lift its legs unnaturally high to take each step. The effect is adorable. We watch until they disappear into the trees and then head back on our way.

After we've traveled a good distance, we stop and take off our skis on the top of a ridge with a nice view of the valley below. Taking a seat on a fallen log, Blake starts pulling food out of his pack.

"So, *not* foldable shovels to bury the body with?" I tease. In my world, that's exactly what would be in a killer's backpack. Luckily, the things I witness in my line of work are not most people's reality.

He pulls out some utensils and selects a spoon. "Might take a while with this."

"Haha, very funny."

He spreads out a small picnic blanket between us on the log and comes up with baguettes stuffed with cheese and ham, grapes, yogurt cups, chips, and brownies. He pulls out water bottles and sets them out too.

"You don't have a table in there too, do you?" I ask, pretending to peer into the depths of the pack.

"Not today. Magic tricks are strictly a third date thing. Speaking of which, I seem to remember that guns were a first date thing for you. Where did you hide yours today?"

A hot flush burns my cheekbones.

"I'm under strict orders from Isabella to leave the gun at home," I manage.

"Seems like good advice." He winks to take the sting out of his comment and passes me a bottle of water.

"She seems to feel I need some coaching."

"Seems like you're doing pretty well on your own."

"Let's talk about something else. Anything else."

The food tastes amazing. We take in the view and polish off most of the food, our appetites revved up from the fresh air and exercise.

"You know," I say coyly, getting up from the log, "I don't have a gun but that doesn't mean I don't have any ammunition."

"Meaning what?" He sounds worried, his brow creasing.

Putting my gloves back on, I pick up a handful of snow and shape it thoughtfully. "Hmmm, well, I don't know..." I take aim and the snowball delivers a glancing blow off his shoulder.

"Oh, I see. That's how it is." He lobs a snowball at me.

I put a hand up to deflect it and get showered with snow for my efforts. Snow covers my face and drips down my chin.

He looks over at me and chuckles. "You've got a little something right here," he says pointing to his forehead and vastly understating the scope of snow cover. He takes off his glove and brushes snow from my hair and cheeks and stops himself as he realizes he's running his thumb over my lower lip.

My breath catches. The reflexive gesture sends tingles zinging along my nerves. If he notices, there's no indication. Damn him for being so oblivious. And sexy. Did I emphasize the sexy part? Damn sexy.

We pack the blanket and remnants of the meal back away. I find myself sneaking glances at him, taking in the view as we clip back into our skis.

"You're just as athletic as I thought," I accuse him jokingly.

"Well, I do like to think of myself as looking like the guy in the Versace commercial, you know the one with the bow and arrow?" He jokes, giving me a wink.

Yep. I know the one. Great. Now I'm picturing the half-dressed god from the commercial. How am I supposed to concentrate on skiing when I just want to find out if he really looks like that? From here he kind of does. My imagination runs away with me.

Blake leads the way back onto the trail. Now we're on a downward incline, much more difficult in these skis. I'm pretty good on downhill skis, where you can push your ski edge into the snow to slow your descent, but cross-country skis don't work that way. I'm not in my element.

I find myself careening down the hill behind Blake and when he stops to turn and check on me, I run headlong into him. I slide under him as he tries to catch me, and we end up in a tangle of skis and body parts. When our tumble comes to a stop, he's lying on top of me.

He pushes up on his hands, his face, with those gorgeous lips, just inches from mine. I freeze, looking into his deep blue eyes, his warm breath brushing my cheek. So close. He hesitates and I can almost feel the heat from his lips moving closer. Or am I just wishing for that? He stops abruptly and pulls himself up and off me, standing back up. He extends a gloved hand toward me to help me up. I'm dazed by the near-kiss and lie there for a moment.

"You okay?" He looks concerned.

No, you bloody man. Kiss me already!

"Fine," my mouth says, but my body says other things entirely as it agrees with my thoughts.

I take his hand and let him pull me up. He looks maybe a bit dazed too.

"*You* okay?" I ask with what I hope is a playful smile.

He nods and turns to head back to the trail, leaving me standing there. I set off in pursuit. A little way down the trail, he stops again to check that I'm following. I sure am. I run smack into him. This time he anticipates it and I run into his solid form as he stops me in his arms. I'm not leaving it to him this time. I wrap my hands around his neck and pull his head down toward me. He leans in and then our lips meet, and we're kissing, deeply. There's nothing tentative about it.

We're all in. The warmth and built-up anticipation put me in a tailspin. I'm clinging to him.

"Wow," he says with a sexy half-smile, when we finally pull apart.

"Yeah, wow," I echo dreamily.

A couple of skiers appear around a bend in the trail and we guiltily spring away from each other. Blake chuckles. "Hazardous trail," he murmurs under his breath.

We manage to finish the rest of the trail without mishap and the rental store comes into sight. My muscles are complaining loudly by then. We return our rentals and climb back into the car. It feels good to relax into the seat. I turn on the seat warmer to ease my tired limbs.

We head back to Seattle, not talking much. I'm lost in the heat of that first kiss all the way back. I may literally catch fire. *Stop looking at his mouth,* I tell myself. I need a fan, a cold shower, something.

When we reach my apartment, Blake parks and I turn toward him. Clearly, he's been thinking about the kiss too because his eyes are smoldering. He pulls me in close and we revisit that first kiss.

"Do you want to come up?" I ask.

"I really do," he says. "But I have to work tonight. I need to get home and shower and then head over."

Drat. Okay. It's probably a good thing, because I want this exciting phase to last and if he came upstairs with me now, I know I would have no self-control.

"Okay, I'll let you get going. I had a great time," I say, opening the car door and smiling back at him.

"Me too. Let's do it again soon."

He pulls me in for one more kiss. He grins. "Couldn't resist."

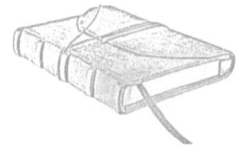

CHAPTER SEVENTEEN

I facetime Isabella as soon as I get back to my apartment. Her image comes up with her kitchen in the background.

"Hey, Kait! Just wait a sec. I have to turn off my stove. I need to hear everything. No distractions." Her face is lit up with anticipation.

She comes back on the screen. "Okay, now spill!"

"We had a perfect day! I really hope this is going somewhere."

"You have those dreamy eyes! I don't remember you ever swooning over a date. Tell me everything!" She props her phone up and sits with her chin propped on her hands. Rapt attention.

"I'm not swooning," I reply with indignation, but secretly I'm pleased. First to be feeling this way and second that she noticed. "We went up into the mountains and tried out cross-country skiing. The scenery was beautiful and I'm not just talking about the landscape." I laugh. While we're talking, I heat up some hot chocolate. I still feel a little chilled.

"No doubt! Sooooo...get to the good stuff. Any chemistry?"

"The man is an excellent kisser."

"Now you have my attention!"

"Yes, a great kisser! Left me wanting more..." I take my phone and hot chocolate to the living room and turn on my gas fireplace, snuggling into the soft couch.

"I take it he left you with only hot chocolate to keep you warm?"

"Yes. He had to work. Left me with only delicious anticipation."

"Oh man, isn't it making you crazy?" She rolls her eyes.

"Honestly, yes. But I think this could be something really good. Maybe it's okay to take it slow."

"True," she draws out the word. "Speaking of slow—the 'most oblivious man in the world' wants me to get all bundled up for some sort of romantic date tonight. He must be borrowing the idea from Blake." Isabella's referring to Darius' distinct lack of a marriage proposal. She thinks he's oblivious to her desire to get engaged but I know the opposite is true. And I also know what he has planned for tonight, and he didn't get the idea from Blake.

"Let the man romance you a bit."

"I will, but it better be good."

Oh, it will be.

"Have fun tonight. Want to run tomorrow morning?"

"Yep. I'll call you."

I give her a thumbs up sign then hang up. Pulling a cozy throw blanket over me, I curl up on the couch in front of the fire and sip my hot chocolate. I really wish Blake was here to snuggle up with. The cat burrows in beside me. He's no Blake, but he'll have to do for now.

I pull out Josie's journal, and open it to where I left off, at the transition from 2019 to 2020.

JANUARY 10, 2020

Stalker seems to have made this his home now. It's nice to come home and find him waiting for me. Sometimes it's a little lonely living alone. I've been trying to keep up with my high school friends, but they're all off at college now and we don't have much in common anymore.

I'm trying not to worry about my mental health because I'm in a good place right now, but that dream thing is happening again. Last year, I kept having that dream about the ocean over and over, and now I'm having a different dream on repeat. In this dream, I'm in a police car with a police officer. We seem to be waiting for something important, I don't know what. We're parked in front of a white house. Is it my house? Did the officer bring me home? There are lots of trees and a big hedge in front of the house so I can't see it very well.

I don't know why I keep having this dream over and over. Is it supposed to have some meaning for me? Last time I had recurring dreams, I was suicidal. I just drifted off into the ocean and let myself be taken by the waves. When my head was in a good place, I thought I just loved the ocean but when I started having thoughts of suicide they seemed tied to those ocean dreams.

With my training for the suicide line, I'm learning all about how the subconscious mind can bring things to the attention of the conscious mind, and one of the ways is through dreams. So, what's the message? Does it have something to do with my parents' death? Am I revisiting something about that time because I'm supposed to help the police? Do I know something that I haven't realized yet and it's stuck in my subconscious? Ugh! I wish I could figure it out.

Hmm, that's interesting. I make a mental note to look into her parents' death and see if there could be any connection to Josie's murder.

FEBRUARY 5, 2020

I put together a little bird house kit today. I'm planning to hang it in the back yard where I can see the birds from my kitchen, but high enough that Stalker can't get to it. I think I'll paint the roof red and the bottom white. I've seen some chickadees in the trees in the neighborhood. I love their little "chick-a-dee-dee-dee" calls. It reminds me of the nest some chickadees made in an empty flowerpot outside my bedroom window when I was a kid. I watched them for months as the eggs hatched and the birds learned to fly. I hope they'll nest in the birdhouse.

Last night, I had the same dream again. Same exact scene. I can't seem to get past the hedge to see the house. What does this mean? Is the hedge a metaphor for something? Am I worried about something happening and the hedge symbolizes something I have to overcome in real life?

FEBRUARY 15, 2020

I put a little cat door in the back for Stalker. That way he can come and go as he likes. Mostly he stays inside where it's warm. He's made himself a little bed on one of my couch cushions. It's nice to have him to snuggle up with on the cold days.

MARCH 10, 2020

Today I saw a chickadee flying into the birdhouse with some pieces of dried grass. I'm excited to see if they make a nest there!

Same dream again. I'm so over it.

I know what it's like to have weird dreams you can't always find the meaning of. I wish I could have talked to her about hers.

MAY 9, 2020

I haven't written for a bit because the world has gone crazy. This virus called COVID-19 has everyone scared. People are dying from it. Everyone stays in their homes and wears masks if they go outside.

I was at the grocery store the other day and I looked around at the people wearing masks. There was this big plastic partition in front of the cashier, and spots on the floor marking off six feet between customers. I felt like I was in some weird sci-fi movie. It doesn't seem real.

MAY 18, 2020

The chickadees are oblivious to everything going

on in the human world. They've built a nest in the bird house, and I can see the female sitting on her eggs. I'm so excited to see the baby birds when they hatch!

I'm lucky to be able to continue working at the hotline. Some people can't go to their jobs right now because this COVID virus has everyone scared and staying home. The hotline put up plastic panels between our desks so we can keep ourselves safe while we work, and we all wear masks. Well, SAFER, at least. I'm still scared. The hotline is going crazy with all the people worried about catching COVID. The people stuck at home are sad and depressed, and some people call us every night just to hear another person's voice. I hope it will end soon.

JUNE 15, 2020

There are baby chickadees learning to fly in my backyard! I won't let Stalker out right now. I'm afraid he'll try to make a meal out of one of them. I've been sitting by the back window, just watching the birds. The parents are squawking at the baby birds, trying to keep them safe. But the babies are little daredevils, jumping out of the nest and flying off just before they hit the ground. It makes my heart skip a beat every time!

I had that dream again. It's been a while since I had it. So long, in fact, I was hoping I wouldn't have it again. I've never gotten past the hedge, but this time a SWAT team runs through the hedge ahead of me and then I'm running in behind them with the officer from the car. Could I be an officer too? It seems like it. I feel scared, like I'm part of the raid. Could the police officer be my partner? Once we are past the hedge, I can tell the house is huge and expensive. We stop at the front door and the SWAT team breaks in. All of us storm through the front door and then it's chaos! Everyone running everywhere. Then I wake up.

JULY 6, 2020

I woke up this morning to Latesha pounding on my door just to tell me Stalker left a mouse at her doorstep again. That cat's a good mouser. Too bad Latesha doesn't appreciate the gifts. I started letting Stalker back out now that the chickadees have left the nest. I can't believe they all survived learning to fly. It was a nice distraction during this time of COVID, since there's nothing else to do. All this staying home is starting to get to me.

It doesn't look like COVID will be gone anytime soon. I've started to go for long walks just to get some air and see people, even if it's from far away.

I remember those COVID pandemic days. It doesn't feel too long ago. But now that the world has returned to normal, I can't imagine going back to quarantining. If I'd known how long COVID would last, it would have been harder to stay home at night, month after month, and wear masks all the time. I too was fortunate that my job was considered essential, and I was able to keep working. It helped me keep a sense of purpose.

I log into the police database and look up the accident involving Josie's parents. The other driver tried to speed through an intersection after their traffic light had already turned red. Josie's parents were going the other way and were t-boned. The other driver died at the scene. If this was an intentional act, I would've expected the other driver to survive. Looks like a dead end.

Reassured, I fall asleep.

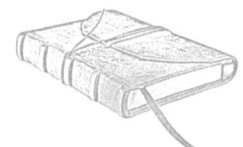

CHAPTER EIGHTEEN

I follow Jeremy's horse with my own as we ride up to the gate and onto the private property.

The day is dreary with patches of fog just starting to burn off as the sun rises over the coastline. This area, the Jurassic Coast, is named for the fossils discovered here. With some luck, today will be our day to find one.

A little girl found some strange looking bones while she was playing in the fields of this farm. Her mother brought the find to town to see if anyone knew what creature left the bones. Our boss, Mary Anning, told them the fossils were those of a giant sea creature, an ichthyosaur. She asked the family to mark the location of the skeleton with a stake. Now we're here to investigate the spot.

Miss Anning has discovered a lot of fossils and become pretty famous for it. This has made her a target for charlatans trying to mislead her with false claims. Once a man asked her to look at his land where he had reportedly discovered some fossils. He wanted to sell her the land for a high price, claiming there would be more fossils where that came from. Miss Anning didn't have the money to purchase the land but asked us to go with her to look at it. She hoped the man would allow her to dig out the fossils for a price. But when we got there, she recognized that the trickster had buried the bones to try to fool her into purchasing his land. He didn't know exactly how the bones should be placed and even I could tell they weren't lined up like any fossil we'd dug up before. When my boss saw how the bones were aligned, she looked more carefully and noticed that a chip on a rib bone was from a slip of her own pickaxe on a previous dig. It was a fossil she'd already excavated and sold.

We don't want to run into another deception, but this location seems to have the hallmarks of a legitimate fossil site. Supporting this, the property owners only asked for a portion of whatever we might make on a fossil sale, not an exorbitant upfront fee.

We head onto the property, careful to close the gates behind us so the livestock won't wander off. Jeremy leads the way, following the directions given to us by the family. We pass a few cows and a herd of goats bleats anxiously as we pass. My horse Champ whickers in return.

Jeremy reigns in his horse at the bottom of a hill. Beside him is a painted stake marking the spot where the bones were found. Champ trudges down the hill, shovels and water canteens swinging with every step. We hobble the horses and set out stakes, connecting them with string to mark the boundaries of the new site.

Now the digging begins. We start removing the topsoil, watching for fossils as we go, careful not to damage anything with our shovels. It's not long before we start to uncover fossilized seashells and then ichthyosaur vertebrae, correctly aligned. The site appears to be authentic after all. Mary will be pleased.

Clearing the topsoil is heavy work and we remove a large area to determine the extent of the finding. We sweat through our clothes in spite of the cool weather. Stopping for a water break, we lean on our shovels and rest a bit.

"That Champ turned ou' to be a good 'orse after all, didn' he?" Jeremy remarks.

"Took a bit o' effort but now 'e's a good worker."

"I thought 'e was full o' beans to begin wi'."

"That 'e was."

"My Charlie's just a plodder now. Gettin' too ol'."

Suddenly, Jeremy makes a strangled sound and flings himself down in the dirt. His quick movement puts me on the alert for danger. I crouch and look around the area. I don't see anyone with a sling shot or a gun, or any other signs of danger. What the bloody hell?

I crouch down beside Jeremy. "What's a matter?"

Jeremy is scrabbling in the dirt, and I'm considering that he may have gone quite mad until he holds up a shiny chunk of rock. I look at it, stunned.

"It's gold!" Jeremy jumps to his feet and begins dancing around. "We found gold! Look! We're rich!"

My heart begins pounding in my ears. Gold! I have a glimpse of myself strutting through London in fine linens, with a gold pocket watch. I can finally propose to my girl. And buy a stable full of beautiful horses...

"Let's see it." I grab the chunk of rock out of his hand. My heart sinks when I see it. "It's iron pyrite, ye damn fool!"

I wake smiling at George's antics from my dream. I know why I'm dreaming of shiny gold things. As if on cue, my phone buzzes with a text.

"I'm at your door. Open up." It's Isabella, just as I expected.

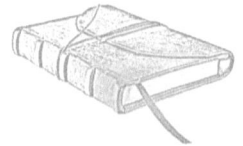

CHAPTER NINETEEN

I traipse to the door in my yoga-pant pajamas, tripping over a stuffed mouse as I go. Looking through the peephole out of habit, I spot a large, glittery object held up to it. Chuckling, I open the door to Hurricane Isabella. She blows into the apartment, jumping up and down and screaming, "Look! Look! Look!" Stalker dashes to hide under a chair.

I take her proffered left hand and gasp appreciatively at the huge diamond ring on her finger, not even having to pretend. It's truly a wonder to behold.

"How can you even hold your hand up with that on it?" I tease.

"Isn't it beautiful? He did so well!"

I coached him a little on what style she would like but Darius really did nail it. I hug her long and hard and then pull her over to the couch to get the full story.

"Okay. Tell me everything."

Darius and I've been discussing each detail of his proposal for the past few months. Isabella's obsessed with the

Northern Lights, and Darius wanted to catch a dramatic aurora as a backdrop for his proposal. It hasn't been easy since one can't always predict when the lights will appear. The winter months are best, which is why it's taken so long.

Darius purchased the ring last summer and has been waiting for the right moment to propose ever since. He attempted a trip to Mount Rainier in September when the lights were forecast to be present; however, a last-minute overcast sky made him abort that attempt. Now finally, we're in prime Northern Lights viewing season and Darius has been diligently following the forecasts to find the best time. Isabella has no idea the lengths he went to but I'll be sure to let her know, now that the event has occurred. A woman should know when she's been loved like that.

"So, he told me to dress warmly and wouldn't explain himself. Said he wanted to surprise me. At first, I thought he got the idea from your date with Blake, but then I realized he was planning it for a while."

Oh yes, a long while.

"He brought out some blankets and this picnic basket, and he wouldn't let me look in it. So, we head north in the car, and he's so mysterious. Won't tell me where we're going. We get all the way up to Deception Pass and he takes me to this secluded little spot with a beautiful view out over the water. We wrap up in the warm blankets, and he pulls out these little thermoses of lobster bisque—it's so good with the cold air, and it's just steaming." She wiggles her fingers to illustrate.

"And the sun is going down. Then he has little mini crock pots of fettuccini alfredo, with mushrooms, just like I like it. It's so romantic sitting there with our gourmet picnic meal in crock pots, looking out over the water at sunset. He keeps checking his watch, and I'm starting to wonder what he's up to. And then, you won't even believe it, just as it gets dark, we start to see flickering greens and pinks in the sky and the most amazing Northern Lights start to dance out over the water." She waves her hands, mimicking the undulations of the aurora, caught up in the drama of the moment.

I definitely believe it.

"I've always wanted to see them like that, in a spot with no light pollution. So, then he gets out chocolate-covered straw-berries and champagne, pops the cork, and pours it into crys-tal flutes that come out of that bottomless picnic basket. He puts everything down on a rock beside me and when I look up, there he is, down on one knee, with this!" She gestures to the huge diamond on her hand.

"What did he say?"

"He says, 'I wanted the perfect moment to ask you to spend the rest of your life with me. I love you. Will you marry me?'" Her eyes are full of happy tears.

Good for Darius. He could have gone for corny but he kept it simple and beautiful.

"Did you just want to melt?"

"It was the best moment of my life. I love that man. I can't believe how much trouble he went to."

Believe it, girl, I think. Darius knows exactly how lucky he is. And she's just as lucky. I'm deliriously happy for them both. Isabella literally bounces on the couch cushions in her excitement. I hug her again as we savor the moment.

"How do you feel?"

"Excited. So in love. Weirdly sad to say goodbye to my young-unmarried-persona."

"Seems about right."

144

"Go get in your running gear. We haven't run together in so long. I thought it would be nice to get out there together this morning."

I recognize this for the gesture it is. She wants me to feel a part of her happiness and to know that no matter how good things are with Darius, she won't forget our friendship.

"Hey, you haven't met Stalker yet." He's hiding, what with the screaming and the bouncing. I coax him out from under the chair.

"Awww, he's beautiful..." Isabella's cut off by a hiss and swipe of a claw. She pulls her hand back and laughs, "...but not very friendly."

"Nope. He'll get used to you, but his personality is decidedly 'slow to warm up.'"

I pull on my running items, still slightly dazed by the news. The shift in our lives is disorienting. Isabella's engaged. Even though I've been aware for months that this was coming, it's going to take a moment to get used to it.

We drive a short distance to a small lake. The weather is cooler today and we have to force ourselves to emerge from the warm cocoon of the car to the crisp fall air for a couple of laps around the lake. It doesn't take long for our muscles to warm up as we ease into a comfortable pace. Our breath mists the air as we chat.

For a moment, I can forget about bodies dragged down a deserted street, murderers, and suicidal teenagers. Life at this moment on a sunny fall Sunday is about new boyfriends and engagements and running with a friend.

Isabella interrogates me on all the details of my date with Blake and I tell her everything, including my fears that this fragile fledgling of a relationship won't take off.

"What if Blake doesn't contact me again?" I'm already doubting my instincts. I thought we had a great connection on our date. But what if I'm wrong? What if he didn't feel the same way and he never calls?

"Don't do this to yourself! I know exactly how great you thought the date was by how over the moon you were when you got back. I'm sure he felt the same way. Just be patient." Isabella tries to make me see reason.

"I hate waiting for contact. Maybe I should reach out to him..."

"Just wait a bit. Didn't he work last night? He's probably sleeping right now. Just give him a minute."

"You're right. You're right. I know, you're right," I concede.

When I get back, I check my rudimentary security system. Yep, the napkin I put in the door is still present. As I remove the napkin, I notice a text from my mom: "See you at 3:00!" I had volunteered to drop my parents at the airport.

I reply, "Yep. I'll be on time."

"Perfect. See you then."

I sit down with Josie's journal pages, determined to do some work today before I head over to pick up my parents.

AUGUST 25, 2020

I've started doing some night shifts at the call line and taking some supervised suicide calls. I always have someone on with me in case the call isn't something I can handle.

I've completed the training course, and I'm taking some college classes, but I still have so much to learn. All my classes are online right now because of

COVID. I find myself craving more human contact, even with my job at the call line.

All that book learning doesn't really prepare me for when a caller says they want to end their life. I can't help but remember when *I* felt like that. It wasn't very long ago. I have to be strong for the caller. That's the hard part. But I love that I can help someone. It makes me feel like something good came out of that time in my life.

SEPTEMBER 1, 2020

I've started having the police dream more often again. It's always the same. I seem to be getting farther into the dream each time now. Maybe this means I'm working things out. Every time I enter the house, I go to the left with the police officer. I've decided he must be my partner. I follow him through the house, always taking the same route.

Each time we come to a new room, he stops beside the door, looks in quickly, then sweeps the room with his gun first before entering. He yells "clear" to tell me it's safe before I follow. In each room, we open drawers and cupboards, looking for something. I don't know what. Maybe drugs? Then I wake up.

We've been talking about dream interpretation in one of my classes. I wonder if this dream is me trying to "clear" my mind of my own suicidal memories so I can focus on the caller. I think I might ask my professor for help analyzing this dream sequence. I just want to get out of this perpetual dream loop.

OCTOBER 15, 2020

There's a guy at work I kind of like. Eli. He sits at the cubicle beside me.

Last night, I answered a call that was hard. The person was talking about how they wanted to drown. It reminded me of the dream I used to have of drowning when I wanted to end my own life. I'm so glad I'm not in that place anymore, but talking about drowning kind of triggered me.

When I got off the call, I just started sobbing and I couldn't stop for a bit. Eli just sat with his hand on my shoulder until I could get under control. I was glad he was there. He said sometimes he feels sad after a call too but it's important to talk about it. We talked it out, and I felt a lot better after.

NOVEMBER 25, 2020

I emailed my professor about my police dream, and he said he wasn't sure what to think about it. He was impressed at some of the details I could remember, like the inside of the police cruiser, the items in the house, things that were said. He said it almost seemed like I had some past traumatic experience in a police cruiser that made me recall actual details. They seemed too authentic for my mind to be making them up.

Maybe it was the ride I took with the police after my parents died and this is my subconscious working through the trauma of it. I guess I might remember more than I think I do from that day. Did I repress some of the memory of it?

> The dream always feels so real, so maybe I just tend to notice the details. I've had this dream so many *f-ing* times, why *wouldn't* I know every detail of it by now?!?

I'm no stranger to weird, vivid dreams. I know how frustrating it is when I can't figure out what they're trying to tell me. But *my* dreams aren't like anyone else's.

It's likely Josie's dreams are just her mind's way of working through her daytime issues. Her hotline job will continue to bring her back to how she felt to be suicidal but, in many ways, this seems to be helping her come to terms with it.

I wish the journal was more helpful in finding a direct threat to Josie, but at least I'm finding out more about her. That could be helpful as well.

At exactly 3:00 p.m. sharp, I arrive at my parents' home. No way I'm going to be late picking them up. SeaTac airport will be crammed with holiday travelers today. My little Prius seems even smaller than it actually is with my parents' luggage jammed into the trunk and their warm coats and carry-ons stuffed in beside them.

"Are you sure you need these big coats?" I ask.

My mom is quick to respond. "Yep! You know Nebraska. The weather is unpredictable. It could be seventy degrees or below freezing. We used to say, 'If you don't like the weather...'"

"Just wait five minutes!" we all say together, laughing. I remember sitting outside with short sleeves one Thanksgiving and another making snowmen in my grandparents' yard. I've always loved the randomness of it. In this world where so much is as expected, it's nice to have some manageable surprises.

The last few years, we've made it a tradition to go to the lighting of the holiday lights in downtown Omaha. It's magical to see the lights all blink on for the first time in the season. I'll miss watching it with my family this year.

"Kaitlyn, I'm so glad you'll be with Sandra and Joe," my mom says. "Next year maybe you'll be free and can join us again."

"I hope so. It all just depends on if we are assigned a case or not."

Wanting to change the subject, I mention the journal to my parents as we make the drive to the airport.

"Is that hard, Kaitlyn? Reading the thoughts of someone you know won't survive past the end of the journal? It seems so odd that after you read the last page, she will die." My mom is a writer, and this is an interesting perspective. I hadn't thought of it that way exactly.

"I guess you're right, it's like reading a novel when you've already read the last page and you know it won't be a happy ending. That does make me feel sad. I've gotten to know Josie better through the entries. If only I could change the ending. At least I can bring her some justice if we can figure out who did this."

"Any leads?" my father asks.

"Jerry! You know she can't tell you that!"

"Shhhh, Rachel, maybe she'll forget." Dad laughs.

"I wish I could tell you more."

"Seems like the murderer usually ends up being someone the victim knows," Dad comments.

"True enough."

"No family to investigate?"

"Her parents died when she was young. There's just an aunt. And a cat. Which, by the way, is staying with me for now."

My parents exchange knowing looks.

"For now," I repeat.

"Right," they say in unison, then laugh.

"I know, I'm already getting attached," I admit, laughing with them.

I don't bring up Blake. The relationship is too new, and I don't want them asking me questions I haven't even asked myself yet.

Stopping curbside at the airport drop-lane, I give them both big hugs and wish them safe travels. Watching them drag their luggage and winter gear into the busy terminal, I'm relieved not to be joining the pre-holiday travel craziness, even though I'll miss not being with them for the holiday.

Once I'm alone again in my apartment, I go back to worrying that Blake might not have had as great a time as I did yesterday. I haven't heard from him all day. I try not to think too much about it as I heat up a microwave dinner.

I've finally distracted myself streaming a movie when my phone buzzes with an incoming Facetime.

It's Blake! He appears on the screen, his hair adorably mussed up, his eyes sleepy. "How are you?"

"Pretty good." *I miss you already,* I want to say but I don't dare. I don't want to seem needy.

"What did you do today?"

"I went for a run with my friend, Isabella." I don't mention Isabella's engagement. It seems like a taboo topic for so early

151

in a relationship.

"It looked like perfect weather for running. My shift was over this morning, and I went home and slept. Just got up. Last night we had a number of victims from a motor vehicle pile-up. Some were life-flighted in. A few didn't make it."

"Wow. That must've been a tough night. I'm sorry."

"Yeah. Glad to put it behind me."

"When can I see you again?" we both say at the same time.

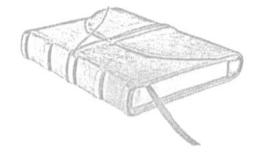

CHAPTER TWENTY

"Dr. Goodman," I greet my mentor as I enter the doctor's lounge and find him struggling to sit down in a chair. It's been a few months since the car hit him out front of the hospital. His legs are mending well, but it's likely he'll have a permanent limp, and I can tell they still cause him pain. Just last week on rounds, the pain forced him to sit at a patient's bedside while we discussed the case. The patient commented he needed a folding chair to take with him on rounds. Dr. Goodman tried to be a good sport, but I could tell he didn't appreciate the comment. He'd always prided himself on his robust health, often taking the stairs two at a time on rounds with the rest of us trailing after him.

Dr. Goodman tries, unsuccessfully, to sit down while holding his patient records. He needs both hands to ease his weakened quadriceps into a sitting position but the manila file folders he's holding are preventing this.

"Here, let me help you with that." I take the files and papers from his hands and pick up a few that have dropped to the floor.

"Thanks." He gives me a self-conscious smile, sinking into the chair with the help of his now unencumbered hands. He reaches to take the papers back, once he's seated.

"How are you doing?" I ask.

"Well, thanks to you, my legs have healed pretty straight, but they ache something terrible and they're still weak from disuse."

I nod in sympathy. "Did they find the man who hit you?" The police had come by after the accident to question me and some other witnesses. I had a good description of the man and the car that hit Dr. Goodman, which I related to the police.

The driver was distraught at the time of the accident, and it appeared he would stay to take responsibility. But then, mysteriously, he fled the scene and couldn't be found in the days following.

"Well, the police came by a few days later to talk to me about it. They told me they suspected the man was a bootlegger and the car was so heavily loaded with alcohol, it was difficult for the driver to stop in time when he saw me. He was probably making a delivery to a speakeasy." He shifts his legs to a more comfortable position. "They thought that was why he didn't stick around. He was worried about them finding his illegal payload or following him to the secret bar."

"Well, that's interesting. I gave them a pretty good description and the license plate number. I'm surprised they didn't find him with that."

"I thought the same thing, so I asked my sister about it. She's a secretary at the precinct."

"Did she know anything?"

"Well, here's the thing. She said word among the secretaries *is, they were paid off."*

"Who was paid off? The police?"

"Right. The rumor is it was Al Capone who paid someone to keep the accident quiet."

"Al Capone? He was here?" The name itself instills fear.

"The man himself. I guess he has a brother that lives in the area and Capone oversees some shady business here. He even visits now and then."

"You mean his brother James? But isn't he a prohibition agent?"

"Yes, that's right."

"Do you think they're in on it together?"

"Could be. Who knows. Personally, once I heard that name, I decided not to pursue it any further."

"I don't blame you."

The dream dissolves. Something's bothering me. It's hovering in my subconscious, so close I can almost grab it, but the thought is just out of reach. Is there something relating to a suspect? We know the killer left the scene. Is there something about the car or the accident I need to pay attention to? A mob tie? Bootlegging? I'm missing something.

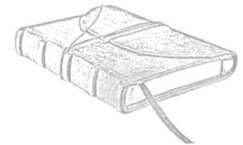

CHAPTER TWENTY-ONE

It promises to be a busy Monday. As we accumulate more leads, we'll have more motives and evidence needing exploration. The work will only increase from here.

First up on our agenda is interviewing suspected narcissist Jennifer Klein. Should be an interesting conversation. Jennifer is a forty-two-year-old with a master's degree in counseling. She lives alone in a nice suburb about a thirty-minute drive from the hotline. Her house is the smallest on the street, but it's well taken care of; well-tended landscape, green lawn, fresh lavender paint on the siding.

Jennifer opens the door at our ring, peering out at us with a quizzical expression. She's short and portly with a tenuous smile and tight curls framing her face. "Hello?"

We introduce ourselves and show our badges.

"We have some questions for you about a former colleague of yours at the suicide hotline," I explain.

"I'll help if I can. Please, come in." She stands aside so we can enter. The living space is open concept, with an eye-pleasing flow into the space from the entry. A few upscale pieces of furniture are arranged around a briskly burning gas fireplace. Large picture windows look out on a lush green backyard. The home is cheerful and tastefully decorated.

"Please, make yourself comfortable." She gestures to a couple of chairs. "Is there anything I can get you?" She's pleasant and hospitable, fussing over getting us settled. We decline any refreshments.

"Who are you here to talk about?" she asks, settling in a chair facing us, her curiosity evident.

"Jocelyn Miller," Joe says.

She nods absently, like she doesn't know the purpose of our visit. "Oh, well, I wouldn't exactly call her a colleague. I have a Master's, and she hasn't even completed an undergraduate degree." Ah, *there* you are, Jennifer. Your sense of superiority is showing.

"You worked with her at the hotline?" I ask.

"Yes."

"What did you think of her?"

"I thought she was allowed to take calls that were above her training. Calls that should've been given to me." Her voice has a note of condescension.

"Did you have disagreements with her over this or anything else?"

"Yes. I don't mince words, detectives, I told her exactly what I thought."

"How did she respond to this?"

"She didn't say much to my face, but then she must have told my boss because he fired me. It wasn't fair at all." She looks petulant.

"She got you fired?"

"Yes."

"Did your boss tell you Josie complained?"

"No. He didn't have to. I knew it was her. That cowardly little girl, she didn't have the guts to say something to my face." And there's the narcissistic attitude coming out. Gotcha.

"Did you get a new job after you left the hotline?"

"Yes, I found a job at a family counseling office. They asked me to do some training before I started seeing my own families."

"How did that go?"

"I thought it was going well, but then one day, out of the blue, they just told me they didn't have a position for me anymore."

"When did that happen?"

"Three weeks ago."

"Were you angry?"

"You bet I was."

"Were you angry when you left the suicide hotline?"

"Yes, very angry."

"We spoke with your boss, Brad Dunford. He said you made some threats."

"Yes, I...I said things I didn't mean."

"What sorts of things?"

"Oh, something about a bomb—I didn't mean it, of course. I just said it in the heat of the moment."

"That's a very serious threat."

"I realize that now."

"Did you do anything else?"

"I called the hotline a few times and got angry with the workers when they said foolish things. I can't believe they fired me when they have so many idiots that still work there."

"You called and pretended to be suicidal?"

"Well, yes." She at least has the integrity to look a little embarrassed. "I was trying to prove a point, you see. The hotline workers that still work there are not as good as I was. I knew if I pretended to be suicidal, I could catch them in their mistakes and prove how wrong they were to fire me. Me! I was the best one there."

"Did you know Josie was killed last week?" Joe takes over the interview.

"What? I hadn't heard. I don't pay much attention to the news and I don't work there anymore. That's shocking. What happened?"

"She was run over on her walk home."

"Terrible." Her face is carefully blank, her sincerity difficult to determine.

"Can you tell me what you were doing last Monday night?"

"I went to a lecture on family therapy techniques." In that moment, Jennifer realizes she's a suspect. The bravado slips away.

"What time did the lecture end?"

"At 10:30."

"Where did you go after the lecture?"

"I went straight home."

"Can anyone confirm that?"

"No."

"What color car do you drive?"

"Red."

"That's the car you were driving that night? The red one?"

"Well, no. I guess it wasn't. I borrowed my sister's car because mine wouldn't start."

"What color is it?"

"White."

We get contact information for her sister. Our plan is to collect a paint sample from her car if she'll consent.

After leaving the house, we head back to the station while discussing Jennifer. She doesn't have a solid alibi and she has motive. She blamed Josie for the loss of her job, and then she was faced with these feelings again when she lost her new job. She's a credible suspect. It seems unlikely she'd bring a smashed-up car back to her sister, we'll need to check into it.

When we arrive back at the station, Bob is waiting to talk with us. "I looked into the addresses from Josie's trash bin." He holds his phone up for us to look at.

"Oh yeah?" Joe peers at the addresses on Bob's phone screen. "What'd you find?"

"At first, I couldn't figure out the connection. They're all houses located within a few miles of Josie's but I wasn't sure why she was looking into them. Then I noticed that one of the houses was an address I already looked up."

Now he has our interest. "Which one?" I ask.

"It's Josie's landlord, Bill Crawley."

"Oh, so was it just a list of important addresses? Her landlord, her plumber, etc?"

"No, not quite. I noticed one of the addresses was on her street. Turns out it's the house that James White lives in."

"Jimmy, interesting," I muse. "Do they have some sort of connection?"

"I wondered that too. I cross-referenced them and it turns out that Jimmy and Josie share a landlord, Bill Crawley. So, I checked the other five addresses and they're all rented by Crawley."

"Huh. I wonder why she was interested in them. Maybe

she wanted to gather all the renters to complain about the poor upkeep."

"Could be. One of the other rental addresses flagged in our system. Guess whose it is."

"Her admirer? Eli?"

"Nope. It was Prince Charles himself, Chuck Thornton."

"That can't be a coincidence. Maybe we better go talk to Chuck," I say. Turning to Joe, I ask, "Is he still in lockup?"

"I checked, thinking you might want to talk to him. He's had some trouble making bail, so he's still here," Bob says.

We have Bob set Chuck up in an interview room. I run over and get him a burger and a Coke from Barrett's. His eyes light up when he sees me walk in with the take-out bag.

"Chuck, I got you a little something. Thought you might be sick of jail food. We just have a few questions for you first." The burger does smell pretty enticing. Even my mouth waters.

"Now, Chuck, we're curious what your relationship is with Bill Crawley."

Chuck manages to tear his eyes away from the burger. "He's my landlord."

"How often do you see him?"

"Just for repairs and what not." He's much more coherent now that the alcohol is gone from his system.

"What about James White—Jimmy? You had his phone number on a piece of paper at your house."

He shrugs. "We'd have a beer sometimes."

We're really flying blind here. I'm not sure how to tease out if there is some reason Josie had the addresses. I decide to try the tack that maybe she was trying to see if Crawley let all his properties fall into such a state of disrepair. "Did you know Jocelyn Miller? She went by Josie." He looks blank so

I try again. "Twenty-two, dark hair, green eyes, lived in the white house, three houses in on the next block."

A flash of recognition registers. "Yeah, I know who you mean but I never talked to her."

Had she just not had a chance to talk to the others yet? "Do you know why she might have your address and some others that Crawley rented to?"

"No," he draws the word out, hesitant. There's something here. "Can I see what addresses?" he asks, a little too urgently.

"Sure." I turn the list toward him. He looks through the addresses and there is a definite change in his demeanor. His pupils are dilated. Sweat appears on his brow. He's afraid. We must be on to something. *Josie* must've been on to something.

"Anything you want to share with us, *Prince Charles*? Is that your street name?" I give him the burger and soda. I had intended to use it as an incentive to answer our questions expeditiously before the burger got cold, but now I think a token of goodwill might make him see that we'll work with him. "If you've got anything to tell us, now's the time. Before we start going down this list and bringing everyone in for questioning."

He takes the burger, hungrily biting into it. "I got nothing to say," he says through the mouthful.

"Okay then. Guess we'll just have to go and ask Jimmy if he'll tell us what you've been up to. Maybe he'll want a deal," I say, standing up.

Chuck freezes. "*I* want a deal."

"Oh yeah? You got something to tell us?"

"Yeah, but only if I get off. No time."

"We can't promise that, Chuck, but we can tell the DA that you cooperated. If the information is good enough, you might get a reduced sentence in exchange for your testimony."

He contemplates this as he eats his burger, washing it down with the soda. He finishes the meal and sits for a moment with his head in his hands, clearly torn.

"Chuck, if you're just playing a minor part in this, it would be in your best interest to come clean now," I say, making a guess that Crawley and Jimmy are likely the ringleaders.

"I just have the weed and a bit o' hash. I don't have no fentanyl," he says suddenly. He just said the magic word. If he has inside information on fentanyl distribution, he just might have a get-out-of-jail-free card.

"So—Jimmy and Crawley—*they* have the fentanyl?" Joe asks.

"Right." He pauses, then seems to make up his mind to distance himself from this hornets' nest. "Crawley set it all up. He inherited the rental homes, turned some into grow houses. I sold the stuff out of mine. Worked just fine but then he had to go and get greedy. Saw how much money fentanyl brought. I tol' him...no way I was gettin' into that stuff. But he just found others to make it. I wanted out after that. Fentanyl kills people. I don' want nothin' to do wi' it."

A tap sounds from the window behind us. I leave Joe with Chuck and enter the observation room. Bob has the phone in his hand. "I called over to the narcotics division as soon as he said 'fentanyl.' They'll be down straight away to take his statement."

"Good work," I tell Bob.

When the narcotics officer arrives I fill him in on what Crawley told us. His eyes widen at the magnitude of the discovery. They'll want to make sure this is dealt with correctly, which I suspect means we will be told to back off.

As if on cue, he says, "You need to leave this to us now. If your murder ties into this, we'll look into that *after* the arrests are made. We don't want to spook them. This is very delicate." He heads in to take over the interview from Joe.

"Bob. The connection you made with those addresses was fantastic. If they can break up this fentanyl ring, it'll save many lives," I tell him. The puppy-dog grin is back. I clap him on the shoulder. "Nice work. We'll make a detective out of you yet."

I wonder how this ties into Josie's death. Did they know she was on to them? Seems like a likely motive but while the DEA sorts this out, we'll have to pursue other avenues of investigation.

I have a sudden thought. How did Crawley's wife die? He sure came into a convenient inheritance. From what I remember, she had poor health. I wonder if that's the whole story.

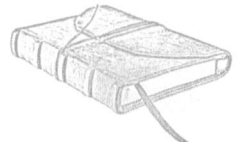

CHAPTER TWENTY-TWO

Since we're forbidden from investigating the suspects in the drug ring we decide to continue down the suspect list with an interview of Josie's admirer, Eli Rodriguez. He lives in an apartment not far from the suicide hotline where he and Josie worked evenings together.

We buzz his apartment a few times before he finally answers, coming to the door with rumpled clothing and heavy-lidded eyes. Looks like we woke him sleeping late after his shift at the hotline last night. Perfect. Catching him with his defenses down will put us in control, just where we want to be.

He's wearing hastily pulled on sweatpants and a hoody, his hair sticking up in several places. Eli looks to be early twenties, tall, dark hair and eyes. Nice looking.

"I'm Detective Riley and this is Detective Kruse. We'd like to ask you some questions about Jocelyn Miller." He blinks at us, slowly, uncomprehending. "Josie?" Joe prompts.

"Oh yeah. Okay. Why? She wasn't the girl on the news who

was killed, was she?"

"Yes, it was her. We are looking into her death."

He stands in stunned silence in his doorway.

"You going to invite us in, Eli?" Joe asks.

"Uh, sure." He steps backward and then leads us inside. As he goes, he picks up discarded pieces of clothing from the furniture in a futile attempt to tidy up.

His apartment is disgusting. A week's worth of dishes are stacked in the sink. Plates and bowls are scattered about with crusts of dried food in them. Pizza boxes and other trash are on the couch. Dirty clothing litters the surfaces. I grimace at the dirty socks on the kitchen counter. Mouse droppings are visible in a corner. No way I'm sitting on anything in this room. It's all I can do not to gag or hold my nose.

"Clean anytime this century, Eli?" Joe isn't going to let him off the hook. "Put a coat and some shoes on, we're going to take this down to the precinct." Thank goodness.

Eli looks for a moment like he might protest, but then he complies, heading off to find a coat. As we leave the apartment building, Joe says, "Eli, which vehicle is yours? Could you point it out to us?"

Poor kid. He's still a bit fuzzy on what's going on. He points to a battered white Kia. White paint, low profile. It could be the vehicle that hit Josie. There's no front-end damage though. We look closer to be sure. I notice some paint overspray on one of the front headlights and point it out to Joe.

"Eli, this paint looks new." I indicate the overspray.

"It does?" He looks confused. Joe and I share a glance.

"Yes. You didn't just paint it?"

"Uh uh." He shakes his head, no.

Why would he lie when the recent work is so obvious?

Must be too tired to come up with an excuse. Once we get a warrant, we'll get a paint sample to check against the paint on Josie's umbrella.

We set up in an interview room and begin the questioning in earnest. We don't want to give him too long to wake up and realize he needs to come up with a cover story.

"Eli, what was your relationship with Josie?" I start in.

"We just worked together."

"Were you two friendly at work?"

"Sure. She was pretty cool. We would talk sometimes between calls."

"Were you attracted to her?"

"Yeah, I guess so."

"Did you ask her out?"

"Not on a date or anything," he says.

"Did you offer to walk her home?"

"Well, yeah, I did."

"Just a nice guy wanting her to get home safe, or were you hoping for a little more?"

"Both, I guess." He scratches his unshaven jaw and gives us a lecherous grin. Gross.

"But she never took you up on that?"

"Nope."

"Did that make you mad? I'd be mad if a girl was nice at work but then didn't want me to 'walk her home.'" Joe uses air quotes. He's attempting to win Eli over by acting sympathetic, but the lewd comment coming from someone I care about makes me want to heave up my lunch.

"I guess a little," Eli says.

Interesting.

"Did you ever follow her home?"

"Yeah, a few times. To see where she lived."

Even more interesting.

"How about last Monday night, the night she died?"

"No, I was tired. Went home and went to sleep."

Sure.

"Did you see her leave?"

"I went home before her that night."

"And you went straight home?"

"Yes." He looks as if he has a sudden realization. "Am I a suspect?"

No shit, Sherlock.

"We're just trying to establish a timeline, see if anyone saw her that night," Joe says.

We excuse ourselves and step out of the interview room, into the observation room where we can see him through the glass. Ray and Bob have been watching our progress. They're both waiting with news. "I got that paint sample from Crawley's vehicle this morning, we should know if it's a match in a day or two," Ray reports. Good news there.

Bob has been looking up Eli's history to give us some background. "Eli's criminal record was pretty clean but it looks like he has some prior issues with a girlfriend," he says.

"Great work, Bob. What did you find?" Joe asks.

"In 2021, Mandy Perkins took out a restraining order against him. She says he was stalking her and once chased her in his car. She had some injuries relating to that."

Sounds like a classic escalation of behavior. Going from chasing to running down.

Joe goes back into the interview room.

"Eli, tell me about Mandy Perkins. She had a restraining

order against you. What was that about?"

"That bi..." He rethinks the expletive. "Mandy was a real pain. She broke up with me and when she left, she took my watch and some money. I tried to get it back, but she said she didn't take it. Didn't know anything about it. I knew she was lying so I followed her a few times...until she got a restraining order."

"She had some injuries. Care to explain that?"

"I was following her in my car, and she saw me. Started running and then tripped over some lady's dog. Got scraped up. The lady called the cops."

Joe rejoins us in the observation room.

"What do you think?" I ask.

"A lot of things fit. The prior stalking. The white car. He knew when she would leave. And he might have motive if he thought she was turning down his advances. But still..." He rubs his temples. "...I don't know. I could see him hurting her in the heat of the moment if she turned him down, but I have a hard time seeing the rage it would take to mow her down and drag her body a block with his car."

"Agree. But you never know what might cause someone to lash out. He thinks, *I've been holding her hand all this time, helping her at work. I've put my time in, and I deserve better treatment.* Not what a normal person would think, but the person who did this would have to be a narcissist or a socio-path, or both." I'm thinking of my dream.

"Maybe. We really don't have any specific evidence to hold him more than twenty-four hours. Let's keep him over-night and get a warrant to search his place and vehicle."

When I get home, I sit down with Josie's journal again, hoping to find out more about Eli. There are only a few copied pages left.

FEBRUARY 10, 2021

Stalker did the funniest thing yesterday. A bird was trying to eat some sunflower seeds I sprinkled out in the backyard for it, and I guess I didn't put them far enough away from the house. Stalker saw the bird in the yard and went flying out through the cat door. He kept pouncing at it, and finally the bird got up in a tree right beside our fence and was squawking at Stalker. That silly cat, he climbed up the fence and took a flying leap at the bird. He looked like one of those flying squirrels. Of course, he missed and sent pine needles flying everywhere as he tried to hold onto the branch. The bird flew off without a scratch. I caught it all on video on my phone. It got over one hundred thousand likes on Insta.

Come on Josie, let's get to the important stuff, I think.

MARCH 1, 2021

I'm having that dream again. I wonder when I'll ever get to the end. I find I'm dreading entering the house each time, there's so much chaos. At least everything's the same each time, so I know nothing new will happen until the part I ended at the last time. We search through the same rooms and never find anything. Does this mean I'm searching for something in my life? I'm kinda over trying to analyze this dream. The last couple of times I've had it, we stop a man trying to run and put cuffs on him. Then I wake up.

The other officers in my dreams call me John or Officer Bowen. Is it weird to keep having these dreams about the same person? A person who isn't me?

APRIL 10, 2021

Eli was really nice to me again yesterday. He makes me feel better when the calls are hard.

There's a new guy on the night shift and I try and help him, just like Eli helps me. Eli doesn't seem to like me helping the new guy. I guess he might be a little jealous. I don't think of Eli that way though. There was a time when I thought he was cute, but now I just think of him as a friend.

One time he offered to walk me home. He seemed a little mad when I told him no. Then I thought I might've seen him drive by my street later and it creeped me out.

MAY 19, 2021

I'm still dreaming about being Officer Bowen. Now I seem to be dreaming about times before the raid. John and his partner seem to always look out for each other and they have a lot of fun times together outside of work. Now I'm dreaming of them going out with other officers to have a beer after long shifts. I like these dreams a lot better.

JUNE 20, 2021

I'm so freaked out, I had to write this down to try to make sense of it. I looked up Officer John Bowen and it turns out he was a real person. And guess when he died. June 20, 2001. That's right. On my birthday. How can that be? Why am I having dreams about someone else's life?!?

This is the last copied page. *WTF?* So many thoughts are coursing through my brain that I close my eyes to try to sort through them. Josie had dreams about a past life! Or maybe more than one past life? I've never met anyone else that had that ability before. I always assumed I was alone.

Bob only copied off a portion of the journal pages so I could start reading it on the first night. I need to copy off the rest of the journal!

My chest aches with the knowledge that I'll never get to share this experience with Josie. If only I'd met her before she was murdered. I could've helped her to understand her dreams. And just to know we weren't alone would have been such a solace. To both of us.

Her dreams really don't seem to be helping her though. They're almost a menacing presence with the suicidal ocean dreams and now the raid.

This unexpected discovery of another person with the same ability is mind-blowing. I need time to process it. I'm not ready to go to sleep and have one of my own past-life dreams again.

Sensing my inner turmoil, the cat brings its favorite stuffed mouse over and drops it on the couch beside me. He puts his paw on my leg to get my attention.

"You're worried about me, aren't you?"

I throw the mouse, and he retrieves it over and over. But I'm craving human companionship.

I try facetiming Blake, but he doesn't answer. He's prob-ably working tonight. I try not to read too much into it. When we talked yesterday, we both wanted to get together again but we weren't able to come up with a day that worked with both our schedules. We decided to try again in a week or so, after the holiday. Or maybe he wasn't really interested and was letting me down easy, pretending he couldn't find a day that worked. Ugh! New relationships are so hard to interpret.

CHAPTER TWENTY-THREE

I'm in my home therapy office with one of my regular patients. He sits like a deflated balloon in the chair opposite my desk.

"Dr. Steel, I just can't seem to shake this feeling. I'm tired all the time. I can hardly get out of bed, and this sadness weighs heavy on me no matter what I do to try to lift it," he says. "Why can't I get excited about anything? Even my daughter's wedding coming up doesn't interest me. This should be a happy time in my life, but I just don't have the energy to enjoy it."

"I'm sorry you keep experiencing these feelings. I wish I could help more. Your symptoms all fit with those of depression. Not getting excited about an event that would normally make someone happy is one of the hallmarks."

"Right," he sighs, his voice listless. I'm worried about him. We don't seem to be making any progress.

"Our therapy sessions haven't been helping you enough. Do you think it's time to consider medication? There are some new ones on the market, Selective Serotonin Reuptake Inhibitors, such as Prozac, that are more effective than the previous ones."

I don't prescribe medications since I didn't undergo medical training as a psychologist, but I can recommend a psychiatrist who can. Maybe it's time for him to move on.

"I really don't like the idea of taking a pill. Won't it mess with my mind?"

"I understand your hesitation, but sometimes we need to consider that brain chemistry is different from person to person. For some, it's hard to work through depression without some help to normalize that brain chemistry."

"I'll think about it." He doesn't look optimistic. But then, he never does. He's always pale and apathetic.

He gets up slowly and I walk him to the door. It's late. He's only able to come to sessions after working hours, so I've been seeing him at night in my home office.

I sit down on the office couch and take off my shoes, intending to just lie down for a minute. The day has been busy and exhausting.

I start to dream as I drift off on the couch. I'm dreamin of Dr. Abrams again....as if I am him.

Peering through the eyepieces of a microscope, I adjust the focus. Disc-like red blood cells come into view on the slide below. They are so big and pale, I think. There's a large textbook open beside the microscope. "Pernicious Anemia" is the title of the page. After seeing the blood smear I'm certain this is what my patient suffers from.

Walking down the hall to the patient ward, I summon the nurse. "Mr. Tuttle has pernicious anemia. Please see that he gets liver with every meal. And make sure he eats it."

"Of course, Doctor," the nurse responds.

Mr. Tuttle turns over in bed. He's weak and pale. "Doctor, why do you torture me? I can't abide liver. It's the devil's own food. Now that I'm weak and frail, must you also torture me with foods I abhor!"

"Mr. Tuttle, you have pernicious anemia, the appearance of your red blood cells confirms it. Dr. Whipple discovered that eating liver can treat this disease. He got a Nobel prize for it a few years ago."

"Oh, bother! The cure is worse than the disease."

"Now Mr. Tuttle, a little liver never hurt anyone, and you'll be feeling better in no time."

I awaken from the dream as Sam and find myself lying on my office couch. Rubbing my eyes, my first thought is the lateness of the hour and that I should make myself something to eat and then get to bed.

Then suddenly the meaning of the dream hits me and I sit up, startled. Going to my library shelf, I pull out the Merck Manual. The section on Pernicious Anemia lists the typical symptoms of fatigue, pallor and depression, just like my patient. It's a more unusual form of anemia, so maybe his doctor has missed it. I grab my calendar and write in a note to call the patient in the morning to ask about other symptoms.

I wake up as Kaitlyn. *Woah!* This is blowing my mind! Clearly my subconscious was preoccupied with Josie's dream about her past life, John Bowen. I've never encountered another past-life-dreamer like me before so maybe this is why I've never dreamed of one of my past identities dreaming of one of *their* past identities before. I didn't realize Sam had this ability, but it makes perfect sense, now that it's occurred to me.

Sam dreamed about Dr. Abrams, and the content of her

dream helped her in her job. Just like dreams help me sometimes. I wonder if all my past lives could do this. After all, they're all just different versions of me.

The idea is a cosmic shift in my reality. I wonder if Sam ever told anyone about her dreams.

It's time for a run to clear my mind. I don't even trip over the stuffed mouse offering outside my bedroom door anymore, I just walk right over it.

Setting an easy pace, I mull over last night's dream of Sam and Josie's discovery that she was dreaming about the experiences of an actual person. Suddenly, I don't feel so alone in the world. It's an enormous relief but there's no one I can share this news with. I'm almost bursting to tell someone.

But who? Who could understand?

It takes me most of the next day to arrive at the answer.

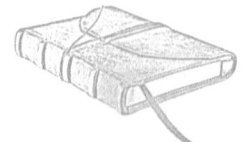

CHAPTER TWENTY-FOUR

I arrive at the office early to copy off the rest of Josie's journal. It's been in the evidence locker, but now I'm a little nervous that someone will get hold of it and read about the past-life dream. Even though I'm in a position to understand that her perception of dreaming about a past life might in fact be true, when viewed by anyone else, this might put her sanity in question. Even the suggestion of mental instability might nullify other useful information if it's thought she didn't have a firm grip on reality. So I can't let anyone else get hold of it until I've read the rest, not even Joe.

Checking out the journal, I take it over to the copy room. I put on gloves and remove it from the evidence bag. I'm hoping I'll be uninterrupted so the presence of the journal doesn't reinterest someone in it. Just as I find the page where I need to resume the copying, Joe bursts into the room. "There you are, Kruse. The captain wants us in the board room for an update on the case. Better stop whatever you're doing. I'd like to run through things with you before we meet."

Shit. I don't want to draw attention to the journal, so I don't say I'll join him when I'm done copying, like I want to. I put the journal back in the bag and bring it back to my desk, placing it in a drawer, out of sight.

Joe updates me. "The captain has gotten wind that we have a number of possible suspects, and he wants to divide up the remaining tasks to help move things along." Again, I find myself appreciating his approach. This kind of team-work could help us to quickly rule out some suspects and determine where our focus needs to be.

When Joe and I enter the conference room, Bob, Ray, Clint, Sean, and Sally are already pulling up chairs. Even Ethan and Ravi are in attendance in case we need their assistance.

Captain Bennett takes a seat at the front of the room. "I'm hoping we can narrow down these leads," he says once we're settled. "Joe and Kaitlyn, how about you give us a run-down on what you have so far and what items need attending to."

I start in, "Currently, we've been forced to suspend the investigation into Josie's neighbors, Jimmy White and Chuck Thornton. We uncovered a fentanyl distribution ring led by the landlord, Bill Crawley. The DEA is working on arrests there, so our hands are tied until they bring everyone in. Josie had a list of addresses that suggest she had some suspicions about these individuals and their connections. This knowledge may have gotten her killed.

"Ms. Washington also mentioned Josie's landlord was repeatedly looking in Josie's windows. He seems like a plausible suspect even if he didn't think Josie suspected the fentanyl distribution. He claims she owes him for letting her lease the property with a poor credit history. If he had a romantic interest in her and felt snubbed, he's likely to react badly. He also has a white car with the front end under repair. We already had Ray lift some paint from the vehicle yesterday on a warrant issued before the DEA got involved."

"Ethan, could you follow up on the paint sample?" Ethan nods in response to the captain's request.

"I also think we should look into Bill Crawley's wife's death. He inherited the rental properties from her. It just seems suspicious." Wanting to give Bob a task with more interest since he's shown some promise with his detective skills, I say, "I think this would be a good task for Bob."

"Okay, Bob," the captain agrees. "Why don't you look into that?"

Joe takes over. "We interviewed Josie's aunt, Mable Frank, and her boss Brad Dunford. They both mentioned a coworker, Eli Rodriguez, who seemed romantically interested in the victim. He seems suspicious. We have him in short-term custody. He has a white car with a recent paint job which may cover up repairs. A warrant was submitted to search his home and vehicle."

The captain looks at Ray. "I want you and Clint to go by and collect that sample once the warrant is approved." Ray nods.

I take up the report again. "A disgruntled employee, Jennifer Klein, also made threats after she was fired. She blames Josie for losing her job. She borrowed her sister's white car the night of the murder. We need to find the sister to see if the car had any damage."

"Sean and Sally, why don't you look into that?" Captain Bennett sits back in his chair and looks thoughtful. "It seems like Eli's the most plausible suspect that we have access to. Are we searching his home and vehicle today?"

KAROLINE ANDERSON

"As soon as we get the warrant," Joe responds.

"I sent the paperwork off yesterday. We should hear soon," Bob says.

"Does anyone have any additional ideas? Other areas to investigate? Suspects we haven't thought of?" Joe invites everyone to contribute.

"Any past boyfriends that might hold a grudge?" Bob asks.

"We asked her aunt, and she didn't have any serious boyfriends in the past few years," Joe replies.

"Okay. Let's wrap this up," the captain says. I'm grateful he's giving us so much help.

We disperse. The captain meets with a few officers to discuss their assignments. Joe suggests we head over to Barrett's Cafe to regroup. I keep thinking of the journal, but I don't want to copy it now and risk bringing it unwanted attention. Its presence in my drawer is like a pebble in my shoe—I'm persistently aware of it.

We sit down with coffee in a booth at the back of Barretts, well away from any other patrons.

"You still planning on coming for Thanksgiving?" Joe asks. "Sandra asked me to check. She has half the precinct coming over." His eye roll is tempered by his chuckle.

"Right, of course I'll be there. Tell Sandra thanks again for the invitation. I have a couple of bottles of white wine I'll bring along. I can't believe it's only three days away, it kind of snuck up on me."

"Me too. But not Sandra, she's already making pies and thawing the turkey."

"Bless that woman." I take a sip of my coffee and sigh happily.

I decide this is a good time to bring up Josie's past life, John

181

Bowen. I have a few questions Joe may be able to answer, I just can't admit where I got the information.

"Did you ever know a John Bowen on the police force?"

"John…Oh, yeah. I knew him more than twenty years ago, worked with him in a different precinct. We did some training together. Why do you ask?"

"Oh, I came across his name somewhere and wondered whatever became of him."

Joe looks surprised at the seemingly random inquiry, but he doesn't question it. "I remember he died in the line of duty. It was pretty tragic. He was only in his thirties. About the same age as I was then. I remember feeling like it could've been me. Shook me up a bit."

"Wow. I bet." I sip on my coffee, feigning innocent interest. "How did he die?"

"The way I heard it, John and his partner went to arrest a suspect in a bank robbery at his girlfriend's apartment. The suspect thought he was safe hiding out there, so he wasn't very cautious. When they knocked, he just opened the door right up. When he saw two police officers at his door, he tried to get away by climbing out a back window to the fire escape. He was too far away, and he ended up hanging by his fingers from the window, trying to swing over to the fire escape. John tried to pull him back in, and they both ended up falling six stories. A real hero's death. I think every officer in the whole city showed up for his funeral."

"Wow. That's sad." What a tragic death. It hits me like a punch in the gut and I struggle not to let on how connected I feel to it. This was Josie in her past life.

Joe's phone rings. He says "Yep" a few times and then hangs up.

"That was Ray. We got the warrant to search Eli's apartment and vehicle."

"Oh man, I'm not looking forward to searching his place." There were layers of trash when we were there before. "Might need to double glove. Oh, and good thing you have green shoelaces today—it'll match the fungus."

Joe laughs. "Lucky choice."

We round up the team and head to Eli's address. Sally and Sean are following up on Jennifer Klein's sister, so Ethan and Ravi come along instead.

When we arrive, Ray and Clint take charge of impounding and searching Eli's car.

We don't have any physical evidence from the scene that we can match to the apartment contents. Instead, we'll be searching for any evidence that Eli had an obsession with Josie or he meant her harm.

I draw the short straw and start in the bathroom. Joe heads to the kitchen while Bob and Ravi start to excavate the main living area. Ethan braves the bedroom.

I actually do decide to double my gloves. I also stuff tissue in my nose and put on safety goggles. I briefly consider a HAZMAT suit. Who knows what toxins are in that bathroom? I hold my breath and enter the room. It's every bit as revolting as I expect. There are layers of algae in the tub and sink and the toilet has unidentifiable muck. Yuck!

I start with the relatively muck-free medicine cabinet above the sink. Ibuprofen, antacids, a razor, and toothpaste are all I find. On top of the pedestal sink is a glass with a frayed toothbrush and some liquid hand soap. Well, I couldn't be more surprised Eli has heard of soap, much less that he owns some. I gingerly inspect the rest of the bathroom and check behind the towels. I peer into the shower, behind a plastic curtain that could stand up by itself, it's so full of fungus. I find some shampoo and a bar of soap. Despite the ick-factor, I may have lucked out with my search assignment. At least the bathroom doesn't have layers of trash to pick through.

When I'm done, I remove my nose plugs and goggles and join Joe in the kitchen. He's checking the few boxes of food in the cupboards for anything hidden.

"Nothing in the bathroom. Find anything in here?"

"Nope. I'm almost done. Why don't you check on the others?" He flinches as a large black bug scurries out from behind a box.

I head to the living room to check in with Ravi and Bob.

"Any luck?" I ask. Ravi shakes his head, while he continues to painstakingly sift through the layers of trash, a look of revulsion pasted on his face.

Bob's going through Eli's computer. He waves me over.

"I've been going through his search history. He searched directions to Josie's address, and he's noted in his calendar which days Josie works."

"Great, Bob. Keep on looking."

I head to the bedroom, but I don't see Ethan. "Ethan?" I call out, confused.

"In here." His voice is muffled, and he's bent over behind an excavated pile of clothing which he's moved to access the back of the closet.

"Look at this," he says, standing up. Several photos are stuffed behind the clothes. Ethan reaches in with a glove, retrieves the photos, and turns them over to me. I flip through. The first photo is of Josie leaving work, and there's a series of photos of Josie walking alone at night on her route home. A whole stack of photos show her street and her house. Ah ha, it looks like he *was* stalking her after all. I stick the photos in an evidence bag.

We drive over to the impound lot where Ray and Clint have taken Eli's vehicle. Ray is carefully removing a paint sample from the front end.

"Anything interesting?" I ask them.

Clint's removing items from the back seat. He's going to need decontamination after being in that car. I peer inside at the pile of discarded fast-food wrappers and other trash. No big surprise there. Suspicious stains are on the back seat. Gross.

"We found this in the left front wheel well, wrapped around the axle." Ray holds up an evidence bag with a clump of long dark hair.

It's not looking very good for Eli.

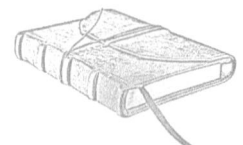

CHAPTER TWENTY-FIVE

As we drive away from the impound lot, we get a call from Bob. His voice comes through on the car interface, sounding both excited and anxious. "The DEA contacted us. They want to raid the rental houses before the drug ring gets word that Chuck talked. There are so many houses to cover, they asked for our help."

"Yeah, we can help. What do they need us to do?" Joe asks.

"Each of us are assigned to a team with DEA agents and an assembled SWAT team. The plan is to enter the houses all at one time, so we have the element of surprise on our side."

"Which house are we assigned to?" I ask.

"The three of us are assigned to Bill Crawley's house. Ethan and Ravi are headed to Jimmy's. Clint and Ray and Sally and Sean are assigned to other rental addresses."

"Okay we'll head over there now and meet up with you."

We make a brief pit-stop at a restroom to change into more practical pants and shoes we keep in the squad car for just such an occasion. Stripping off our jackets, we throw them in the trunk.

In Crawley's neighborhood, we park out of sight around the street corner awaiting the arrival of the SWAT team. It's not long before the unmarked van pulls up the street and parks a distance behind us. I can't help but think of the similarity to Josie's dreams. We join the SWAT team, Bob, and the DEA officers, in the van.

"I'm O'Sullivan." The SWAT leader gives us a hand up into the van. He introduces his team as they hand out gear. "That's Granger, Howe, and Rashid. They're SWAT. Officers Green and Cortez—they're with the DEA." Cortez is the only other woman. They all nod, welcoming us to the hastily assembled team.

"Riley and Kruse," Joe responds, taking a bulletproof vest and helmet.

O'Sullivan nods at us. "We're on full protection protocol for fentanyl. Make sure you put on eye protection, masks, and gloves. Comms are over there."

We suit up and then gather around a map of the home's layout, spread out on a tiny table folded out from the wall.

"There's one entry in the front and two back exits—one through the garage and one out the back of the kitchen." O'Sullivan points to the areas on the map. "I think he'll attempt to leave through the garage to get to his vehicle, so Bob and I'll cover that exit. Riley and Kruse, you cover this back kitchen exit, and Granger, Howe, and Rashid, you'll enter through the front, followed by Green and Cortez."

The intensity of the planning rattles me a bit. Everything is happening so fast. Just an hour ago, we were leaving the impound lot and now we're all suited up in a SWAT van. It feels rushed and that makes me uneasy. But I'm not in charge. The urgency is understandable, I just hope we've covered all our bases.

"We'll wait for the signal. All the raids will start at the same time," O'Sullivan says as he puts on his mask.

We find spots around the edge of the van and squat, shoulder to shoulder. And then the wait begins. I'm sweating in my vest and helmet. There's not much talking as we listen for word from dispatch. The wait is agonizing.

Then...finally, we get the go ahead. It's time. My heartrate climbs steadily.

O'Sullivan takes the lead as we exit the van and creep down the street silently, one following the other, as we've been trained. Rounding the corner, we head along Crawley's street. O'Sullivan stops as we reach the driveway and looks back to ensure everyone is ready. Satisfied, he heads down the driveway, all of us following one by one, guns drawn. Crawley's truck is in the drive and there's a light on inside the house.

Rashid and Granger approach the front door with a battering ram, followed by Howe, Green, and Cortez. O'Sullivan and Bob head to the side of the garage. Joe and I veer off through the side gate to the back yard, taking up position near the back door. My heart pounds. I wipe my sweaty palms on my pant legs as I position myself beside the back door, across from Joe.

I look over at Joe and he nods, reassuring. "Kaitlyn, you stay hidden, come over here," he whispers and indicates the laurel bush behind him.

"No way. I'm not hiding behind you..." I protest in a harsh whisper. I know he wants to protect me, but he'll be right in harm's way if Crawley comes out the back door.

Joe's eyes narrow and flash with irritation. He rarely shows anger. It hits me that I'm not obeying him...again. I'm allowing my concern for his safety to cause me to contradict a direct order.

I move behind him as directed, hiding behind the bush. Safe, like Joe wants, but feeling like a coward.

The sound of the front door being breached reaches us through our ear pieces. Those entering the front of the house make calls for surrender.

We've barely had a chance to register that the raid has begun when the back door flies open. Bill Crawley appears, carrying a gun and making a run for it.

Joe launches himself at Crawley, missing his body but managing to grab Crawley's right foot in his outstretched hands as he falls to the ground.

Crawley wrenches his foot away, then angles back toward me, accessing his only means of escape from the back yard, a path that runs past me, through a gate and down between the two houses. He doesn't see me. Now I recognize the brilliance of Joe's plan. He didn't have time to explain it to me. All this runs through my mind in the split second that Crawley takes to turn my direction.

As he passes the laurel bush, I spring out at him, causing him to fall face-first on the ground with me directly on top of him. I put my knee in his back and fight to pull his hands around and cuff him. His wiry body is strong, and he tries to right himself and launch me off his back. Joe is beside me now, using his weight to help pin Crawley, and together, we get the cuffs on him. He's spitting and swearing liberally at us as we haul him upright.

Howe runs through the back door and sees us with

Crawley cuffed. "Clear!" he yells to those inside. "The suspect is apprehended," he says into his comm microphone as he takes possession of Crawley.

My neck stings and I raise my hand to it, removing it to find a smear of blood. My flight or fight response is still so high, I don't trust myself to feel an injury, so I take a moment to take stock. Nope. It seems I'm intact. No major wounds. Just some scratches and bruises. I sigh in relief when I see that Joe is also uninjured.

Entering the house from the back door, we find Bob and the other officers searching the house with gloves and face masks still in place to prevent any accidental exposure to fentanyl. The super-potent narcotic is a killer. Just a small amount inhaled, ingested, or absorbed through the skin could put us at risk of overdose.

Joe and I join the search. We look through the bedroom and living room, then the bathroom. No white powders or tablets to be seen.

"Got something," Cortez says into her comm and indicates a floorboard with a carved notch. It was revealed when she pulled back a throw rug. Using a gloved finger, she pulls the board up and looks down into the space under the floor. Bingo. Thousands of individual packages of white tablets in clear plastic bags are visible under the floor.

While Cortez and Green investigate the large stash, the rest of us continue searching. Joe and I head outside, thinking we might find something in his truck.

"Do you think Xavier's wife got fentanyl from one of these dealers?" I ask.

"Yeah, I bet that's right. Jimmy lived right beside them. Could've been him."

"It's sad she was a victim in all this. And Destiny and Xavier too, by extension."

"So many victims. Every time one of these people gives someone a pill, they started a possible addiction. That's a lot of addicts."

The scope is indeed staggering. I'm determined to find all of the drug so it can be safely disposed of. So how would he hide it? I try to think like him.

We look through the glove box and remove his toolboxes and some building material, checking the back of the truck. The side panels are removed from the truck doors. Nothing. The toolboxes are full of tools. We rifle through them, searching for pill packets but there's nothing there.

I pull out all the tools, checking each for handles with secret compartments. Once the tools are all out, I compare the depth of the bottom of the toolbox with the outside dimensions. Sure enough, the bottom inside the toolbox is noticeably higher than the underside of the toolbox from the outside. It must have a false bottom. But how can I access it? I feel around, try to pull the floor up. Then I see it. A tiny latch at the back. When I push it, the floor pops up, revealing the hidden compartment. Inside are more packages of pills.

We bring the toolbox inside and turn it over to Officer Green.

Bob motions to me and Joe from the floor space. "Hey, look at this." He indicates the excavated space under the floorboards. We crouch down to have a look. "They found quite a bit of fentanyl under there. Enough to put the Crawley drug ring away for quite some time." The space under the floorboards is large and now empty of pills. Some trash is left that likely has fallen in when the board was removed time and time again to access the stash. Some candy wrappers, a few pull tabs from beer cans, an old used tea bag, a rook.

"Crawley doesn't strike me as the type to drink tea," Bob comments, using tweezers to put the items in an evidence bag.

"He doesn't seem like the type to play chess either," I remark.

Green enters the living room trailed by the other team members. "I've heard from the other teams." We stand and gather around him for the report, drawn like moths to a flame. "Fentanyl was found at four of the properties Crawley rented. Drug detection dogs are making the rounds to see if the other tenants they searched are just better at hiding the stuff. All the raids went off without much in the way of collateral damage. All the tenants involved are being brought in for questioning."

"What do you mean 'without *much* in the way of collateral damage?'" Joe asks.

"Well, it seems at one of the houses, a Doberman took a bite out of someone's ass."

It must be Jimmy's charming dog.

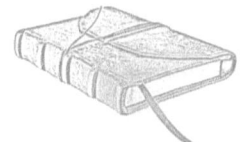

CHAPTER TWENTY-SIX

Now that the raid is over, my stress hormone kick wears off and I'm exhausted and depleted. It's been a crazy day. As we drive back to the precinct, thoughts are swirling around in my head. Eli still seems the likeliest murderer but I'm not ready to rule out Crawley and his group. Not yet.

The dream from last night has been troubling me all day, always returning to my thoughts. It's shaking the foundations of what I thought I knew about the world that both Josie and Sam had dreams of their past lives. I always thought I was alone. Maybe this ability isn't as rare as I thought. After all, I ran into evidence of someone else with it who lived in the same city. It's not the kind of thing anyone is likely to admit to, except in a journal. Maybe that's why I haven't discovered it before.

I'm bursting with the need to share my discovery with someone, and it comes to me suddenly that I know the perfect person. I'm not sure why it took me so long to think of her. When we get back to the precinct, I head toward her house.

I'm tired but now that I've thought of someone to share this with, my mind won't rest until I do.

During my last big case, I had to ask some questions of Sam's sister, Tina, who still lives in the home Tina and Sam grew up in. It was very disorienting to visit Sam's childhood home, a home I knew from Sam's dreams but which I'd never visited before as Kaitlyn. Tina was very helpful, but I didn't feel I could share my dreams with her at that time. Too much relied on me being a credible witness, and I didn't know how Tina would respond. She might have dismissed me if she thought I had a tenuous grip on my sanity.

I still don't know how Tina will respond to what I have to share so I'm nervous, but at least the outcome of a case doesn't depend on her response.

When I drive up tonight, I have the same odd sense of déjà vu. There's the basketball hoop where Sam played ball, the glass window by the door Sam broke as a child. I have so many dream-memories that involve this house that it feels like *my* home, and yet I've only been here myself a few times. The incongruity is as dizzying as it was before.

When I ring the bell, Tina is visible through the window panel as she approaches the door. Same auburn hair shot through with grey, same ample frame as when I saw her last. I give her a little wave and her face breaks into a smile. The same beaming smile I remember. It's a comfort to see her. Through Sam's memories, she's come to feel like a sister to me, and I have to keep reminding myself that while I have memories of her from Sam, she doesn't have any such memories of me.

Tina throws the door wide. "Why, Kaitlyn! What a lovely surprise!" She envelops me in a huge bear hug. My ribs protest. "What brings you by?"

"I'm struggling with a case. I was hoping you might be able to help."

"Surely, surely. You just come on in and sit yourself down." She ushers me back to the small table in the kitchen. It feels like home. There's a smell of freshly baked bread. I sink into the comfort of the cozy kitchen and the warm company.

Tina fixes us tea and puts out a plate of still-warm bread and some butter.

"Now, what can I help you with?" she asks, sitting in the chair opposite me.

I've been stewing about how to bring this up with Tina, and I have an idea that might work. I tell her, "I'm reading through a victim's diary, and it seems she has some very strange dreams."

"Oh, that's interesting. What kind of dreams?" Tina sips her tea and holds the cup in both hands, warming them, a posture I remember well from Sam's memories.

"She's dreaming that she's a police officer named John Bowen. It seems very real to her, and she keeps dreaming of him over and over. Then one day she googles John Bowen and finds out he was a real person."

"Wow! That *is* an unusual dream." If Tina knew about Sam's dreams, she's covering it well.

"When she looks up John Bowen, she finds out he died many years earlier. And here's the weird part, the day he died is the same day she was born."

"Huh...what do you think that means?"

"Well, *she* thinks it could mean her dreams are actually a memory of a past life she experienced as John Bowen."

I need to get Tina to trust me if I want her to talk to me

195

about Sam's dreams. What will build that trust?

Tina's giving me an intense look. Either she thinks I'm a few sandwiches short of a picnic or she's trying to decide what she herself can safely share. "What do *you* think?" she asks.

"Well, I'm open to the idea that our world may hold more than what immediately meets the eye. Maybe some people are more in touch with past realities." *Damn, damn, damn!* If only I could just be honest.

"You came to me because you know Sam had these kinds of dreams, didn't you?" Tina asks. And there it is. The truth now suddenly out there for me to grab hold of. My eyes meet hers and see the openness there, waiting to be met. Relief floods through me.

"Yes," I half-whisper. Not daring to say more.

"How did you know? Did she tell your mother?"

Oh no, I'm about to be caught up in a necessary lie I told Tina before; that my mother was Sam's friend. This is how I chose to explain that I knew some things about Sam's past. Is this lie going to keep us from sharing now?

"No." I get up and start to pace the small room.

"She didn't tell your mother?" Tina looks confused. I couldn't have met Sam so how else could I know these things? She hasn't put it together yet.

"Sam told *you*, didn't she?" I'm going to have to push her to tell me the truth.

"Yes. It was hard for her to share it with me, to trust me to believe her." Tina seems to consider for a moment. "After all we've shared about Sam, I don't see the harm in telling you about this. You know a lot more intimate things about her than that."

I stop pacing and sit back down across from Tina. "Thank

you for sharing that."

"I did believe her, you know, when she chose to share it. I have to admit, it sounds far-fetched, but I really did believe her. The first time she told me was when I was having a problem at work at a retail store. I'd seen a regular customer take an item and when I told my boss about it, the customer said I'd been inappropriate with him, flirting and making advances. This wasn't true, of course, but the man said he had turned me down and now I was making things up to get back at him. I'd told Sam the story, asking her what to do. She told me about a dream she'd had where she was a nurse named Abby and was accused of allowing herself to be alone with a man named Mr. James and how she'd been found at fault even though *he* was the inappropriate one. She almost lost her job. Sam warned me to be very careful because she suspected my boss would side with his regular customer."

I remember this dream well. I've had it too. I stop pacing and sit down again to hear her story. "So what did you do?"

"I wrestled with it for a while. I felt I had to be true to myself but I wanted to keep my job. In the end, I stuck with the truth and got fired for my efforts, just as Sam warned me." She rolls her eyes at the unfairness. "When I shared it with Sam, I was marveling over the fact that she'd had such a related dream. That's when she chose to share with me that it wasn't just a random dream at all but a memory of a past life. She said they would happen sometimes, often related to something she was dealing with in her current life. She said our talking about my dilemma had brought that memory out. I suppose I should've questioned such a fantastical notion but to be honest, I just believed it from the start. It was Sam, after all. She was as straightforward as they come. I just never believed she would make something up.

"After that, she would tell me about some of her dreams and it became obvious she was right about them being past lives. She would learn something medical she didn't know before, or later, when she was a psychologist, she would suddenly get insight into a patient that came from an experience I know she didn't have. Some of her dreams were even about places she'd never been to but could describe in great detail. When we looked these places up, her descriptions were very accurate."

I reach out for her hands, for her reassurance. They're still warm from her tea. "I knew you would believe her."

"How did you know Sam had dreams like that?" she asks softly.

"I knew because I have dreams like that about Sam."

Tina's eyes fix on mine. I can see she's working this through. "So, you're..." The penny is dropping. "...you're *my* Sam...in her next life." Her eyes fill with tears.

I nod, unable to speak. Tears start to track down her face.

"Don't cry," I tell her gently.

"You either," she tells me, wiping the tears off my face. Tears I didn't realize I'd shed.

She hugs me, and the embrace is so familiar and comforting, I never want to let go. Finally pulling apart, we just sit for a moment lost in our own thoughts.

"So, did your mother really know Sam?" Tina asks.

"No."

She gives me a reproachful look, but she can't hold on to it. She ends up smiling wryly. "I never really believed that story, but I couldn't work out how you would know those things otherwise."

"I couldn't tell you the truth then."

"I understand. But I can't abide lying so only the truth from now on, okay?"

I nod.

"So, I'm not sure I understand. You had dreams about Sam's life, but how did you know she had the dreams too?"

"I read in the victim's journal yesterday that she dreamed about *her* past lives, then last night I dreamed of Sam, dreaming of *her* past lives. When my subconscious is working through something, I tend to dream about it. The idea that others could do this had never come up before." I take a sip of my tea, and grimace, finding it now cold. "I didn't know until my dream last night that Sam could do it too, although it makes sense now, since we are one and the same. Anyway, it made me hope she might have shared this ability with you. That you might not think I'm crazy."

"No, I believe you."

"It's such a relief to tell someone. You can't imagine."

"You've never been able to tell anyone?"

"No, and it made me feel very alone not to be able to share such an important part of me."

"It's an unusual ability, that's for sure. It requires a certain change in perspective to be able to accept it." Tina gives me a kind smile and squeezes my hand. "Since Sam told me about her dreams, I've wondered if others have these dreams too but just don't have a good memory of it when they wake up. My own dreams disappear like mist in the sun when I wake up. The more I try to remember details, the more they slip away. Maybe what makes you different is your ability to *remember* what you dreamed every night."

"I hadn't thought of it that way. Do you not remember

dreams every night?"

"No, not at all. They rarely stick with me. Sometimes though, a dream will have a different *feel* than how I feel in my current life, even if I don't remember it well. Does that make sense? It's like the background 'me-ness' is not the same."

"Yes, it does! I can tell if I'm dreaming of a different life by the feel of it. Sometimes even when I'm awake, I'll smell something that seems associated with a memory or I'll think of something, and it just *feels* different than I feel as Kaitlyn. Even if I can't quite place it, I'll know it's not from my current life."

"I've always noticed that too, but I didn't have a way to explain it." She looks shyly at me. "What things do you re-member about me?"

"I have so many fond memories of you. Do you remember when we were walking home from school one day and that mean girl Anna tried to take my lunchbox?"

"Oh yeah! You had that blue one with Roy Rodgers horse Trigger on it. Everyone wanted it, including me."

"Right. Anna tried to grab it, but I was holding on tight. And you were younger than me, but you pushed that big mean girl to protect me. You were so feisty. And she fell and ended up running off crying."

We laugh at the shared memory, mine from a dream, hers from her life. It all tumbles out then in a jumble of stories. I tell her about playing together in the backyard when we were young, about when she lost her first tooth and when she got her first cat, Snowy. I remember posing for that stiff family photo on the wall behind her and making all those pencil marks on the wall every year to mark our heights with an S or a T, as we grew. I tell her about the seven stitches I got in my hand when I broke the glass beside the front door, racing her to greet someone. I describe memories from the vacation at the beach that's immortalized in one of the photos on the wall. Dad got such a bad sunburn, his back blistered. Sam's dad, I mean. The lines are starting to blur.

"You know, I've felt very comfortable with you from the moment we met," Tina shares. "Now I understand why. You are so very like her, it's as if Sam is here with me now, and I guess, in a way, she is."

"I've felt the same way. We have a connection, partly because I have so many memories of you that it's as if I know you already, and partly because it's as if I still remember you. Even though I'm now Kaitlyn, your connection with Sam is still there."

"I feel like I have my sister back," Tina says softly, through fresh tears.

"Me too," I whisper.

It's very late by the time I head home.

Glancing at my phone when I get in my car, I see Blake texted me earlier. "Let's find a time to get together earlier. I know we said after the holiday but I'm missing you already." Relief floods through me. He *does* want to make this work. My rollercoaster of emotions soars back up.

I text back before I start up my car. "I'd love that." It's so late, he likely won't see it until tomorrow. The emotional evening and long day have me wrung out. I suppose that's why I'm hanging on his every word. Or maybe I'm already that hung up on him. All I know is I'm already daydreaming about reconnecting with him. All the way home.

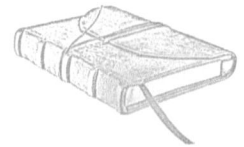

CHAPTER TWENTY-SEVEN

Devin the narcissist is back. He's agitated today, pacing the room before settling on the couch.

"How are things going at work?" I ask when he finally comes to rest. "I know you've enjoyed making your lunch for a while now. Do your coworkers seem to appreciate this change?"

"Well, Dr. Steel, you'd think they would, wouldn't you?" The question comes out as a snarl. "But these stupid people, they never learn."

"Okay, stop for a minute. Take a deep breath." I wait until he literally takes a breath.

"Why don't you start from the beginning and tell me what happened?" I glance toward the office door, planning my escape route should it be necessary. This guy's behavior makes me nervous. Thank goodness we're meeting in the counseling office with many others around, and not in my home office.

"I started bringing my lunch, just like we discussed last time. I make these great little finger sandwiches with the crusts cut off, just like I had for tea when I lived in London for a year.

Some are egg salad, some cucumber, some curried chicken. I bring a variety. For appetizers, I make little mini quiches and rye bread toasts with smoked salmon and capers. It took me a while to perfect the quiches, but now they are exactly how I want them with Swiss cheese and thyme. I bring a bottle of Perrier too. Oh, and then the desserts—I make little brownies with cherries and chocolate shavings on top, and the other day..."

He has a dreamy look on his face as he describes the feast of carefully prepared foods. It must take him hours to prepare this each night. It's amazing the lengths he'll go to prove to those he works with he's superior. But we're getting off-topic. "It all sounds very delicious. So now you're getting to eat these foods you like every lunch break. Are you enjoying that?"

"I did. I really did. I even had a little tiered serving platter and a wine glass at work to eat it with the elegance it deserved." I cringe inwardly. His coworkers must just love that.

"You're speaking in past tense. Aren't you enjoying it anymore?" Did his coworkers "accidentally" drop his serving plate? Or hide his wine glass?

"Not for the past two weeks." Devin is sullen, crossing his arms in a defensive posture and pouting like a toddler.

"What changed?"

"Well, last week Brian..." The name is uttered with a derisive sneer and drawn out with a contemptuous whine, "...started sneaking in and stealing my lunch before I could get there to eat it." Uh oh. Brian, why would you challenge this man? Don't you have any sense of self-preservation?

"How do you know it was Brian?"

"When my lunch went missing for a couple of days, I put a nanny-cam in the break room, disguised as a plant."

"Oh no. Tell me you didn't."

"What? Why shouldn't I do that? Someone was stealing from me." He crosses his arms again in a huff.

"Don't you think your colleagues might feel that was a violation of their privacy?" What am I thinking, asking a narcissist to take another person's feelings into account? Of course, he won't be able to see my point.

"I think they would want me to find the perpetrator." He's unaware of the situational irony of his statement. Just a few weeks ago, he was the person taking lunches from others.

"So, you found out it was Brian. What did you do?"

"I told him I knew it was him. And you won't believe what he did!"

"What did he do?"

"He denied it! Said I was mistaken. He made me look like a fool in front of everyone else. So of course, I had to point out I hid a camera there and I saw him!"

I'm seriously regretting suggesting Devin bring his lunch. Who knew it could go this wrong?

"What happened then?"

"No one will talk to me because of the camera. But Brian was stealing my lunch. They should be mad at him, not me."

The lack of insight is staggering.

"So did you take away the camera?"

"I replaced it with one in a picture frame." I'm mentally banging my forehead in frustration.

"Did Brian stop eating your lunch after you confronted him?"

Please, Brian, be smart enough to stop provoking this narcissist.

"No!" The anger is back, and I find myself eying the door

again. "He took my lunch out of the fridge, brought it over to the frame, and winked at me! Winked!"

My shoulders are tight with the tension his revelations cause in me. I'm bracing for what he'll say next.

"How will you handle this conflict with Brian?" *I ask, afraid of what the answer might be.* Please have a reasonable solution. Please.

"I've been poisoning my lunch for the past week."

He looks smug. Smug! If only he were joking. My hands start to sweat. How do I deal with this? He's poisoning someone! Okay. Think. *I don't want things to escalate in the office.*

I pick up my phone and glance at it, pretending to have a new notification.

"I'm so sorry, Devin, I have a personal emergency. I'm going to have to address it. Please wait here for a moment." *He looks perplexed, but I don't give him a moment to respond. I leave the office and head directly to the open door of a colleague for help.*

I take my time returning to the room, but I know I have to go back in so he won't leave. I dry my sweaty hands on my suit pants. Breathe normally, Sam, stay calm. *When I open the door, Devin looks unperturbed. He believes what he's doing is appropriate, so he isn't suspicious of my actions. At least there's that.*

"Everything okay, doc?" *Devin looks at me questioningly. For a split second, I think he knows what he said upset me, but then I realize he's referring to me declaring a personal emergency.*

"Oh yes, all taken care of," *I say smoothly.* My voice is calmer than I expected. I can do this.

"Now where were we?" *Devin asks.*

You were poisoning someone. *"You were telling me how*

you planned to get back at Brian."

"Oh yeah. I started putting poison in my lunch. The lunch he's stealing."

"Don't you think that might harm Brian?"

"If he didn't steal my lunch then he wouldn't have anything to worry about, would he?"

A misplaced sense of justice. He's checking off all the narcissist boxes.

"What exactly are you putting in your lunch?" If he says laxatives or something else that might cause embarrassment, but no real harm, then I'm about to look like a fool. But a relieved fool. I'm holding my breath, awaiting his answer.

"Cyanide. You can get it from peach pits, you know?"

Nope, not laxatives. I've never been so relieved to have followed my instincts.

At that moment, the door to my office opens and two uniformed officers enter. The first addresses Devin. "Sir, we are detaining you due to evidence you're causing harm to a coworker. You will remain in custody until the validity of that threat can be determined." The handcuffs are placed on Devin before he understands what's happening. They start reading him his rights.

"What's going on? Dr. Steel, tell them I did nothing wrong." At first, he thinks it's a mistake, but then the realization dawns. His face transforms with hatred. "I trusted you, Dr. Steel! You'll regret this!" He's still fuming and spitting threats at me as he's taken off by the officers.

My hands are trembling when I wake up, shaken by the dream and the reliving of Sam's fear—struck by how quickly a routine task such as bringing a lunch to work becomes a dangerous situation in the wrong hands.

Sam had a professional obligation to report anyone that might be harming another, the only reason she's allowed to break patient confidentiality. However, it's scary to make an enemy of such a dangerous person. I wonder if she'll come to regret it.

Did Josie's murderer feel justified in some way, as Devin did about Brian? Felt she deserved it? Our murderer has taken things exponentially farther than Devin though. Putting cyanide in a lunch is a passive act compared to dragging a person down a street under a car. Cyanide is no joke though, someone could die, but we're looking for a narcissist of a much grander scale.

A couple of our suspects ring all the narcissist alarm bells—Bill Crawley and Jennifer Klein. Inflated sense of self-importance and entitlement, check and check.

So, if we're looking for a narcissist, Eli doesn't fit this personality profile. I try to picture Eli driving into Josie in a self-entitled rage. I could see him feeling jealous or slighted by Josie turning him down, but I have a hard time picturing him in a rage. Still, one thing I know from my job is people sometimes do things you wouldn't expect them to be capable of. And all the evidence points to Eli.

I arrive at the precinct a little earlier than usual, still lost in thought about Eli. When I get to my desk, I notice the papers on top are tossed about haphazardly. I know that's not how I left them. Weird. Did someone search through them? What was the person looking for?

Suddenly my breath catches. The journal! Is it still there? I wrench open the drawer I'd sequestered it in. It's not there! Desperately, I search under papers and files. I check all the other drawers just to be sure. It's definitely not there.

Someone has taken the journal. What does this mean? Why would they be interested in it? Is there something incriminating in the part I haven't read yet?

It strikes me like a physical blow that now I won't be able to read about Josie's past lives. The thought is devastating. I finally find another person who dreams about past lives and now I won't be able to find out more about it. I sit for a moment, absorbing the upsetting news.

Bob comes in carrying a cardboard cup of coffee. "Can I bring you some..." He stops abruptly as he sees my face. "What is it?"

"I can't find Josie's journal. Have you seen it?" I ask hopefully.

"Yeah, I got it out of your drawer yesterday morning."

"Oh, thank goodness, I thought I'd lost it." I sigh in relief, realizing belatedly that I should try not to seem too invested. To Bob, it's just a piece of evidence. To me, it is a window into the life of a past-life-dreamer like me.

"I took it out to copy the rest of it for you." He looks perplexed. "I put it back though. It's not there?"

"No. I can't find it. Are you sure you put it back?"

"Positive. I'll get you the copies if you like."

I nod. He leaves his coffee on my desk and heads off to his desk to retrieve the pages. Huh, I'm not sure what to think. I'm glad I'll get a chance to read the rest of the journal but who took it? Bob? Did he really put it back? Making copies would be the perfect excuse to take it. No one would question him.

My thoughts drift back to my dream of Devin from last night. At least I don't have to worry about someone poisoning me at work. Although, that work coffee is so bad, it's almost like poison. I glance at Bob's cup sitting on my desk, steam rising from it. How can he drink that? The precinct drip coffee is so weak it's like drinking tea. Suddenly a thought grips me. How could I have missed this? The tea bag. Poison. Did Crawley poison his wife? We suspected him of benefiting from his wife's death. Did he in fact kill her like we suspected? Is this what my subconscious was working through in my dream about Devin last night?

Bob returns with the copied journal pages. Setting them on my desk, he picks up his coffee, taking a sip. Before I can stop myself, I say, "Don't drink that!"

He stops mid-sip and turns to me, alarmed. "What?"

"Sorry, that's just terrible coffee," I cover. "But it made me think about the tea bag we found under Crawley's floor last night. It looked ancient. Could it have been his wife's? He doesn't strike me as a tea drinker."

"Me neither. I looked into him yesterday morning after our meeting. He definitely benefited from his wife's death. She died of some sort of wasting disease. The doctors couldn't figure it out. Do you think he poisoned her?"

"I wouldn't put it past him."

"I'll have the tea bag checked for poison. Wouldn't they have found that at his wife's autopsy though?"

"Not necessarily. They would have to suspect it. If the doctors didn't suspect poisoning, they may not have even requested an autopsy at all."

"I'll look into it," he says. "Did you hear, the DEA thinks they've managed to find most of those involved in that fentanyl ring. Once they brought the dogs in, they found fentanyl stashed in more of the properties. The suspects started turning on one another after they were brought in for questioning last night. It looks like Crawley and his buddies are going away for a long time."

"Great, that's good news. Hopefully they'll let us interview them now so we can see if they had any involvement in Josie's death. I wouldn't put it past Crawley to be involved in that too."

"I'm sure they'll let us start interviews once the arrests are finalized." Bob turns to leave, heading back to his desk.

"Oh, and Bob?" I call after him. "At some point today, could you just check if you might have put the journal in your desk?" This will give him a plausible excuse to return it if he really did take it, either intentionally or inadvertently. Regardless of his intentions, I want it back.

"Sure." He nods, walking off, lost in thought.

I pick up the copied journal pages he left, excited to finally get back to them. What else does Josie have to say about her past lives?

NOVEMBER 27, 2021

Work has been really rewarding. I'm finally making a difference. They're starting to trust me to take tougher calls. Yesterday I talked for an hour to a girl who was feeling suicidal, and I got her to agree to counseling. I feel like we really connected.

It's hard working so late though. I miss out on half of the daylight because I sleep so long after a shift. When I get up, everyone else has left to start their day.

I've decided that maybe I *was* John Bowen in a past life. Why not? I like the idea that I was a police officer in a previous life. Maybe I did some good, helped some people. Just like I do in this life. That tracks.

I'm glad Josie seemed able to accept this idea of being in touch with past lives. It's something I'm still wrestling with, even today. The talk with Tina last night was therapeutic though. It's going to be amazing to have someone I can talk to about my dreams.

DECEMBER 2, 2021

Last night, I had the police dream again and something new happened. After we searched all the rooms and then put the man in cuffs, my partner told me to take the man back out to the squad car. When I went back into the house, I walked past a bedroom and saw an officer taking cash out of an open wall safe and putting it down the front of his uniform.

He started to turn around and then I woke up. Of course I woke up right at the important part! Who took the money? And did he see me? This dream is making me crazy. Maybe I need to go back to my therapist.

DECEMBER 12, 2021

I keep having the dream about the other officer taking the money during the raid. Over and over. If he would just TURN AROUND before I wake up!

JANUARY 18, 2022

I helped my aunt move today. She's moving so far away, it makes me sad, but she says I can come stay with her any time. I borrowed my neighbor's car to help her move and wouldn't you know, I got a stupid parking ticket. I parked in front of her apartment to load up, and when I came back down with a box of her stuff, there was a ticket on the car. Ugh! So annoying, now I need to get it paid off before my neighbor finds out.

I'm going to miss my aunt. She's the only family I have.

JANUARY 25, 2022

The weirdest thing happened today when I went to the police station to pay my parking ticket. I was standing there paying my ticket and a few officers were walking by and I recognized one of them.

He looked so familiar that I just blurted out "Hi!" like an idiot.

Of course he didn't know me.

He looked confused and said, "Do we know each other?"

It was then that I realized who he was, and it freaked me out. I swear he looked just like John Bowen's partner in my dreams, only older. It was such a surprise, I couldn't help but just stand there and stare at him. I told him I thought he was someone else.

Now I *know* I'm having dreams about a past life. I'm not crazy. Bowen's partner is a real person that I've seen with my own eyes.

So, she's certain it's true now, she's dreaming about her past lives. And these dreams might be leading her to witness another officer doing something illegal. Maybe she'll find out who it was so I can track them down.

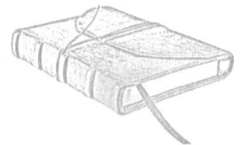

CHAPTER TWENTY-EIGHT

Joe arrives at the very moment I'm grappling with the fact that an officer at the raid stole money, and he was possibly never caught. Even though we have an active murder investigation that should be taking all my time, I just can't let the idea of the dirty cop go. He might still be out there committing crimes. He needs to be caught and brought to justice.

Unfortunately, I'm not sure I can figure out who it was from what little Josie knew about him. I'll have to read through the rest of the journal when I have time later. For now, I can discuss it with Joe. Bowen worked at the same precinct as Joe before Joe was transferred here. Maybe Joe will have some idea who it was. It's possible they were already discovered.

Discussing dirty cops is sensitive business though. I don't want anyone to overhear. I'll have to get him to a location where we won't have to worry about surveillance in the precinct or through our cruiser or body cams.

"Ready for a huge Thanksgiving dinner tomorrow?" Joe

puts down some bagels and coffee, oblivious to my inner turmoil.

"You bet. I've got the wine chilling," I respond while I'm trying to think how I can signal Joe. Several officers have arrived now and are sitting at their desks.

Ethan Carter walks by with a slight limp. I'm about to ask him about it when another officer says, "Carter! I heard you took getting your ass chewed to a whole new level. Don't worry, you've still got a little left." This is met by laughter and comments from the other officers.

"Very funny," Ethan responds, irritated.

I look at Joe for explanation. "He was the officer that Jimmy's dog took a bite out of," Joe says.

"Ah," I respond, still distracted. Waiting for the other officers to go back to work. When they're busy, I get Joe's attention and put my finger to my lips, motioning for him to follow me. Worry creases his brow, but he follows without comment.

We leave the precinct and get in our patrol car. Signaling that we can't talk yet with another finger to the lips, I drive to a trail I know from a previous case involving a serial killer, purposely parking the cruiser so the camera points away from the trailhead. We leave our body cameras in the patrol car and begin a leisurely walk up the scenic trail.

"So secretive, Kaitlyn. And we're back to the haunting grounds of a serial killer. What's up?" Joe says, his voice full of concern.

"It's just a spot I knew where we could get away from surveillance."

"What's with all the cloak and dagger stuff? Are you worried about someone at the precinct overhearing?"

"Yes, I might have some information about a dirty cop."

Joe raises an eyebrow. "That's a pretty big deal."

"Yeah. And when I came in this morning, I discovered someone had taken Josie's journal." As I say this out loud, I suddenly realize that if the journal is gone then someone must think it has something in it that would implicate them. Someone *knew* that she knew. Something about this is bothering me, pulling at my subconscious, I just can't quite put it together yet.

Joe looks surprised, and then troubled. "Does it have something incriminating in it?"

"I've been reading through it, and I wouldn't have thought so in the beginning, but I think it might. I haven't had a chance to read it all yet."

I turn away, pacing, then turn back to Joe, realizing I have to share something from the journal with him so he can understand what's worrying me, but I don't want to get into specifics that discuss the idea of past lives. If I do that, I'll lose all credibility. "She mentions John Bowen, says he knew something about another officer taking money at a raid. Were there any rumors about an officer at your old precinct?"

"No, at least, I never heard about it. What did Josie know?"

My mind's racing. How am I going to explain Josie's knowledge? The answer comes to me. "Her father knew Bowen. They must've talked about it." *Forgive me for the lie,* I think.

Then something clicks into place as I realize what's been bothering me. It's an idea far worse than a dirty cop going without detection. I'm almost afraid to say it out loud. "Do you think it's possible Bowen's death wasn't an accident?"

"Wow." Joe runs his hands through his hair, a sure sign of agitation. He looks up at the sky and blows out a big breath. "Well, let's think about this. Bowen died trying to help save a suspect and they both fell to their death. He was a hero."

"So that's the other officer's version of how he died, right?"

"Yeah. True. What are you thinking?"

"I'm thinking, what if that's not how it went down?"

"What do you mean, like maybe the officer lied about it?"

"Okay, so go with me on this, I know it's a stretch, but Bowen knew another officer was stealing money, right? Maybe he gets partnered up with him that day. When Bowen was trying to save the suspect, he's holding the guy's hand, trying to pull him back. He's off balance and maybe the other officer sees his chance, if he just nudges him out the window, problem solved."

"Kaitlyn, do you realize what you're saying?"

"Yes. If Bowen was murdered by another officer, then there's a murderer in the police department. And that person may have killed Josie because of what she knew. We might be working right alongside him and not even realize."

"Okay, but you're forgetting that the evidence that Eli is Josie's murderer is pretty strong. I was going to tell you; I got a call this morning and the paint sample from Eli's car matches the paint from the umbrella. It's all but certain Eli did it."

"Well, that does seem pretty condemning." I think for a bit. "But it just doesn't feel right somehow. Eli doesn't fit the personality profile of the narcissist that would kill that way, so blatantly, so brutally."

We're both silent for a moment, taking this in. Joe's face transforms as a dark thought occurs to him; it's as if the shadow of a thundercloud suddenly crosses his features. "So, you think the evidence against Eli might've been planted?"

"I'm beginning to wonder that."

"*Shit,* Kaitlyn, this is a big deal." Joe paces.

His reaction brings this home to me. We might be in danger. This person has possibly already killed two people to cover his tracks. What would stop him from killing again?

"Okay. So, let's work through the evidence," Joe says. "The paint on the umbrella matches Eli's car. How could this have been faked?"

"Well, a number of ways. Someone could've altered the test results, so the paint on the umbrella may not actually be a match to Eli's Kia at all."

"True. So, the report might be fake. Or the sample may not be from Eli's car at all. Someone may have submitted a sample from the actual car that hit Josie. Or—someone might have painted Eli's car with a matching paint."

"So, the paint match evidence could be untrue in a number of different ways. What other evidence do we have?" I pause. "Let see. What about the photos of Josie in Eli's closet?"

"Right. Those may have been planted but maybe they really were Eli's. If that was the only evidence against him, it would be incriminating but not conclusive."

"Okay. What about the hair in the wheel well of Eli's car?"

"Could have been planted too. Okay, so the car evidence, the hair, and the paint. Who had access to it?"

"Ray and Clint collected the samples."

"Do you think one of them is a killer?"

"I don't *want* to think that."

"Okay. I'm going to have to let this settle for a bit and see how it fits."

"Right. This is all just conjecture. Eli could be guilty. I don't think we can let on we think he might not be the killer until we *know* if someone in the department is involved."

"Agreed," Joe nods.

"Should we talk to the captain? Let him know our suspicions?"

"Not yet, but soon. He might be able to help."

"Maybe we could resubmit the samples, take them ourselves, and make sure they're valid. We could get the ME involved, tell her our suspicions. Keep it on the down low."

"I like that idea. We just need to be careful. The more people involved, the more likely someone will be on to what we're doing."

"How do we deal with the body cameras and the one in our patrol car?"

"Let's take your car and leave our body cameras in the patrol car. We can come up with some excuse for not wearing them. I know they only record when we activate them, but I worry someone could access them for GPS location or hack into them in some way. I'd rather not have to worry about that."

We walk back to the patrol car in silence, the troubling information hanging over us.

I nod to Joe as we get into the patrol car, signaling that we need to keep quiet until we pick up my car. Driving to the precinct, we switch to my car, leaving our body cams in the cruiser. I just hope someone doesn't find this suspicious in and of itself. We drive a circuitous route, keeping an eye on the cars behind us and ensuring no one's following.

"Which evidence should we re-collect first?" Joe asks.

"Let's go by Josie's house," I say.

The surveillance was called off since Eli's our prime suspect and he's in custody. Parking a block away, we walk to Josie's house and slip past the crime scene tape. Only Joe has a key, so no one has access to the house besides us. However, Ray and Clint were in the home when we searched it. One of them could've collected hair to plant at that time. We collect another sample of Josie's hair from her hairbrush and slip back to my car as covertly as possible. We know Latesha notices everything, so we can only hope we slip past her now.

Next, we drive by the impound lot. The security officer is sitting in the access area. We park a short distance down the street and wait. Joe nudges me when he sees someone bringing a vehicle in with a tow truck, stopping at the access area to register. While the security officer is distracted with the new registration, we slip in, flashing our badges in front of our faces when he looks our way. He nods and returns to the tow truck driver.

When we get to Eli's car, we inspect it carefully.

"Joe, it's only the paint on the front end that's new, and it looks like it doesn't match the rest of the body perfectly. I didn't notice that before. Let's get a sample of the original paint from the back as well as the new paint on the front to compare them." I examine the transition of the paint from the front to the back. If I can tell it's not the same shade just with my naked eye, the paint must be different in composition. Looks like amateur work. Maybe Eli tried to match the paint himself. Or maybe someone painted the front end to frame him.

We take the paint samples and slip out before the tow truck driver is finished with the paperwork. There are security cameras, but we are mostly wanting to avoid the security officer recognizing us and warning someone. We aren't too worried someone will check the footage.

Next is the tricky part. We think we can trust Dr. Mitchell, the ME. The fewer people we bring in on our suspicions the better, but we need to access the forensic work, and she has that access.

Beth Mitchell once had me do a background check on a man she was dating. They had just started seeing each other and he had unexpectedly asked her to go with him to his remote cabin for the weekend. She was interested enough to consider going but wanted to make sure she would be safe with him, alone in the woods.

Dr. Mitchell and I have never been close, but I was glad she trusted me enough to come to me with the favor. She technically could have run the check herself but thought it might catch attention since she doesn't typically run them. When the background check came back, we discovered her boyfriend had been involved in a domestic violence dispute a couple of years earlier. A neighbor called the police when they heard arguing and sounds of physical violence. When police arrived, the victim had bruising on her face and arms and a split lip. She said she had tripped and fallen on the stairs and refused to press charges. Dr. Mitchell broke it off with the guy. She said she owed me one. I thought I might have to call in the favor during our last case but luckily, I still have the debt in my pocket.

I call her. "Dr. Mitchell, I have a favor to ask you."

"Sure, what is it, Kaitlyn?" She sounds wary. She's not one to bend any rules when it comes to evidence. I like this about her.

"Can you meet me at Kerry Park in an hour?" To her credit, she doesn't ask questions. Clearly, she remembers the favor. I can't be sure my phone isn't being monitored so I say as little as possible.

Joe and I wait at Kerry Park, enjoying the view of the Seattle skyline until Dr. Mitchell arrives. The view of the Space Needle is perfect from here. While we watch, some clouds drift in, obscuring our view, and the first snowfall of the year starts, large white flakes drifting down. They melt instantly when they hit the still-warm pavement, but the effect is still beautiful. I feel a momentary sense of peace, as if the danger we face is momentarily on hold.

"I love the first snow," I comment.

"It's pretty. As long as it doesn't interfere with everyone arriving for Thanksgiving, I'm all for it."

We're interrupted by the arrival of Dr. Mitchell. She parks her car a couple of spaces away. I get out, taking the new paint samples with me. As I walk to her car, I look into the parked cars and check the couples huddled on the park benches, checking for anyone watching us. No one looks my way.

I slide into the passenger seat beside Dr. Mitchell, shaking snow out of my hair.

"What's up?" she asks, brows raised.

"Joe and I have suspicions that some of the samples in our current case may have been tampered with."

"You're kidding! That's just wrong." I knew this would resonate with her beliefs that the evidence is sacred. It must speak for itself. The very idea that someone would alter the results has her hackles up.

"Right. We need to see what the true results are so we can determine who may have altered the other results."

"Who do you suspect? Not someone in forensics, surely."

"We can't rule that out yet, but we trust you and knew you wouldn't be involved."

"Damn straight I'm not."

"Could you run these for us on the down low and let us know the results directly?"

"Sure. Count me in. I want to find out what idiot thought they could get away with manufacturing evidence. Just let me at 'em..."

"Please just call us with the results. We need to be very careful to have proof before we accuse someone. If they find out what we're up to, we could all be in danger."

"Of course. It just has me all riled up." She shakes her head.

I laugh and get out of the car. Looks like we have an ally. I slide back in beside Joe. "She'll run them."

"Perfect. While you were talking, I called Sally to see if she and Sean had any luck contacting Jennifer Klein's sister."

"What did they find out?"

"She said the sister got her car back from Jennifer the next day. No damage. They even had a look at the vehicle themselves. Seems unlikely she could've repaired it that fast."

"Well, at least we can rule someone out."

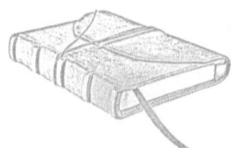

CHAPTER TWENTY-NINE

The possibility someone in the precinct might be watching what I'm doing is messing with my sense of security. I all but tiptoe to my desk to get the rest of Josie's journal copies from the precinct. And when I get home that night, I confirm the napkin is still in my doorframe and double check the door is locked and the dead-bolt secure.

If someone is framing Eli, I just hope they think we bought into Eli's guilt. And maybe Eli is guilty after all. I'll admit, all these thoughts about a dirty cop are pure conjecture.

I text Blake. "Sorry I've been hard to reach. Work is crazy right now." The last thing I want is for him to think I'm blowing him off. These long days might just tank our fragile new relationship. I need to do damage control.

He doesn't text back right away.

I pick up Josie's journal, anxious to find out more.

JUNE 10, 2022
    I've still been dreaming about John Bowen. Mostly

it's just routine days on the police force. He's just trying to do his job and be a good cop. I guess my mind is still trying to work through something.

Seeing Bowen's partner in real life kinda freaked me out. Now when I dream about him, I know he's a living, breathing person.

JUNE 15, 2022

I finally had a breakthrough on the dream about the raid but it wasn't the good kind. This time when I saw the officer taking the money, he turned around and I got to see his face. It was my partner! How could he do that? I thought he was a good guy.

Even worse—he saw me seeing him! The look he gave me felt like an electric shock. I could *feel* it. I knew if I said anything about the cash, I was dead. I knew it right in my core. I woke up and my heart was pounding. It was the scariest dream I've ever had.

Knowing that he's a real person makes him seem even scarier. I know what he did. And it's something he should go to jail for. No way he should be out there pretending to "serve and protect."

Shit! The dirty cop is Bowen's partner. We need to find out who this was. He's probably still working for the Seattle PD if he hasn't been discovered.

JULY 20, 2022

I've finally moved on from the dream about the raid. In last night's dream, I went to a girl's apartment looking for her boyfriend. He was involved in an armed bank robbery, and he was holed up in the apartment, thinking he was safe. I really surprised the guy. He didn't even check the peephole. When he opened the door, he took one look at me standing there and booked it back into the apartment. He opened one of the back windows and was trying to make it over to the fire escape to get away. He didn't make it and ended up hanging from the window. I put out my hand to help him back in, but he didn't trust me. He didn't want to take my hand.

Then I woke up. Ugh! So frustrating. I can sense something important is about to happen. I want to save this guy.

AUGUST 18, 2022

Eli has been really nice to me at work, and I think he's forgiven me for not letting him walk me home. We have some new people on the night shift, and we're busy training them. One of the new girls, Penny, is making a lot of mistakes. I'm trying to help her. I remember how it was when I first started. This girl Jennifer is also new and pretty smart, but she's so bossy. She thinks just because she has a degree, she knows everything.

I had the bank robber dream a few more times. The guy still won't take my hand. What can I do to make him trust me? Maybe this is a dream metaphor for me figuring out how to save suicidal people at the hotline. I have to figure out how to get them to symbolically take my hand and let me pull them out of danger. I think I might know why I'm having these dreams!

OCTOBER 19, 2022

Holly shit! I have to write this down right now! I had the bank robber dream again and this time the guy finally trusted John enough to take his hand. When his hand is gripped in mine, I start to lean back, trying to pull the guy back into the apartment. The guy is heavy, and I'm off balance. Just as I'm getting my footing, I feel this push from behind.

I've never experienced the kind of fear John has in that moment, when he realizes he's about to die. I start to fall forward, and I see this incredible fear on the face of the suspect too as he realizes the same thing. I try to grab something with my free hand, but I can't get ahold of anything. I find myself free-falling out of the window with the suspect's hand still clenched in mine. We both fall. It's like the bottom falls out of my stomach. I see the ground rushing up as I fall head-first toward it. I know I'm going to die.

I wake up before I hit the ground, but I'm sure this is how John Bowen died! There's no way I would've survived that fall. It had to be like six stories! I still have the sickening feeling of falling in the pit of my stomach. Even now that I'm awake.

And someone pushed me!!! Was there another person in the apartment I didn't see? Or was it my partner that pushed me?

Stunned, I put the journal pages down. My hands are trembling with the revelation. Bowen's partner may have murdered him. And whoever stole the journal might be reading

this too, might know that I know. I force myself to keep reading, knowing I need to find out the rest so I can find out what
I'm up against.

NOVEMBER 1, 2022

These dreams about John Bowen are consuming
me. At first, I thought his ghost was trying to commu-
nicate with me about the dirty cop. That seemed crazy
enough, but now I think I used to *be* John Bowen and
these memories are coming back to me now, reminding me of what I experienced.

In my dreams, I remember being John Bowen and
I want justice. His killer is still out there, and no one
suspects a thing. Now I find myself actually hoping to
dream about John so I can find out more about the fall
that killed him. I need to make things right.

JANUARY 22, 2023

I don't think I'm going to be able to get out of
this dream-loop until I find the person who pushed
John. I looked up newspaper articles about his death.
They all said he was a hero. He was trying to save the
suspect, trying to pull him back in through the window. He died in the line of duty. I'm the only one that
knows someone pushed him, someone killed him. But
how can I get proof?

Yes, this is the question? What proof can we find now, so
many years later? They didn't have body cameras back then,
so no one else would know, except the partner. It was the perfect crime.

FEBRUARY 17, 2023.

I looked through all the information about John Bowen I could get my hands on to see if it would help me. I've been searching for months now and I finally found one that mentions a witness to the window incident. It was a tiny article written the same night and it mentions police interviewed a witness, Darcy Rollenstein, who saw the fall. I need to find out what she saw.

I flip past the personal entries, desperate for more about Bowen's death. *Come on Josie, I need more to go on.*

MAY 12, 2023.

I found Darcy Rollenstein! It's an unusual name so it wasn't hard to find her. She's a software developer who lives in Everett now. I contacted her and made up some story about wanting to interview someone in the tech industry about how their job has changed over the years. Said I got her name from an employee list. She bought it. I'll be meeting her next week!

I can't wait to find out what she knew. Did she see the person who pushed John? If she did, why didn't she tell someone?

MAY 17, 2023

The interview with Darcy was crazy! I set up a recording on my phone and pretended to interview her, just so I could ask her the one question that's been burning a hole in the center of my being.

It was hard to answer all the interview questions about her job, just so I could make the interview look legit. Finally, I got to the end and while we were still recording, I told her I googled her, and I found the article about her witnessing John Bowen's fall. I asked her what happened that day. My heart was pounding so hard. I was praying she would remember. My nails were digging into the palms of my hands. I wonder if she could see how nervous I was.

Darcy said it was a weird day; one she would never forget. At first, I thought she might not tell me anything, but then she said it was so long ago, she couldn't see how it would hurt to talk about it now. She said the police had interviewed her, just like the article said. She told them the officer was pushed by someone inside. She'd been sitting right at her window. Saw the whole thing. Thought it must've been another bank robber or the guy's girlfriend.

The officer thanked her and told her they would be sure to look into it. He took down her contact information and said they would reach out if they needed anything else. Darcy said the officer emphasized that she shouldn't talk to anyone about what she saw since the case was still ongoing. She assured them she wouldn't tell anyone. She never heard another word about it.

I recorded everything Darcy told me. The file is on my computer, and it feels like a ticking time-bomb. I made a copy and saved it on a USB drive as a back-up. Now I have proof John Bowen and the suspect he was trying to save were both murdered.

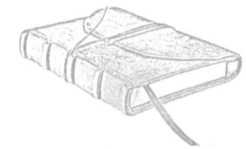

CHAPTER THIRTY

Mr. Ross is recovering from a below-the-knee amputation of his left leg. I've been nursing him for a while now and today he's pale and listless, his pain requiring larger and larger doses of morphine with each passing day. But it's his fever that has his doctors concerned today. Even though his wound is covered with leeches to reduce the swelling and withdraw the ill humors, Dr. Elliot is still worried about advancing infection. He keeps letting blood, trying to improve the patient's chance of survival.

Yesterday, Dr. Mallory declared too much blood had been drained already for the health of the patient. He told the family it wouldn't be a good idea to blood-let again. We nurses are left to try to reassure the family when there's controversy among the physicians about whether or not bloodletting is helpful. Some physicians believe there are new, better ways to do things, and some are certain the old ways are best. Dr. Mallory feels too much bloodletting is detrimental. He tells everyone he thinks George Washington would've survived his sore throat if his physicians hadn't drained over forty percent of his blood volume.

Dr. Elliot doesn't agree and he's the one here today. He gets to make the decisions. And I can tell he's been drinking. Again. Just like at the picnic. He smells like alcohol and his gait is unsteady. It's going to be a long shift. We nurses have all learned to redirect him to tasks with no consequence when he's like this, but right now, he's decided Mr. Ross needs his attention. I was busy with a little girl with the whooping cough and had no chance to distract him.

"Get me a scalpel," he instructs the head nurse, Edith. She glances at the rest of us nurses. We all know this is exactly what Dr. Mallory instructed us not to do. But even the head nurse won't dare to question the doctor directly. It's the first thing we learn in training. The doctor is always right.

"Right away please, nurse." He sounds cross, his words slightly slurred.

Edith supplies him with a clean scalpel. He proceeds to make an incision in the man's forearm, and when he has a good blood flow, he turns the arm, so the blood drips into a pan on the floor. The pan has quarter pints marked on the sides. We watch as the blood volume reaches one pint. Edith is noticeably agitated, muttering under her breath. It doesn't seem like Dr. Elliot is watching the pan.

As the blood in the pan reaches two pints, Edith's sense of duty to the patient overtakes her sense of self-preservation. "Doctor, I'm concerned..."

He cuts her off, "Not to worry, nurse, I know what I'm doing."

Edith looks desperately around for something to distract the doctor from his task. "But doctor, I just noticed the patient over by the window is in need of some attention. The one with the head injury. He's been calling out." It's partly true. The poor man has been calling out routinely for hours now.

Dr. Elliot mutters to himself. He gets up unsteadily and heads off to check on the other patient. Edith grabs a cloth and presses it against the wound, holding pressure to stop the bleeding. "Abby, please take that pan away." When I bend to pick up the pan, I'm interrupted by the arrival of the patient's family.

"What are you doing?" exclaims Mrs. Ross. "Dr. Mallory said no more blood should be let. He was very clear about it."

"Sorry, ma'am," splutters Edith. It's one of the few times I actually feel sorry for the strict head nurse. She's been put in a difficult position, but there's no chance she'll blame the doctor.

"I don't understand." Mrs. Ross is beside herself. She looks at us, as if for explanation.

"Bloodletting is an acceptable practice, ma'am. Many of our doctors prescribe it," I say, omitting the fact that Dr. Mallory doesn't agree with it, and Dr. Elliot has taken more blood at one time than would be considered safe.

"Well, I don't want any more blood taken! I plan to sit right here and make sure it doesn't happen again."

I'm relieved we won't be forced to cover for the doctor again.

When I arrive for my shift the next day, Mr. Ross's bed has been stripped and his family is absent. The other nurses tell me he passed peacefully in the night. No one can say whether it was the infection or the loss of blood that took him.

Bloodletting? I'm not sure what connection my exhausted brain is trying to make. I roll over in bed, wishing I could sleep just a little longer. I fell asleep late last night while I was reading Josie's journal. I'm anxious to read more now, but I slept late and need to get ready to head over to Joe's place for Thanksgiving. Joe's family eats their Thanksgiving feast at midday, just like Sandra's family did. Everyone will gather before the meal. I need to get moving.

I throw back the warm covers and check my phone. Blake texted back late last night. "Sorry. Just saw this. Busy night shift at work. I know. I'm looking forward to seeing you too. Let's find some time ASAP."

CHAPTER THIRTY-ONE

Snow has continued to fall overnight and I emerge from my apartment building to find everything transformed by a fresh blanket of white. The new-fallen snow brings a comforting quiet, the only sound the squeak of snow under my feet. In the distance, Mount Rainier is resplendent in the same fresh white coating.

I warm up my Prius as I brush the snow off, breath misting in the air. Such a pretty day. But cold. I give my scarf another wrap around my face for warmth. I've chosen a red sweater and black skirt to go with my black leather boots.

The bottles of wine clink behind my seat with every turn as I carefully pick my way through the partially plowed streets to Joe's home. My sleep-deprived brain is still wrestling with the anticipation of a day spent in a cozy world of celebration with Joe's family, juxtaposed with the underlying possibility Joe has invited a killer into his home. A murderer may be talking to his children and holding his grandchildren. We can't let on we know anything, or it might put his family in danger.

After reading Josie's diary last night, I'm even more certain we have a murderer in our midst. I need to let Joe know the danger is real.

When I reach Joe's block, there's a line of cars parked on both sides of the street from the guests already at his house. I turn my Prius around and park a block away, struggling to get close to the curb in the snow pushed up by the plow. Grabbing the wine from behind my seat, I head to his front door, sliding precariously in the snow, unaccustomed as I am to wearing boots with such an impractical high heel.

Joe's Christmas lights are already installed and brightly lit, and a decorated tree sits in the front window. The rumble of laughter drifts out to the street. A freshly cut wreath on the front door smells deliciously of pine, and I find myself inhaling the sharp scent, drawn in by the cozy scene. The peacefulness of the surroundings grounds me. I tamp down the slight twinge of foreboding.

Joe's daughter Chloe answers my knock. "Kaitlyn!" Chloe throws her arms around me. I've become an honorary part of the family over the past five years. Their Golden Retriever, Clouseau, winds around our legs, whining in excitement. I give his ears a rub.

"Come on in," Chloe says, standing back. "I think Mom invited the whole police department over."

"Sounds like your mom."

"I'll take those." She grabs the wine from me.

Her partner, Liz, drapes an arm around her shoulder. "Kaitlyn! So good to see you. Now, you know better than to give the wine to Chloe. There won't be any left for the rest of us by the time she's finished with it."

I laugh. Liz takes the wine and heads to the kitchen with it. Chloe takes my coat. "Great sweater," she says. I kind of love her for it because I'd been wrestling with what to wear.

"Are you keeping my dad out of trouble?" she asks with a raised eyebrow.

"Always."

"Any juicy cases you can tell me about? Dad will never share."

"Nope." I mime zipping my mouth shut. She pretends to pout in response, making me laugh.

We pass through the living room where clusters of officers are chatting. It looks like Sandra has cajoled Joe into inviting all the single officers. She doesn't want anyone alone at Thanksgiving.

The room is dominated by the brightly lit Christmas tree and other festive decorations. A fire cheerfully burns in the fireplace, fresh pine boughs on the mantle.

It's always odd to see everyone in street clothes when I'm used to seeing them in uniform. It makes them seem more human, more vulnerable somehow. Ethan is chatting with Captain Bennett. Sally and Bob are sitting cozily by the fireplace, laughing easily. Hmmm, maybe a relationship developing there?

Clint and Ray are standing by the window, deep in conversation. Prickles form on the back of my neck. Ray looks over and gives me a nod as he catches my eye. I nod back. Keeping up pretenses is going to be a strain.

Joe's sons, Bryce and Connor, sit on the couch, laughing and smiling as they talk. Bryce bounces a baby in his arms while simultaneously entertaining a toddler and keeping up conversation with Connor. Talent. That must be baby Ella and little Greg. Joe's always telling me cute grandkid stories about them.

I follow Chloe into the kitchen where there's a flurry of activity. And oh, the divine smells!

"Kaitlyn!" Sandra bustles over and folds me into a huge hug.

"Happy Thanksgiving," I tell her. "How can I help?"

"Here, you can be in charge of warming up the rolls." She pulls out sheet pans and hands me the partially risen rolls in large Tupperware containers. The smell of yeast wafts out when I open the lids. I inhale deeply. Heaven.

Chloe and Liz are busy taking the turkey out of the oven. It's a two-person job with the size of the turkey. Sandra must've been up in the wee hours of the morning getting that bird in the oven. And if I know Joe, he was up early helping, cleaning the turkey, placing the stuffing. I can picture it. The scene reminds me of my own family and Thanksgiving at my grandparents. I have a momentary twinge of nostalgia. I'll call my parents later.

The turkey looks mouthwatering. "Should we start carving it yet, Mom?" Chloe picks up a rather lethal-looking carving knife.

"No, no. Let it rest a while first." Sandra adjusts the oven racks to accommodate the casseroles waiting to warm. Trisha and Sara, their daughters-in-law, are putting the finishing touches on the green beans and sweet potatoes. They greet me with smiles. "Okay, ladies, the oven's ready for you," Sandra directs. "Here, Kaitlyn, those rolls can go in the second oven in about twenty minutes."

Joe appears from the back patio along with a gust of cool air. He's wearing a flour dusted apron and looks tired but happy. There's flour in his hair. He catches my eye and motions for me to join him on the back patio. I've finished laying out the rolls on the baking pans, and it's not time for the oven yet. I follow him out.

The air is chilly without my coat, but it's refreshing after the warm kitchen. It's a sunny day and the sunlight sparkles on the fresh snow. Joe has beer and the white wine I brought nestled into the snow on his back patio.

The comfortable family setting, the beautiful weather, the promise of amazing food. It all has me feeling somewhat blissful.

Joe offers me a beer but I decline, wanting wine with the meal instead. We wipe snow off the patio chairs and sit looking out at the back yard. I update him with another half-truth, telling him that I read some more of the journal and Josie remembered that her dad said the person that took the money at the raid was Bowen's partner.

His face is suddenly grave. "I looked up who John's partner was." He says it in a near whisper, even though no one's around to hear. And there it is. The thrill of fear I was suppressing. I'm not sure if I want to know. Not today, when I just want to absorb the good feelings of his family life.

"It's Ray." We thought it was likely Ray or Clint, based on their involvement with the evidence taken from Eli's car. This seems like damning information, but we have absolutely no proof.

"He seemed to take a big interest in the case," I say. We're communicating in covert whispers now.

"I thought so too."

"And do you remember Ray was mysteriously sick the day after Josie died?"

"Right, I forgot about that. And he looked just fine the next day when we searched Josie's house. But how are we going to prove he might be involved?"

"I found something else in Josie's diary when I was reading it last night. It seems like Josie was very curious about the case after her dad told her about it. She found out that there was a witness to John's death and she interviewed her. The witness told Josie that John was pushed out the window."

"Ray."

"Ray. Covering up for being dirty."

"We need to find this witness."

"Let's look her up. I have her name."

We slip back through the kitchen into Joe's office, closing the door so no one will surprise us.

He searches Darcy Rollenstein.

What comes up is frightening.

An obituary for her death November 4th, 2023, less than a month ago, and just shortly before Josie was killed.

"Well. That rules out Darcy as a witness," Joe whispers.

Joe and I exchange a long look. John's killer is getting more desperate to cover his tracks. He's dangerous. And now we know it's Ray, sitting in the living room right now with Joe's family.

"Josie recorded the interview. We just need to find the recording. She said she put it on her computer and also hid a USB drive."

"Did Darcy and Josie get killed right after the interview was made?"

"No, the interview was months ago. It must have taken Ray a while to find out about it."

"Ray must have wiped the computer. Do you think he did

it during our search of Josie's house the next day?"

"Well, no, because the captain noticed the computer was wiped. Maybe Ray did it after he killed Josie, maybe he broke into her place that same night."

"Do you think we can find the USB dr..." We're interrupted by the door opening and my heart leaps into my throat. I couldn't be more relieved to see Sandy standing there. A waft of warm air with the smell of turkey and sweet potatoes accompanies her.

"No more shop talk, you two! Kaitlyn, please warm up the rolls. Joe, I need your help getting dishes on the table."

We follow her back inside and get back to our assigned tasks. I slide the rolls in the oven and then help Joe carry dishes. Their large dining room table has two leaves added to accommodate everyone. The table is already set with pretty dinnerware, white with a gold rim. Centerpieces of lit candles are set on mirrors, and gold chargers and napkins with gold rings complete the ready-for-a-magazine look. Guests are making their way to the table. Chloe and Liz pour wine into the large goblet-like glasses. Trisha and Sara place seasonal trivets for the casseroles.

I go back into the kitchen and pull out the rolls, putting them in a basket covered with a cloth napkin to keep them warm.

"Perfect, Kaitlyn," Sandra says. She grabs my hand, and I look up at her. "I'm so glad you came today. I know you usually spend the holidays with your own family, but you are so important to Joe. You're a part of our family too."

I pat her hand and smile. I love this woman like a mother. "You've always made me feel that way, Sandra. I appreciate it more than you know."

We bring the last of the food to the table, and Sandra takes her place across from Joe. I look for an empty spot and find myself squeezing in between Ethan and Ray, of all people.

Joe clears his throat, and everyone turns their attention to him. "It makes me so happy to be able to combine my two families for the holidays. Sharing time together during this time of thankfulness brings me great joy." He says a quick grace and then the delicious food begins circulating. *Nice job, Joe,* I think. Ray will never guess we're on to him. We just have to keep up the pretenses until we have some evidence.

Conversation simmers around the table. Ethan tells me stories of bad first dates he's had using a dating app. It's entertaining, but often he crosses the line between tasteful and offensive. I nod along, pretending to be interested. I hope he'll take the hint and start up a conversation with Joe instead.

Ray is quiet throughout the meal. Does he know something? No. I'm being paranoid. How could he know? He talks a little with Chloe, sitting on his other side.

Baby Ella starts fussing in the middle of the meal, and Trisha leaves to feed him. Greg toddles after his mom, bored with the adult conversation.

The captain entertains everyone with a story about a drug bust where the marijuana smoke was so thick in the home, the officers from the bust had a very relaxing afternoon.

Dessert is brought out and pies are passed around. I'm glad I wore my skirt with the stretchy waistband because I'm ridiculously full already. Why does the pie seem like it'll still fit in my too-full stomach?

Joe's phone rings and the room quiets in respect as he answers it. My instincts register danger even before my food-numb mind can decipher the threat. Joe's face registers that the caller is Dr. Mitchell, at the same time we all hear her loud voice coming through the phone. "Detective Riley, sorry to call you on a holiday but I knew you…" Joe glances at me and there's naked fear in his eyes. Then, as if in slow motion, he's turning out of his seat, trying to make it to the kitchen before anyone can overhear her, fumbling to adjust the volume, mute it, anything. "…would want the results of the rerun on the car paint…" Too late, Joe manages to quiet his phone.

A second of deadly silence follows. Joe glances back at Ray to see if he overheard.

Oh, he overheard alright. Before any of us can respond, Ray jumps to his feet, pulls out his gun, and drags Chloe out of her chair. He starts pulling her backwards toward the front door. Chloe yells in surprise, struggling against Ray's strength. Several officers stand and draw their guns, including me. Clouseau sits up, barking and growling. Liz tries to run to Chloe's aid, but Bryce grabs her and holds her around the waist. She fights him and I'm afraid she might get away from him. Liz is a ninja, and a provoked ninja at that.

Ray points his gun at Chloe's head and all movement stops instantaneously. Even the dog stops barking. "Put the guns in the center of the table." His voice is deadly calm.

No one wants to follow his instructions. They hesitate. "Now!" he yells, pulling back on the safety of his gun. Everyone complies immediately. "No one follow me, or I *will* kill her. Don't test me." My brain's flashing images of Josie's broken body lying in the street. He *will* do it. He's proven to be a deadly, ruthless killer.

Ray pulls Chloe out the front door and drags her down the stairs to his car. We hear Ray drive off and it's like a bomb goes off in the house. Officers are yelling. Guns are grabbed.

The captain directs officers, attempting to coordinate the effort. There's a race for the door. Everyone is in their car and peeling out in the direction Ray disappeared.

My car is down the block. I don't have time to get there. Racing back through the house, I see Joe heading for the garage. I run after him and reach the car as the garage door opens. I'm barely in the passenger seat, my door still open, as Joe hits the gas, screeching in reverse. He tears after the other cars.

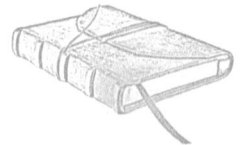

CHAPTER THIRTY-TWO

My heart pounds as Joe accelerates down the street. He screeches around a corner, the car tires fighting to find traction in the snow. It occurs to me to tell him to slow down, but I'm so anxious about finding Chloe that I don't really want him to go slower. Instead, I wrestle my seatbelt on, catapulting across the seat with every turn. We have to find her. The alternatives are not contemplatable.

Think, Kaitlyn. Where would he take her? Where would he go? Maybe his apartment? He'd probably need to get some things if he's planning to get out of town. But that would be too obvious, it's the last place he'll go. Or will he think we won't go there because it's too obvious? *Ugh!* It's impossible to know what he'll do.

My phone buzzes with an incoming call. I'd almost forgotten it was in my pocket. Fishing it out, I see the captain's number. He's calling with directions, attempting to organize our search. We need to make a coordinated effort to ensure Ray doesn't double back on us, that we cast a tight enough net he can't slip through. I wonder if he'll release Chloe at some point but I doubt it. She's his insurance policy if we catch up with him.

Fanning out, we search the neighborhoods in the direction Ray drove, painstakingly checking all side streets and alleyways, parking lots, and parks. As time goes by, it becomes evident Ray's gotten away from us.

I call the captain, and we agree Ray's apartment is a good place to start a more directed search. He's shocked at Ray's abduction of Chloe and confused about the motive, so I update him on our suspicions about the planted evidence. I have some misgivings about not involving him before. Maybe we could've avoided this situation if we had.

We assemble at Ray's address, all of us still in our civilian clothes. What I wouldn't give to be in my work clothing. They give me a feeling of authority, a sense of assurance. The boots with heels now feel like an encumbrance.

There's little conversation as we congregate in the parking lot. The captain continues to coordinate the efforts to find Chloe. With a loose plan we stealthily approach the apartment, with SWAT team mentality. We break in his door and swarm the apartment, searching every room, in every closet, under the bed. Nothing.

There's no sign of him. It doesn't appear he's been here since he left with Chloe. A dead end. "Shit." Joe punches a cabinet in frustration.

We hastily search the apartment, desperate for clues. At the very least, we might find something about friends or family he might turn to. He has no family in the area. Clint knows some of Ray's friends and he comes up with a list of possible contacts Ray might reach out to. The captain dispatches officers to those locations.

Joe and I continue to search the apartment, looking for anything that might help in the search. I can't even look at Joe. The thought of Chloe being in danger rips me up inside. I can't imagine what it's doing to him.

One after another the officers call in that Ray hasn't been found at any of the likely locations. Bob returns from an assignment to help us finish the search at Ray's.

"I feel so helpless. It's frustrating." He voices what we are all feeling while he and I sift through Ray's office papers.

"I know, Bob. We're so glad you're here helping. I know Joe appreciates it. Everyone has been great. Ray just knew what our moves would be." As the afternoon turns into night, it's obvious he's given us the slip.

We finally have to admit we aren't going to find Ray tonight. Joe slumps into his car, mentally spent. He sits for a moment and then slams his hands on the steering wheel. I reach out and put my hand on his shoulder. He looks at me and the raw pain in his eyes is searing, like a knife in my chest. I steel myself, absorbing the pain. I'm going to be strong for this man. My partner. My friend.

"Here. Switch places with me. I'm going to drive," I tell him. He complies without a word.

"I can't go home yet," he says.

For a second, I'm surprised but then realization dawns. His family are all waiting at home for him to bring them news that Chloe's okay. He can't face them yet.

Looking for a place of comfort, I drive to Barrett's, the familiar coffee shop across the street from the precinct. We get coffee and sit for a second to let it sink in, to prepare to tell his family the worst.

"I never should've let Sandra invite all those officers over. And I shouldn't have let Ray stay once I knew what he was capable of. Or taken Dr. Mitchell's call. I should've hung up or covered the sound, or..."

"No," I say firmly, giving him a sympathetic look. "I won't let you do this. This is NOT your fault."

I look over at the precinct. For the first time, I don't want this job anymore.

It's then I notice it. There's a light on.

I grab Joe's hand. "Look. There's a light on. Do you think he would go to the precinct?"

"Seems like a strange choice. But maybe he'd know we wouldn't think of it." Which we hadn't.

We cross the street on foot, sliding in the snow, and covertly approach the back door of the precinct, drawing our guns as we go. I swipe my badge and Joe hauls open the heavy door and then takes off running down the hall, heading for the door with the light. He approaches the door with his back to the wall, then enters, leading with his gun. He was so quick, I'm left scrambling to catch up with him.

A commotion erupts in the room he's entered. Thinking the worst, I rush through the door. Chairs have been upended in Joe's haste. He's grabbing someone, collapsing. Is he hurt? Does he need help? I rush to his aid, my mind racing. Then I realize it's Chloe he's embracing. A wave of relief washes over me. My knees feel weak. Chloe is wrapped in duct tape, securing her to Joe's desk chair, the chair handcuffed to his desk.

Joe rips the tape off her mouth. She's sobbing and can't speak for a moment. He just holds her, saying, "Thank God," over and over. Then, when the sobbing dissolves into hiccups, he holds her at arm's length and looks at her. "Are you okay?"

"Yes," she whispers.

"Is Ray still here?"

"No, he left hours ago."

"Do you know where he went?"

"No. He tied me to the chair and then he went off to do something, who knows what. He was gone for quite a while and then when he left, he had a duffle bag with him." So he'd already planned for an escape, had a bag at the precinct for that purpose.

"He didn't hurt you?"

"No." She shakes her head to emphasize it. To reassure her dad.

He hugs her tightly again.

I take Chloe back to the car while Joe calls his wife to tell her we found Chloe and she's okay.

"How did you find me?" she asks.

"Well, we searched half the city looking for you and then when we couldn't find you, we went to the coffee shop to re-group. And then I saw the light on. I'm surprised he left it on."

"He didn't. The light has a motion sensor, and I noticed whenever I wiggled in the chair, it would come on. I kept moving every ten minutes so it would come on again. I hoped one of you might go by and notice it."

"Clever girl." I give her a heartfelt hug.

When we get back to Joe's house, Chloe's family takes turns hugging her tightly. There's not a dry eye. Sandra brings her a piece of pie. Liz brings her some wine. Sara runs her a bath.

She doesn't eat her pie or drink her wine, and she doesn't get in the bath. She just wants to sit with her people and take them in. Getting the pie and the wine and the bath are what helps the *others* feel better. It's all they can do to help her. She knows that, and so do they.

I call my parents, needing to hear their voices. They are festive and chatty about their Thanksgiving meal, the upcoming Husker football game tomorrow, and the tree lighting ceremony. I miss them terribly but am also reassured to hear their voices, unencumbered by worry. Keeping the conversation light, I decide I'll update them on today's events after they get back. There's no reason to burden them.

Joe takes me aside. "Thank you. For being there. And for not giving up, it gave me hope."

"Of course."

"I'm so glad he didn't hurt her." Joe runs his hands through his hair. His hair's left standing up at odd angles. He looks spent. "And yet..."

I know what he's thinking because I'm thinking the same thing. "You don't want to question this gift, this amazing outcome—that she isn't hurt, but...*He didn't hurt her.* Could he really be the same person who ran over Josie and dragged her a city block? I thought of that too."

"I guess I need to call Dr. Mitchell back and explain. And find out the results of the studies we ordered. This isn't over yet."

"Ray must have done something to the paint results, or he wouldn't have run when he heard we double checked them. We'll have to sort it out. *Tomorrow.* Today, just be with your family."

"It'll be a Thanksgiving I won't forget. I've never been

more thankful my family is all okay."

Sandra sends me off with a heaping plate of leftovers. I'm not hungry at all, but I have an idea what I might do with them.

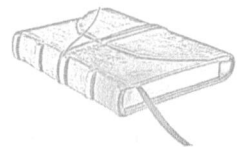

CHAPTER THIRTY-THREE

Blake is still working his shift at the ER so that's where I head. I'm tired of phone tag. Our lives are too busy. If I want to see him, I'm just going to have to meet him where he is.

When I walk in with the plate of food and ask for him, the receptionist says she'll fetch him, giving me a knowing look.

"Kaitlyn!" Blake appears at the waiting room door, smiling broadly when he sees it's me who's summoned him. I love the look of him in scrubs. If I could just get the man alone...

Raising the plate of Thanksgiving bounty, I say "I come bearing gifts."

"Oh, fantastic!" He looks at it hungrily. Then his eyes meet mine and he takes me in. "You look like hell," he says in undertones, concern furrowing his brow.

"I do? I didn't even notice. Thanks though, something a girl always wants to hear." I try to laugh but it comes out a sob.

He steers me into the break room and sits me down. Suddenly it's all hitting me. Exhaustion. Fear. Relief. I put my head in my hands and just let the tears come until there aren't any left.

Blake tries to comfort me and then just gives up and holds me until I'm done.

His scrub shirt is soaked. "Sorry," I say dabbing a napkin at his shirt.

"It's okay. I know where to get more," he says, winking. He pauses and looks me in the eye. "Do you want to tell me about it?"

And so, I do. The whole story. Even the stuff I'm not supposed to share. It just falls out of me as if someone turned on a tap and out it flows. He's a good listener. Doesn't ask questions. Doesn't interrupt. Just lets me get it all out.

The only thing I don't tell him about is the whole dreaming of past lives thing. I don't want to scare him off just yet. I tell the same story I told Joe, that Josie's dad knew John Bowen and they talked about Ray and the stolen money.

After I finish the story, he reaches out for my hand. "I didn't realize before how much danger you put yourself in for the sake of your job. I'm glad you're safe now."

"Me too."

"What can I do?"

"You're doing it. Just telling my crazy story helped me feel so much better. Thanks for listening."

"Of course."

"What was your night like?"

"Oh, just the usual holiday visits. A turkey carving accident where someone cut off part of a finger. We had an entire family in with food poisoning, a burn from molten marshmallow topping."

"You're a good person, working on the holiday." Blake has a big family. I'm sure he wishes he was with them.

A male nurse comes to the break room door. "Doctor..."

"Sorry," Blake says to me.

"I know. You've gotta go." The nurse leaves to give us some privacy.

"Yep." He stands, pulling me up beside him.

"We've had some weird dates, but this might just top all of them," I say.

He tips my chin up and kisses me, tenderly at first, gauging if this is what I want right now. It is. It definitely is. Then he's kissing me deeply, thoroughly, leaving me breathless.

After the kiss ends, I pause for a minute with my eyes closed, enjoying the pure bliss of it. Then I open one eye and see him grinning down at me. "Wondered if I lost you there for a second."

"Oh, I was lost alright." I open both eyes and sigh.

The nurse clears his throat from the door, making us break apart guiltily.

"Just wait until I get you alone some time," Blake growls in my ear.

"Promises..." I whisper back.

When I reach my apartment, I'm deliriously worn out. It takes a couple of tries before my key inserts into the deadlock. It's just before I turn the key, I notice the napkin is missing. I'm certain I placed it in the door this morning.

Someone was in my apartment. The hair raises on the back of my neck. Now I'm wide awake.

I glance down the hall. No one's watching. Both locks are in place. If I didn't have the piece of napkin in the door, I would never know someone came into my apartment. How did they get in? Clearly someone has a key.

It must have been Ray. Did he know we were on to him before Dr. Mitchell's call tonight? It didn't seem like it, but maybe he knew already. Maybe he just knew Dr. Mitchell's information would force our hand, make us arrest him on the spot, and that's why he picked that moment to run.

The day was such chaos as we searched frantically for Chloe. It's occurring to me now how extreme Ray's reaction was to flee in response to Dr. Mitchell's words coming through the phone. He could have denied any tampering or at least let it be investigated. He would've had time to run before we had any evidence against him. Why did he show his hand like that?

We don't even know yet what Dr. Mitchell's report was. But Ray must have suspected it would implicate him. Just the fact that we reran the results was enough to spook Ray.

I enter the apartment carefully, wondering if someone's still here.

The lights are off.

I flick them on.

Stalker is hiding under a chair, and he hisses. Usually, he greets me at the door, so I know something's off.

Fishing him out from under the chair, I pat him reassuringly, saying a silent thanks that the intruder didn't hurt him. The cat has kinda grown on me. I wonder if he went all "guard cat" on the intruder like he did with me at Josie's. The image gives me a brief sense of satisfaction. *Take that, you intruder, you.* My fatigue-addled brain wonders if you can collect DNA from cat claws.

Weapon drawn, I quickly check the kitchen and the bedroom, but the apartment is empty. I look on the bedside table where I've been keeping the journal pages.

They're not there.

Damn!

I immediately feel a sense of loss. The last few entries might have helped more with her case. And I'll never know if she said anything else about her dreams.

Feeling defeated, I go back to the living room to make sure the dead bolt and locks are in place.

If the intruder had a key somehow, then they could still get back in, so I push the couch up against the door and put some heavy items on top.

Then I place a jar of coins I've collected on the arm rest. If the couch moves, the jar should crash on the hardwood, alerting me.

I'll change the locks tomorrow.

Satisfied with my temporary security system, I manage to change into a t-shirt and yoga pants before I crawl into bed.

Fluffing up my pillow, I glimpse something white between the mattress and the headboard.

Did the intruder leave something behind?

I flip my bedside table lamp on.

There's definitely something stuck there.

I reach in and pull out a crumpled loose paper.

What is it?

I straighten the pages and see familiar handwriting.

It's the journal!

I forgot I was reading it last night when I fell asleep. The pages must have fallen out of my hand when I drifted off. It wasn't visible until I was in bed so the intruder probably didn't see it.

The second half of the journal is there. The intruder must have taken the first half from my bedside table. If they check, they'll notice it's not the whole journal. Maybe they'll assume I hadn't copied it all, and didn't have the incriminating part.

Thank goodness.

I'm desperate to know what the rest of the journal says. Re-sorting the journal pages, I start reading where I left off.

SEPTEMBER 10, 2023

I've been wrestling with my conscience for months, and I can't seem to make up my mind. I know I should take a copy of the interview with Darcy to the police, so they know John Bowen was murdered, but I'm scared. I don't want to run into John's partner again.

SEPTEMBER 25, 2023

My neighbor Jimmy is an ass. He lets his scary dog out without a leash, and it chases Stalker. I took some cookies over to Destiny yesterday, a new recipe from Aunt Mable with little toffee bits and chocolate. After I dropped off the cookies, I saw Stalker over in Jimmy's front yard so I went over to get the cat in case his dog was out. Some man left through the front door in a big hurry, opening a pill bottle right there in the open. He ran right into me and little white pills spilled everywhere. He freaked out and started picking them all up as fast as he could.

Jimmy's dumb dog came tearing out of the house, chasing Stalker. The cat ran up a tree to get away from him. I yelled at Jimmy, told him to get that dog on a leash. He got real mean and started yelling back at me. That man's just as scary as his dog. Jerk. Drug-dealing jerk.

SEPT 30, 2023

If I have this dream about falling out of the window one more time, I'm going to scream. I'm not sleeping and I'm so tired, I'm drifting off at work. It's embarrassing. I dream of falling and jerk awake. I guess I need to get justice for John, or I'm going to go crazy.

OCTOBER 1, 2023

I have to face it. It's time to take the Darcy interview to the police.

I'm dragging my feet because the police department reminds me of my parents' death, and I don't want to relive that. And because I don't want to run into John's partner.

I just wish I would stop having the dream of being pushed. It's horrible.

OCTOBER 5, 2023

I had a terrible call today. A woman called in and said she was suicidal, and I was working through things with her. Then suddenly she started yelling and swearing at me. She said if she was really suicidal, I would have killed her because I'm so incompetent.

It turned out the caller was actually this nasty woman Jennifer. She's a real piece of work. She was fired a while ago, and she thinks it was because of me. I tried to tell her that wasn't true. I didn't ever complain about her. But she didn't believe me.

She was so mean on the call tonight. She made me cry. Eli brought me some coffee and a cookie when

I got off the call. He told me I did a good job, and Jennifer was just out to blame someone else even though she should be blaming herself. That made me feel better.

OCTOBER 15, 2023

My landlord Mr. Crawley keeps coming by and peeping in my windows. He says he's here to check on the house, but I don't believe him for one second. It's not like he's here to do any actual work, after all. Just "checking the place out."

We got in a big argument today. He told me I should be thankful he rented to me. I don't see it that way at all. I'm a good tenant, always on time with my rent. And his house isn't so great anyway. It's pretty run down. All his rental places are. Maybe if I contact his other tenants, we can get together to get him to take better care of his properties.

It looks like Josie knew about the drugs but the reason she had the addresses was actually to get the tenants together to complain about property upkeep.

NOVEMBER 3, 2023

I finally borrowed my neighbor's car and took a copy of the interview to the police. I was literally sweating, I was so nervous.

Luckily, a nice officer took me to an interview room, sat me down, and offered me some water. He didn't record anything, but he seemed very interested. He listened to the copy of the interview I brought and then took my contact information. He also took down Darcy's contact information in case he had some questions for her.

He said he'd make sure the right people had a listen to it and he asked me if I had any copies of the interview, so I told him I had one on my computer if they needed more.

What a relief! Now I hope I can finally sleep without dreaming of falling out that window!

NOVEMBER 4, 2023

No more falling dream. I slept like a baby.

NOVEMBER 7, 2023

I'm freaking out right now. I googled Darcy again to find out more about her. Taking in the interview made me think about her again.

What I found was her obituary for Nov 4th. She died the day after I turned in her interview! The obituary says she jumped out of her apartment window. Yeah, right.

I'm scared out of my mind! It must have been the person who pushed John. He must have thought it was some sort of twisted karma to push Darcy out a window, just like John.

What the hell!?! Did someone on the police force tell him? I wish I could go to the police for help, but I don't know who I can trust now.

The person who pushed John must have found out Darcy talked to me. OMG, do they know who I am? Holy shit!

NOVEMBER 8, 2023

I hid the USB drive of the interview. I put it in a little plastic bag and sewed it into one of those little mouse toys. I don't think anyone will find it there. I took the interview off my computer too. I'm scared someone could hack into it. Maybe this whole thing will go away.

I swear I saw a car following me when I was walking home after my shift ended yesterday. I think I'm being paranoid. I'm so jumpy lately. I just need to chill out. I'm sure this will blow over.

So, she did make a copy of the interview, now we know where to look for it. And, Josie, you weren't being paranoid. Someone really was out to get you.

NOVEMBER 9, 2023

I told Eli about the car I saw, and he told me he would walk me home if I wanted. I like the idea of having someone to make sure I'm safe, but I know Eli's looking for a hookup and I'm not interested. I don't want to lead him on. He seemed pissed when I turned him down. Now that I think about it, maybe he was the one who was following me anyway.

NOVEMBER 10, 2023

I saw the same white car following me again last night. I don't want to be too obvious looking at it but I'm trying to get the license plate number. No luck so far.

I think I might take a self-defense course. Walking home alone at night is making me paranoid.

Why did I have to turn in that interview? Now I wish I never did.

The journal ends here. Poor Josie. She didn't have a chance against Ray, a seasoned police officer with resources at his disposal.

The officer that took her interview must have alerted Ray or he came across the information somehow. The fact that the intake officer asked for her and Darcy's contact information isn't incriminating in itself but it sure suggests that officer may have been involved. Maybe it was Clint, Ray's partner. He was also present when Ray collected the car paint and when he discovered the hair in the wheel well. He could have helped Ray plant it. Is Clint involved?

After reading Josie's journal, it's as if I know her. I wish things had turned out differently. I wish I could've helped her. If only I'd been the one to take her interview. And oh, if only I could've talked to her about her dreams. I feel her loss so deeply, it's almost physical, an ache deep in my chest.

Now that I've gotten to the end of the journal, I can finally give in to my exhaustion. I think of my couch against the door as a temporary barricade. I won't feel truly safe until I change the locks tomorrow but I'm so tired...it's as if my limbs are made of lead, pulling me down, down, into sleep...I drift off before the implications of the break-in can re-enter my consciousness.

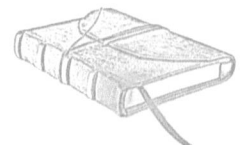

CHAPTER THIRTY-FOUR

While I'm tucking a clean pillow under a patient's head, I spot Edith heading to the back hallway. This is my chance to get her alone! Ever since I learned Mr. Ross passed away, my conscience has been eating me up inside. I find myself pacing and fretting. I can't concentrate on work.

Rushing to follow Edith out into the hallway, I almost run into the back of her as she stoops to pick up a dropped bandage.

"Abby, you scared me," she says, straightening and clutching her chest. "What is it that has you chasing after me?"

"Edith, how could you take the blame for that drunk, Dr. Elliot?"

"Shhhh!" She puts her fingers to her mouth and draws me down the hall into an empty room. "Don't let anyone hear you say that."

"Why? It wasn't your fault. But the family blamed you. Someone should know about Dr. Elliot. He's unsafe."

"Abby, haven't you learned yet? We're a team here. We protect each other."

"What do you mean? Even when patients are put at risk?"

"We don't know the bloodletting was what caused Mr. Ross' death. Dr. Elliot's practice style is just different than Dr. Mallory's."

"But Dr. Mallory told us not to let any more blood..."

"That was just his opinion," Edith interrupts me. "The doctor present has to make a choice that's right at the time."

I cross my arms defensively, "Even so. It was too much blood..."

A noise at the door to the room makes Edith put her finger to her mouth again to shush me. She listens at the door but doesn't hear anyone. She returns to me and speaks in hushed tones. "It's not our place to question the doctors, Edith. They are in charge. You could get in a lot of trouble."

"No one knows Dr. Elliot may have put that patient at risk. If you'd let him keep taking blood, he might have died right then!"

The door to the room opens and Dr. Gregson walks in. The head of the hospital. I've been on the receiving end of lectures from him before. It's not pleasant. Just seeing him makes me stand up straighter.

"What are we doing back here, ladies?" Condescension drips from his words.

"Nothing," we both say in unison. We couldn't look more guilty.

"Edith, you're needed on the ward." Edith scurries out and I make to go after her.

"Abigail, a word please." He stops me. Uh oh. Did he overhear me?

"One of the other nurses overheard you talking to Edith. She was worried you might say something to Mr. Ross' family."

"Of course not, but..."

"No 'buts,' Abigail. We need to support each other. Next time it might be you who makes a mistake and needs everyone's support. You wouldn't want to be blamed, would you?" *This sounds like a threat. Stay in line, he's telling me, or you'll take the blame.*

"Sir, the patient was losing so much blood...Dr. Elliot had been drinking, and he wasn't paying attention."

Dr. Gregson recoils like I've slapped him.

"Abigail!" *His voice is raised.* "How could you possibly know that? Don't forget your place! You are here to aid the doctors. You do not have a medical degree!"

I have two eyes, I think, but I drop my gaze and assume a contrite posture. "Yes sir."

"Dr. Elliot is valuable to this hospital. If you can't support him then I suggest you pack up your things."

"Yes sir."

"I don't want to hear anything more about this."

"Yes sir."

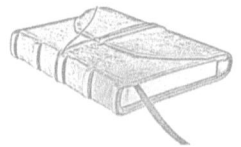

CHAPTER THIRTY-FIVE

I wake up to the buzz of an incoming text. "I'm at your door."

I pad to the door, my mind just starting to wake up. I push the couch back in place and look through the peephole.

Blake's standing there in his work scrubs, his hair rumpled, stubble shadowing his jaw. God, does he look sexy. I open the door, my pulse starting to climb.

He gives me an apologetic look. "I just didn't want you to be alone tonight. I don't want you to think I have expectations…"

I reach out and pull him in by the front of his scrubs, locking the door. I don't want to be alone tonight either. And *I do* have expectations. Our kiss is hot with anticipation. There's too much clothing between us. Pieces are coming off, almost of their own accord, leaving a trail as we stumble into the bedroom. I want to take it slow, to savor it, but my body has other ideas.

Much later, I wake up to the sun streaming in, entwined in Blake's long limbs. I raise my head to look at him. Hmmm.

He *does* look like the Adonis in the cologne commercial. I suppress a smile.

"What are you grinning about?" His voice is still rough with sleep. I guess I didn't suppress that smile after all.

"Last night."

"Yeah...Wow."

"Wow, indeed."

He pulls me in for a slow kiss. This time we take our time. Savor it.

A while later, Blake lifts my head from where I'm dozing lazily on his chest. He slides out of bed and throws on his scrub pants. "I'll make us some coffee," he says, opening the bedroom door.

It's then I realize what's about to happen.

"Wait," I call out, but I know it's too late.

I throw his scrub top on over my head and run to the bedroom door just as I hear a flurry of activity followed by some very creative cursing.

"Don't hurt him!" I reach the door to see Blake holding a very pissed-off cat by the scruff of the neck. I'm not sure who exactly I was telling not to hurt who.

I take Stalker from him. The cat hisses, getting in the last word. "Sorry, I should have warned you—I have a Stalker."

Blake starts laughing and then we just can't stop. We laugh until the tears come.

It's Black Friday and the department is closed, only a few officers are assigned to critical duties. I plan to go over to Joe's later, but the morning is mine to share with Blake. I make us some eggs and toast as he wrangles the coffee machine into producing some serviceable coffee. We sit at my tiny kitchen table enjoying our breakfast and the entangling of our legs under the table.

"I could get used to this." I brush a crumb from his lower lip.

He grabs my hand before I can pull it away and kisses it. "Me too."

"I had this dream this morning..."

"Do tell."

"Someone was kissing my neck and looking for a *third* rendezvous..."

"I think that was real..."

I wink at him. "Ohhhh. Could be. No, seriously, I have a question for you. Before you came over, I was dreaming about a confrontation between a doctor and a nurse because she wouldn't support a doctor's bad decision. Does that stuff happen anymore?"

"I'd say medicine has changed a lot when it comes to stuff like that. It used to just be part of a medical culture that the doctor was revered because they were putting themselves out there to save lives. They were stepping up to do a near-impossible job, and someone had to do it."

"So, no one would question them?"

"No one was really in position to question them. For one, those supporting them likely didn't have the training to always recognize a mistake, and even if they did, they were taught never to question the doctor."

"What's changed?"

"It's more of a medical team with nurses, technicians, etcetera, working together with the doctor to help patients. We're all responsible for making sure the patient gets the right treatment. If a nurse notices that I've ordered the wrong dose of a medication, then I would want them to say so. There are checks and balances these days so a mistake like that would likely be caught anyway."

"How so?"

"If I order an incorrect dose, the computer system will flag me. Or someone like the pharmacist or nurse giving the medication will notice and tell me. We recognize no one's perfect, so we have to always be checking for those mistakes."

"So, the culture of 'not telling' about a medical mistake is a thing of the past?"

"Mostly. Rot can exist in any system, but I think it's much rarer now. There are just too many ways it would come to light."

I'm quiet for a moment, contemplating. Rot can exist in any system. It looks like Ray killed Josie. He was covering up that he stole money at crime scenes and it escalated to murder. A chain of worsening crimes used to cover up past misdeeds.

My thoughts are interrupted by Blake playfully dabbing a glob of jam on my lower lip. "You look lost in thought."

"Hey!" I scoop the jam off and wipe it on his cheek. Then I make a run for the bedroom, certain he'll catch me.

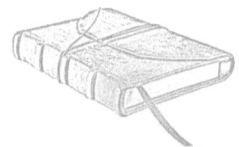

CHAPTER THIRTY-SIX

I need to talk with Joe about all these thoughts running around in my brain. And I want to reassure myself Chloe is okay.

Reluctantly, I wrap things up with Blake. "I'll call you later," I tell him, kissing him goodbye. Then I can't resist sneaking another. And maybe one more for the road. *Focus, Kaitlyn.* There are lots of loose ends that need addressing. I need my wits about me, and I need to get over to Joe's. I finally manage to let Blake go.

As I'm getting ready to head out the door, I can't resist a quick facetime with Isabella. I haven't talked to her in five days but it feels like a lifetime, so much has happened.

She answers, walking outside past a long line of people. "Hey, Kait!"

"Where are you?"

"Out shopping like the rest of the world! I was up at 4:00 a.m. getting in line for a store opening. You won't believe the deals I got." She holds up multiple packages and puts them in the trunk of her car. "You should've come with me."

Sometimes I forget what the rest of the world is doing while I'm absorbed by a case. "Well, that would've been fun but when you find out what I was doing instead, you're going to approve."

"Okay, spill!" She laughs.

"I was sleeping in with your favorite ER doctor."

"You're right, I approve wholeheartedly! Oh Kait, I'm so happy this seems to be working out for you. I've been hoping someone like Blake would come along."

"Well, early days but I'm definitely hooked. And we seem to be...compatible."

"I'm going to have to get all the details on that."

"Definitely but right now I have to get over to Joe's." I relate the details of yesterday. Isabella sits in her car, listening, taking it all in. Exclaiming in all the right places.

"Oh my God, Kaitlyn! I'm so glad Chloe was okay. What a traumatic experience for all of you. I hope you catch Ray soon, so I know you're all safe."

"That's the plan. I'm heading to Joe's now."

"Okay, be safe. Take good care of my best friend, okay?"

"Will do."

Sandra answers the door when I ring. She pulls me into a hug that tells of her recent fear and subsequent relief. It's all there. I hug her back, a mirror of her emotions.

"How's Chloe?" I ask when Sandra releases our hug.

"She's okay. A little shaken up but I think she'll brush it off. She's young. You can always trust the young to go back to feeling invincible." She gives me a weak smile.

"And Joe?"

"It's going to take more for him to pull through this. He's going to feel guilty until you two catch Ray and put him away. He can't forgive himself for allowing danger into our home."

"That's what I'm worried about."

We walk back to the kitchen where the family is gathered, sharing leftovers from the feast the day before. Everyone greets me warmly. Smiles are maybe a little too bright. Overcompensating perhaps.

Chloe gets up and gives me a welcoming hug. "Thank you," she murmurs into my hair.

"I'm so glad you're safe." I give her a smile but my thoughts are in turmoil. I didn't realize how guilty I felt about our job affecting Joe's family until this moment. Seeing his family gathered together, happy and intact, brings it home.

Sandra hands me a sandwich piled with turkey, stuffing, and cranberry sauce. Typical Sandra, feeding us is her love language. The sandwich is incredible.

Joe grabs a coat and gestures for me to follow him outside.

We head back to the old swing set. Shaking off the melting snow that still clings to the seats, we sit down. Clouseau bounds around us, trying to get us to throw his tennis ball. I toss a few throws for him.

"Thanks for everything yesterday," Joe starts, his voice breaking.

"You don't need to thank me. I'm sure you know by now I'd do anything for you or your family. Please, let's just focus on finding Ray."

"Right." Joe clears his throat. I recognize the moment he turns from the father back into the detective. *Good. I need Detective Joe.*

"Someone broke into my place yesterday. It was probably

Ray. He took the copies of the journal but didn't get all of them."

I share the last pages of the journal with Joe, telling him about Josie turning in a copy of the interview, that someone got all her particulars and Darcy's, and it looked like Darcy was likely killed by Ray so she couldn't identify him. "When Josie found out Darcy died, she immediately thought it was a murder. She started to worry about her own safety, thinking she was being followed and getting concerned about hiding the information she had. She took the interview off her computer so it couldn't get hacked, and she hid the USB drive."

"That confirms a lot of what we suspected."

"Agreed. And if we can find the USB, we might just have proof."

"Right. Even though Darcy didn't see who pushed Bowen, we know it had to be his partner," Joe says.

"Yep, the interview would be pretty damning evidence. We have to find it. She mentioned she hid the USB in a cat toy. I wouldn't have thought to look there."

"She's a smart girl."

"Did you call Dr. Mitchell back to find out what she had to tell you?"

"Yeah. Late last night. I had to explain what happened. I think she felt pretty bad she was the cause of the kidnapping. I felt like I had to tell her since it would get back to her eventually. Better coming from me. I told her it wasn't her fault; it was mine. I should never have taken that call."

"It wasn't anyone's fault. No one could've predicted that would happen."

"Anyway. She said the paint from the umbrella didn't match the white Kia. That particular paint mix is from a

Chevy Malibu. The hair in the wheel well did match Josie's, but I'm thinking Ray probably planted it."

"How was the paint evidence tampered with?"

"I suspect Ray submitted paint from the Chevy instead of the Kia, so it came back a match."

"So, he took paint from the white Chevy that killed Josie and submitted it as if it's what he collected from Eli's car?" I ask through a mouthful of sandwich. "Or maybe the killer painted the front of Eli's car with the paint they use for white Chevys."

"That's also possible. Ray could've painted the front of Eli's car to frame him. The guy's not very observant and he sleeps all day."

"And then he takes hair from Josie's hairbrush when he's searching the house, saves it for an opportunity, and eventually plants it in the wheel well."

"Makes sense."

"Does Ray drive a Chevy Malibu?"

"Well, that's the thing. I looked yesterday and the only car registered to him is a silver Ford, the one he was driving yesterday."

Finishing my sandwich, I sit back on the swing for a moment to think. My subconscious is wrestling with something. My dreams seem to be trying to tell me something over and over, but I haven't been able to figure it out.

First, there was George's dream about discovering gold that turned out to be iron pyrite. At the time, I thought I was dreaming about gold because I knew Isabella was going to get an engagement ring, but maybe the dream was warning me all was not as it appeared on the surface.

I think about Sam and her narcissistic patient. He was

poisoning a coworker who was stealing his lunch, and he felt justified doing it. I was focused on the chronic poisoning suggesting Crawley was poisoning his wife. The coworker angle made me think maybe Josie was being stalked by a coworker, but it was my *own* coworker that was dangerous.

Then there was Dr. Abrams' colleague that was run over by the car. The police were paid off by the boot-leggers. The police were in on it. Dirty cops. Again, pointing to Ray.

And Abby with the bloodletting and doctors covering up dangerous medical practices. Her boss was in on it. They were all in on it. She was told to get in line or risk losing her job.

Everyone was in on it! "Shit!" It hits me like lightning.

"What?" Joe says in alarm.

"Do you think Ray might not be the only one involved?"

"What do you mean?"

"Well, do you think he could have tampered with the evidence without Clint knowing?"

"Maybe...but it would've been easier if Clint was involved."

"What about the captain? We don't know him very well. Could he have been the one who wiped the computer that first day when we were in Josie's house?"

"Okay, now I think we're getting a little paranoid."

"Let's check if any of them own a white Chevy."

As we head for the back door, Joe has a thought. "Ray could've planted a bug at your place yesterday or maybe even in my house while he was here."

I hadn't considered this before today, and it feels like an invasion that someone might've been listening in. "I guess we better check and be careful until we can."

We're silent as we log onto Joe's computer and access the DMV.

We pull up Clint's records. No Chevy.

We pull up the captain. We've seen him driving a Black BMW...there it is. And...a white Chevy Malibu.

I look at Joe, and he looks at me. He silently indicates he's had a thought. He switches to articles about John Bowen's death and searches through them until he finds what he's looking for. One article quotes Bowen's partner's account of events. His partner *that day,* was Mark Bennett.

I experience real fear now. My hands are sweating.

We head out to the backyard.

"Oh my God. Oh my God." Am I having a panic attack? I sink into the swing. My pulse races. "All this time, it was him. He met us at the crime scene for God's sake!"

"I know. And he pretended to coordinate the search for Chloe. I bet he was helping Ray escape the whole time. We have to nail the son of a bitch." Joe's calm. Focused. A look of determination on his face. They messed with his family.

"So why did Ray run?" I'm trying to put all the pieces together.

"He's covering up for the captain. He's afraid of him. I think we got lucky. Ray's not a killer. That's why Chloe's still alive."

"But Ray's the one John caught stealing money."

"Right. But I bet they're all in on it. That's how they've gotten away with it for so long. And the captain saw an opportunity and he killed John because he knew he wouldn't be able to keep the secret. John Bowen was a loose cannon."

"And what's to stop him from killing us? He'll just blame it on Ray." I'm fighting down the panic.

"We have to find that USB drive. We need proof. That's our protection."

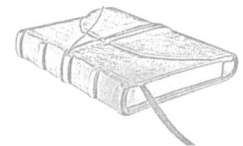

CHAPTER THIRTY-SEVEN

We let ourselves past the crime scene tape into Josie's house.

When we open the door, my heart sinks. There are stuffed mouse carcasses littering the floor, the stuffing ripped right out of them.

"Shit! I forgot that someone took the journal. Of course, they already knew that the USB drive was in a stuffed mouse, and they beat us to it." I look around the room at all the de-stuffed mice. Someone must have picked the lock because we have the only key.

"Let's look anyway. Maybe they missed one. We don't know for sure they found it," Joe says optimistically.

"Okay," I agree but my heart isn't in it. I'm sure they wouldn't have stopped looking until they found it.

We check the destuffed mice on the floor just to be sure. No USB drive there. Looking under the couch, we don't find anything—must've been removed already because I know Stalker constantly loses toys under my own couch. We check Josie's room. Two de-stuffed mice. No USB drive.

We check under Josie's bed and my heart leaps with hope. There's an intact stuffed squirrel. We pull it apart. Nothing. We continue through the house, finding de-stuffed mice on the closet floor, even in the bathroom but all the mice have been checked already. We check behind bookshelves, under her bedside table, all the typical places but the mice were found by the person searching before us. No luck.

I look at all the mouse carcasses littering the floor. "Maybe she moved it after she wrote that."

"Maybe we should bring the cat back to see if he has any hiding places we haven't found." Joe checks under the ottoman. No mouse.

Something occurs to me, giving me a glimmer of hope. "We didn't find any mice that weren't checked."

"Yep, it seems like whoever it was, was pretty thorough."

"Right, but if they found the USB drive then they would've stopped searching. Then we would've found some mice intact, the ones they didn't get to searching."

"That's true. Unless they found it on the very last mouse," he points out.

"True, but how likely would that be?"

Suddenly I remember something Latesha told me. "Joe! Stalker used to bring Latesha little gifts. Dead animals, things like that. He'd put them on her doorstep."

I'm already out the front door, ducking under the tape and heading to Latesha's, Joe right on my heels.

She answers my knock, looking surprised to see us.

"Latesha, we're looking for a stuffed mouse Stalker might've left on your front doorstep. Did you keep anything he brought over?"

"You know, it's funny, I did keep the things that weren't

dead animals. At first, I was just planning to give them back to Josie. When she died, I just couldn't bring myself to throw them away, you know?"

She goes to the fridge, takes a dish down off the top and hands it to me. There are a few hair ties, a plastic bracelet, and two stuffed mice. Oh please, please let one have a USB drive. I pick up the two mice. One is noticeably heavier than the other. I tear apart its seam, making an inarticulate noise of relief and discovery as I hold up the USB drive, encased in a small plastic bag.

"Nice work!" Joe high fives me.

Now that we have the drive, we need to find a place where we can view it unobserved. We decide the precinct is less likely to be bugged than our homes.

"How do you think they got a key to my apartment?" I ask Joe as we walk to the cruiser.

"You leave your keys on your desk sometimes when we're at work. You'd have no reason to worry about an officer having access to them, but I bet someone took a copy. Or maybe someone flashed a badge and your super let them in."

We drive covertly by the police precinct to check if any of our suspects' cars are there. Only a few cars are in the employee lot and none belong to Ray, Clint, or the captain. It's a holiday, so only a few assigned patrol officers will be out in cruisers. A skeleton crew.

We park Joe's car down the block and enter the precinct through the back door. I try to block out images of being here last night. It feels like a lifetime ago.

When we're satisfied no one is around, we plug the USB drive into Joe's computer and pull up the audio file.

There's some static, then what must be Josie's voice. After reading her journal and talking about her to her friends and family, I feel like I know her, so it's strange that her voice is unfamiliar.

"I'm here with Darcy Rollenstein. She's agreed to my recording this interview."

"Yep. I agree."

"Could you tell me about your job in the tech industry..."

We skip forward until Josie asks about Darcy witnessing John Bowen's fall.

"Darcy, what happened on June 20, 2001?"

"I was home having lunch and getting ready for work. I was sitting right here at my kitchen table eating my salad and some movement outside caught my eye. I looked over and there's this guy dangling out of the window. A cop was holding his hand, leaning way out of the window, trying to stop him from falling six stories. Well, I could hardly breathe. I was so scared the guy was going to fall. I opened my window so I could see better. The one cop was yelling at him to stop squirming, he'd pull him up. But the guy dangling was kind of freaking out. I would've been too!"

"Sounds pretty scary. What happened next?"

"I saw another person come over to the window and I just couldn't even believe my eyes, he just pushes the cop out the window and the cop and the other guy fall six stories. It was the most sickening sound I've ever heard when they hit the ground. I just can't un-hear that noise."

"Do you remember anything about the person in the window?"

"I had a bad angle so I really couldn't see him well, just his arms really."

"Did you ever tell anyone about this?"

"An officer interviewed me, and I told him the police officer was pushed by someone inside. I couldn't see who. I thought it must've been another suspect. I remember the officer said he'd look into it, and he took down all my information, saying he'd reach out if they needed anything else. He said it was impor-tant I didn't discuss it with anyone since the case against the suspects was still ongoing. I assured him I wouldn't tell anyone about it."

"What happened after that?"

"I never heard anything more about it."

"Did you ever tell anyone else what you saw?"

"Not a soul."

So, our fears are valid. Mark Bennett was John's partner the day he died, and someone pushed John and the suspect out the window to their death. There was no record of someone else being in the apartment that day. The captain didn't have to cover that up because no one suspected John was pushed. Until Josie came along and brought her suspicions right into his hands.

Now the USB drive is our precious evidence of the crime. Joe slips it into the chest pocket of his jacket.

Grabbing a couple pairs of crime scene gloves, Joe motions

for me to follow him. He checks the captain's office door. It's unlocked.

"I don't think this is a good idea," I whisper.

"Probably not," he says and goes inside anyway.

I roll my eyes and follow him. He flips on the light.

We search the captain's desktop and shelves, looking for anything that might shed light on his activities. I pick up a photo of him standing outside with three other officers, arms around shoulders, very chummy. It was taken at his previous precinct. In the photo with him are Ray Kirkland, Clint Lydiate, and Ethan Carter. Everyone looks a decade younger.

"Joe, look at this, did these four all work together in the past?"

"Yeah, they all used to be at my old precinct."

"We know Ray and the captain are involved. What about Ethan and Clint?"

"I've noticed them talking to the captain here and there. Could be."

I snap a photo of the picture on my phone.

Joe opens the top drawer of the desk. We're now entering dicey territory, clearly breaching the captain's privacy. Joe looks through some papers and pulls out some photographs hidden under the paperwork. "Here, take a photo of these." He hands me pictures of Josie walking home. Copies of the ones we found in Eli's closet.

"Hmmm. It was Ethan who found copies of these photos in Eli's closet. Maybe he planted them."

"Probably. So that means one of these four probably took them. Whoever killed Josie, and my money's on the captain."

This is starting to be a little too real. We're about to accuse a senior ranking officer of murder. We better have proof.

"Well, what have we here?" It's Captain Bennett. His voice is pure steel.

Oh shit! I freeze with my hand in a file cabinet.

"Put your hands where I can see them."

I raise my hands slowly and see Joe doing the same in my peripheral vision.

"Turn around, Kaitlyn. Slowly." I turn to toward him. *This is the face of a murderer,* I think. A person who would drag another human being to death.

His gun is trained on me, just waiting for an excuse to pull the trigger. My heart hammers in my chest, my mind scrambling to find some plausible excuse for our presence in his office.

"You two are really something." His smile is eerily benign, his voice level, friendly even, as if we are just having an ordinary workday conversation. "I knew you'd be trouble. You should've stayed out of it. Now you've forced me to have to deal with you."

I'm trying to figure out if I could duck down behind the desk for cover and grab my gun. Will the desk protect me at all? From his past actions, I know he won't hesitate to kill us, but he'll want it to look like an accident.

"Did you frame Eli?" I try to distract him, trying to buy time.

"That kid was such an easy target. Finding him was almost too good to be true. I saw him following Josie home one night. He was the perfect fall guy."

I slowly start to move closer to the desk.

"I *will* shoot you if you try anything." It's like he read my mind.

He gestures to me, and points to a chair at his conference

table. "Kaitlyn, sit there. Nice and slow. Joe, put your cuffs on Kaitlyn, hands in front and around the table leg."

Joe does as instructed, cuffing my hands to the table leg. He leaves them loose so I can wiggle out of them when the captain isn't looking. A glimmer of hope.

"Joe, you sit here." He indicates the chair across the table from me and Joe sits. The captain cuffs him to another table leg.

He takes our weapons, then frisks us. He finds the USB drive in Joe's pocket and takes it to his desk. He pulls out a heavy tape dispenser and crushes the drive, along with any hope of preserving the evidence. "Thanks for finding this for me," he quips. "I've been looking everywhere for it." Joe and I exchange a glance. Things are looking bleak. But at least I know I can get my hands free.

The captain takes the photos out of his desk drawer and flames them with a lighter, one by one, dropping them into an empty trash can. I'm hoping the smoke detector goes off. I look around, trying to decide what to do once I get my hands out of the cuffs. There's a heavy-looking geode, split open to expose the crystals inside, sitting on his bookshelf. That looks like a good weapon.

Just as I'm about to attempt to free my hands, the captain spots me surveilling the room. "What are you up to?" He checks my cuffs and, finding them loose, tightens them. *Damn.* "Nice try," he says to Joe.

I notice the captain has a scratch on his neck, five long lines. A graze from a cat. He was the one who broke into my apartment. Good for Stalker, it looks like he did attack the intruder, just like I suspected. He sees me looking. "Yep, these are from your little fiend of a cat. Don't worry, I destroyed the journal and the copies you had. The evidence is gone." He doesn't know I still have the few pages from the end of the journal, and I'm not going to enlighten him.

The captain sits on the edge of his desk. "Now what to do with the two of you? A fire in your cruiser? Falling off a cliff? A drive-by shooting? Being a police officer is such a dangerous job. So many accidents could happen." He says it as if he's just discussing the weather. Sunny or rainy tomorrow, what do you think? *Cloudy with a one hundred percent chance of murder,* I think.

We watch as he takes a bottle and cloth out of the bottom of his filing cabinet. *Shit! What's in the bottle?* He wets a cloth with the liquid from the bottle and then covers Joe's nose and mouth with it. Joe struggles, but it's not long before he's unconscious.

My heart feels like its bursting out of my chest. While the captain is busy with Joe, I work frantically on my handcuffs, trying to get them off even though they're too tight now. I slide the cuffs down to the floor, tip the heavy table with my shoulder, and slip the chain of the cuffs under the leg. But just as I get the cuffs free, the captain grabs my hair and pulls my head up, placing the cloth over my face. I fight him, clawing at his hands, but my vision starts to blur and then everything goes black.

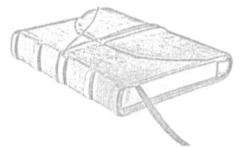

CHAPTER THIRTY-EIGHT

When I start to come around, I find myself somewhere dark and confining. My limbs are aching, and my head is pressed flat against something hard. My senses are coming back but my thoughts are sluggish and fuzzy. Forcing myself to concentrate, I focus on the background roar of a car engine. Attempting to move my arms, I realize they're still cuffed.

Shaking my head, I try to clear it. It's so dark, I can't make anything out, but I can tell I'm moving. I must be in the back of a vehicle.

My claustrophobia kicks in. I find myself taking small, stilted breaths as I fight off the terror. *Don't panic, Kruse, keep it together.* I had a childhood experience when I was playing hide and seek with friends that ended with me stuck in a tight spot. Ever since then, I'm claustrophobic in elevators and other enclosed spaces.

My vision is returning but it's frustratingly slow and spotty. I peer through the dark and see Joe, his eyes closed. "Joe," I hiss. He doesn't move. I try nudging him with my knee.

Nothing. *God, I hope he's alive.* Panic threatens to take over again. *Breathe,* I tell myself. My only way out of this is to keep a clear head.

We continue driving for a bit, and I force myself to concentrate on the route we're taking to tamp down the panic. Joe and I are sliding in the confined space with every turn, unable to put out a hand to protect our heads from banging into the side of the vehicle repeatedly. I ignore the discomfort, concentrating on the movements of the vehicle. There's a left turn, now a stop. Then a right turn. I try to figure out where we are but my brain is too fuzzy. If I could just think straight, maybe I could figure it out.

Slowly, it dawns on me we're riding in the back of our own cruiser.

My mind goes back to the accidental death scenarios the captain was listing off. He's going to fake an accident with us traveling in the car. An accidental swerve off an embankment. Bursting into flame after hitting a tree. Drifting into an oncoming semi. There are so many scenarios he could use. He just needs to get us in the seats up front, unconscious, and out of handcuffs and it's as if we were killed in the line of duty. Problem solved. No one will ever know the truth.

The adrenaline courses through me now as I contemplate the nature of my last moments. Will I wake up burning in an inferno, or with a gut-wrenching drop off a cliff? How will my parents find out? Isabella? Blake? Will they suspect we were murdered? Why would they? No one knows the captain is in on this. He's been far too clever and ruthless at stamping out evidence.

I find myself envying those who never see their final moments coming. Anticipation paralyzes me with fear. I have to keep forcing my mind to concentrate on a workable plan. I can't just act out of panic.

Think, Kaitlyn!

The vehicle pulls onto a gravel road, the gravel crunching under the light snow cover. The captain drives for a short distance and comes to a stop.

This is it.

My next moves will determine if I live or die.

I hear the captain's voice from the driver's seat, talking to someone. "Yeah, just wait back there. I'll be done in a moment." The response is muffled and tinny, likely a cell phone. Someone's helping him. Probably his ride back.

A car door opens and closes.

Footsteps.

Then the liftgate is opened.

I decide at the last second that I should pretend I'm still unconscious. Maybe I'll have a moment to try to run if the captain doesn't anticipate it. I keep my eyes closed but it feels unnatural—I'm trying to fake unawareness while my heart pounds and my hands shake.

Don't move, I command my muscles. I can only hope the captain isn't watching me too closely.

He manhandles me out of the trunk, hitting my head on the side of the car. I grit my teeth to keep from crying out.

"Okay, Kaitlyn. Do you want to be the one who drove over the cliff, or do you want to be the passenger?"

For a terrifying second, I fear he knows I'm awake, but then I realize he's just talking to himself.

I keep my limbs limp and take another blow to the head as the captain wrestles me into the driver's seat.

He removes the handcuffs and buckles the seat belt to

hold my limp body to the seat.

The captain leaves the car door ajar, intent on his task and not anticipating I might try to run.

He heads back to get Joe.

I open my eyes and blink at the searing daylight, eyes adjusting after the dark trunk.

I'm begging my aching limbs to work.

The captain bends down, struggling with Joe's weight. It occurs to me for a second that maybe Joe is faking his unconsciousness like I am, but I never saw any sign he was waking up. I can't rely on it.

I slip out of the vehicle in a crouch.

Even with the light snow cover, the gravel shifts noisily under my weight, and I freeze, looking back.

No sign the captain heard me.

I'm going to have to run for it.

Please work, legs. Maybe all those morning runs will save my life today. Hopefully, I can outrun the captain.

Okay, here's the moment.

I pause to take a deep breath and prepare myself. The captain will hear me the second I begin running, so I have to launch with incredible speed.

I take off running as if my life depends on it—as it does.

As I anticipated, my sudden movement makes alarmingly loud noise on the gravel. The captain drops Joe back into the trunk and starts to pursue me. I realize immediately I have no chance. He's gaining on me. Fast. My muscles scream in protest.

The captain tackles me, and I hit the ground hard. The breath is knocked right out of me. My ears ring with the impact.

I see double for a second, then recover.

The captain flips me over. Pins my shoulders down.

Gravel digs into my back.

I struggle in earnest then.

Clawing.

Scratching.

Bucking.

Fighting like a cornered lioness.

If only I could get his weight shifted and push him off me.

As my strength ebbs, my mind goes to all the victims Joe and I have seen over the years.

This is it. The moment when the victim realizes they are outmatched. When they know their strength just doesn't measure up. The moment they understand they're going to die and nothing they can do will save them.

I'm that victim now.

The captain punches me hard.

My vision swims, my limbs go slack.

It's a struggle not to lose consciousness completely.

He picks me up, standing me on my feet and pushing me ahead of him back to the car. I stumble, trying to regain my vision. He hauls me along and pushes me down into the back of the vehicle, pinning me there.

Joe is still lifeless. *Damn. Wake up, Joe! We're going to die!*

The captain takes out the cloth and bottle, unscrewing the lid.

"Freeze!" a female voice yells from out of nowhere.

Captain Bennett whips around, pulling out his gun.

"You're surrounded. Drop the gun right now or we'll shoot!"

The captain points the gun at something in the distance

and his finger finds the trigger.

Suddenly, he makes an inarticulate noise and his head slumps to the side. Blood sprays on the liftgate and all over me. I watch in fascinated horror as he seems to hesitate in midair, then he's falling, hitting the ground with a heavy thud. Several officers rush toward us now. Are they the captain's team members planning to set him up, double cross him? My eyes are blinded by the sun.

Then Bob's there, lifting me up. "Are you alright?"

"I think so." He helps me up and checks Joe's pulse. Joe's starting to come around.

"They're okay," Bob yells back to someone. "An ambulance is on the way," he tells me, checking me over.

My wrists are raw and bleeding and my face throbs.

A shadow falls on me as someone approaches. "Kaitlyn. I'm glad you're okay. Joe looks like he's going to be all right too." I squint at the voice. It's the same voice I heard yelling "freeze." My eyes finally focus. It's Elizabeth Garcia, our previous captain. I've never been so happy to see anyone in my life.

She looks us over, reassuring herself we are, in fact, okay. She pats me on the shoulder and then turns to walk away. "Wait!" I grab her arm.

"What is it?" Her eyes register alarm.

"There are others involved."

"Who?" she asks.

"Lydiate and Kirkland. And Carter too, I think."

"Okay. We'll pick them up."

I nod weakly. "How..." I try, my voice faltering. "How did you know?"

"Joe emailed me a copy of the interview." I remember it

took him a while to eject it. He must have been sending the email. I underestimated him.

"As soon as I listened to it, I headed over to your precinct to talk to you about it and I saw Captain Bennett putting you in the back of your patrol car. I called in everyone I could reach."

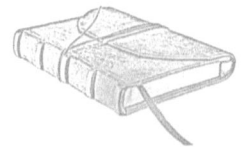

CHAPTER THIRTY-NINE

The ambulance arrives with sirens and flashing lights.

The EMTs shine lights in our eyes, take our pulses and respirations, check for lacerations and fractures, and assess our mental competence. It seems like unnecessary fussing.

"Am I good to go then?" I ask, ready to race off and find Ray the moment I'm cleared.

"No ma'am, I'm afraid we need to take you in for a full medical evaluation."

"Do you think that's really necessary? I'm fine."

"It's protocol after a hostage taking, ma'am. No exceptions." *Damn.*

I take the ride in the ambulance as instructed. The adrenaline starts to wane, and a wave of exhaustion hits me.

I recognize the ER nurse taking my vitals as the one that called Blake back to work from the break room last night. It was less than twenty-four hours ago. It's like a lifetime has passed since then. When he leaves, I look in the mirror and see a large bruise blooming by my left eye. My face is scratched, my lower lip split, my hair sticking up. There are droplets of blood on my face and shirt. Not my own. The spray from the captain's death. Some of my fingernails are ripped, my arms and back are torn up from the gravel, my wrists are raw from the cuffs. I'm a mess. *You thought I looked like hell last night, Blake, you should see me now.*

I fall asleep on the exam table, waiting for the doctor.

When I wake up, I'm startled to see Blake pushing past the curtain. "Hey," he says softly.

"Are you working?" I ask, confused.

"No, the nurse called me." He takes my hand. "Are you okay?"

"They're just flesh wounds," I tell him. He smiles. The comfort of having him there is tearing down my defenses. I can't stop shaking.

Blake brings me a warm blanket and then sets to cleaning the wounds and trimming and bandaging the torn nails. He gives me a washcloth to clean my face and checks out the bruise by my eye.

"Ouch." I pull back from his probing. "Be gentle."

"Yep, still feisty," he comments. "I'll take that as a good sign."

"Damn straight."

"Do you want to tell me what happened?"

I nod and take a deep breath. And then it just pours out, everything that happened, everything I feared might happen. All of it. Like a purge. Like if I can tell it all, I can leave it behind. In this ER. In my past.

When I'm done, Blake just looks at me, speechless. "Wow."

"Yeah…wow."

"Kait! Thank God you're okay!" Isabella throws back the curtain and rushes in for a hug.

"I'm so glad you're here," I tell her. "But how did you know?"

"I called her," Blake says. "She's on your emergency contact list." He shrugs sheepishly. "I knew you would want her here."

Blake backs out of the room as Isabella sets up a litany of chatter. "Thank you," I mouth in his direction. He nods and leaves for a bit so we can talk.

I tell Isabella the whole story. She's uncharacteristically quiet as she absorbs all the details. By the end, I'm yawning.

"Poor thing," she says, smoothing my hair. "I'm so glad you're safe. You need to get home and get some rest."

I nod, feeling sleepy and, finally, safe.

"Here, I brought you some clean clothes." She hands me a bag. "But you should have Blake take you home." She winks at me. I grin back at her.

I call my parents then. They're still in Nebraska, coming home this weekend. I give them an abbreviated version of events, not wanting to worry them. Just hearing their voices is a comfort.

I change into the clothes Isabella brought me and then Blake takes me home. Everything seems surreal. Four officers I worked with were dirty. Just two days ago, we had no idea any of this was going on. Now all of them have been exposed, and one of them is dead.

Black Friday indeed.

When we get to the apartment, I shower, taking my time with soap and shampoo and cleaning off every trace of the day. Every little cut and scrape stings and my body aches from being thrown in the back of the cruiser and fighting for my life. I feel boneless and drained of all emotion.

After I dry off, I get into comfortable yoga pants and a t-shirt. I sink into my bed and pull my comforter around me. Blake lays down beside me and holds me. The weight of his arm across my waist and the solidness of his chest behind me is all I need to drift off into a dreamless sleep.

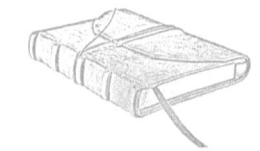

CHAPTER FORTY

FOUR WEEKS LATER

It's a beautiful day. Mount Rainier shines in the distance. It's late in the morning and the parking lot is full. I get out of my Prius and stand looking at the precinct, taking a few deep breaths.

My brain flashes to a memory of finding Chloe here. Then a thought of being taken hostage by Captain Bennett intrudes. I force them away.

The days off were therapeutic. At first, I resisted the leave dictated by Deputy Chief Garcia, but I eventually came to see the value. I've been meeting twice a week with a psychologist hired by the precinct for traumatic event processing. He was very helpful at guiding me through the difficult process. Okaaaay, so maybe it was important. I can admit that now.

I'll keep seeing my therapist as I transition back to duty. I'm sure there will be some triggers as I get back to work. Even the precinct itself and our cruiser are all part of the trauma. I'm confident I can work through it with his help and the help of my friends and family. But it will take time and effort.

My parents are hovering unnecessarily, as parents will. After they returned from Nebraska, I told them the whole story about the captain and our brush with death. They've insisted I come over for dinner frequently in the past four weeks. I've gained five pounds. It's time to put a limit on the comfort food.

I've spent some time with Tina during my time off. We drank tea and talked about Sam and her memories. My time with Tina warms my heart. Sometimes I have to remind myself she's not actually *my* sister. We're getting very close.

Isabella is busy planning her wedding. She asked me to be her Maid of Honor and, of course, I cried like an idiot. A deliriously happy idiot.

Right now, she's obsessing over what flowers she wants in her bouquet. My leave has me so blissed-out that I'm not even slightly irritated that she can't decide. I find myself watching her, noticing the excitement in her eyes, how she's smiling all the time, how truly happy she is. I'm more aware of these things. Ever since "The Event." Since I realized how lucky I am to be alive.

And Blake. I don't mind saying that I'm falling head over heels for him. He has a cozy little apartment with a view of the harbor, and I find myself spending more and more of my evenings over there. The light streams in at sunset in such a beautiful way and it's like the two of us are the only ones in the world as we talk about our futures and our hopes and dreams. Except, of course, about *those* dreams. Maybe someday I'll be brave enough to share. For now, I'm just enjoying the idyllic early days of our relationship, where everything seems possible.

Joe's been waiting for me in the parking lot. His laces are hot pink today. Brave. "Ready?" he asks, and I know he's asking himself, as much as me.

"Ready as I'll ever be."

Together we walk in. As we round the corner to the room with our desks, officers start to notice our presence. Bob is on the far side of the room talking to someone. He looks up and sees us. He salutes us and then begins clapping. Immediately, others take notice. They stand, turn to face us, and join the clapping. We stand, stunned and admittedly slightly mortified, as they acknowledge us.

Once the clapping dies down, we find our desks. Bob joins us. "You two are heroes, you know?" he says.

"Just doing our jobs," Joe mutters.

"You went after a ruthless, hidden network of corrupt cops that no one else could even uncover—and you made it out alive."

"Barely."

"Garcia says they've been suspicious money was going missing from crime scenes for years now, but they thought it was one or two bad officers. They couldn't figure it out because they never suspected it was actually four people. They covered for each other."

"Did they manage to arrest everyone?"

"Yeah, Captain Bennett was the leader. He killed at least four people to cover it up. John Bowen and the bank robber, Darcy Rollenstein, and Josie Miller. The others were just involved in the theft. They all used to be at one precinct together but slowly they started transferring over to our precinct, hoping to go undetected. The captain helped them all get away with taking things from crime scenes. Ray said it started with cash taken from busts. They justified it as a victimless crime. No one would miss the cash so why not take it? As time went by, none of them could turn in someone else without fear of that same person turning them in for their own thefts. As the crimes got worse, they found themselves in deeper and deeper and couldn't see a way free. The captain had them all doing his bidding in the end.

"Now, thanks to you two, the higher-ups know what was going on and who was involved. After the other three were arrested, their properties were searched and cash and some other valuables were discovered. Now starts the work of tying specific raids where money seemed to be missing to those four officers. When the cash was tested, they found traces of drugs, which will tie it to the crime scenes. They will all do time."

"I was Ethan Carter's partner for a while, but I never knew anything about it," I muse.

"I'm sure he knew you wouldn't go along with it."

"Still, the fact that he was doing that behind my back makes me feel complicit somehow."

"Well, at least you found him out in the end."

"Whatever happened to Creepy Crawley and his fentanyl ring? Did they all get time? And did Crawley kill his wife?" I ask.

"They're still bringing all the cases to trial but it looks like they managed to find everyone involved. True to his word, Chuck didn't distribute fentanyl so his sentence will be lighter, especially since he helped the DEA," Bob says. "They tested the tea bag and found high levels of arsenic. Crawley's wife's body will be exhumed and her hair tested to confirm. But for what it's worth, I think he killed her."

I nod. "How did he get ahold of arsenic?"

"The theory is that it was some ancient bag of pesticide he had in his garage."

"How did you find Ray?" He's been on my mind. I've forced myself to stay out of it until now, trusting those still working to find him. Garcia took the precinct back over until a new captain can be named and I trust her. Still, it's been hard to leave it to someone else.

"Believe it or not, he turned himself in. I think he was more afraid of retribution from the others, especially Captain Bennett, than he was afraid of being found out. Once he heard the captain was gone, he came out of hiding."

"What about the evidence? Did Ray say how it was altered to frame Eli?" I ask.

"Ray admitted they intended to plant evidence right from the start. After Bennett noticed Eli stalking Josie, he thought he would be an easy target, but he waited to see what other suspects you had. Once we had the meeting to discuss the case with everyone, he directed the others to plant the evidence. Ethan planted the photos in Eli's closet. Captain Bennett took those photos of Josie when he was planning the murder. Then the captain gave Ray some of the hair from Josie's brush that he took from the sample Joe collected. And a paint sample from his own car, the Chevy that hit Josie. Ray submitted it as if it was from Eli's car. Eli was an easy mark."

"What about the car the captain used? Did they find it?" Joe asks.

"Yep. It's a white Chevy Malibu. He hid it in a storage facility. We found the address of the storage place when we searched Captain Bennett's house. The car had been re-paired. We think he did it himself. He hadn't disposed of the damaged car parts yet though. We found them wrapped in blankets. Likely he was going to put them in a dumpster somewhere. You don't want to know what those parts looked like. It was grim."

Garcia interrupts us and gestures us into the captain's office. She's taken it over again. Boxes of Mark Bennett's things are stacked in the corner. I'm glad the room looks different than when we were last here. I don't want anything to remind me of that day.

"Welcome back, detectives," she says. "I have you assigned to light duty this week. Take your time getting back to work."

"It's nice to see you back behind that desk," Joe comments.

"Don't get used to it," she replies. "It's just until we find a new captain. Now off you go, time to get my best detectives back on the job."

Joe and I head across the street to the coffee shop and find a quiet booth to reconnect with each other. With our shared trauma, all our interactions feel painfully raw and stilted. We need to find a way back to our comfort zone.

"I still can't wrap my mind around the fact that Captain Bennett was a killer," I say.

"All that time we were looking for the murderer, and it was him all along, right under our noses. He dragged that girl all the way down the street and then came back a few hours later to investigate what he'd done."

"I know, it's hard to imagine the kind of person who could do that. And then he acted like someone might be in the house, when he knew all along no one would be there."

"Right, and I bet he wiped the computer right then, while we were searching the house. 'Not very tech-savvy,' my ass!"

"The captain directed all the evidence collection to those that were in on it when we had that meeting. I thought he was being so helpful. Boy, did he have me fooled."

"Me too," Joe says.

"When we were searching for Ray and Chloe, I bet he was telling Ray where we were searching, all the while pretending to help us find him."

"They probably all were, Clint and Ethan were there too. We didn't have a chance except that Ray wasn't a killer. Didn't have it in him to hurt Chloe."

"Speaking of Chloe, how's she doing?" I ask.

"She seems fine. We've been seeing a lot of her and she really seems okay. She and Liz are in a good place, and she doesn't seem worried about her safety."

"She has a loving family to surround her. You can't underestimate that."

"Speaking of family, how are your parents?"

"They're good. Back from their travels. We spent some time together and I have to say it was a nice distraction for me."

"Did you tell them everything that happened?"

"No. I didn't want to add to how much they already worry about me, but I told them the basics."

"So, did they get to meet the new man in your life?"

"Not yet. I need him all to myself for a bit. Soon though."

"So, when do I get to meet him?"

"Oh, pretty much never. I can't have the two of you telling secrets about me."

"So, you don't want me to tell him about the time you slipped and fell into a fountain when you were chasing a suspect?"

"Not unless you want me to tell him about the time you

couldn't find the key for your handcuffs..."

And there it is. We've found our way back to each other. To the comfort zone.

Some bonds, even the worst of crimes can't tear apart.

ACKNOWLEDGEMENTS

I am indebted to so many who were involved in the polishing of this novel, reshaping it into the version it is today.

Thank you to my family, Dan, Ashdyn and Jordan, for your feedback and patience with many readings and rereadings. Most of all, thank you for your continued encouragement; it keeps me going.

Dan, my husband, continues to be my steadfast partner and committed fan. If he comes with me to the post office to send off a book, he tells all the staff I'm a writer and even finds my webpage on his phone to show them. If someone at his job mentions the book, he recruits them to be a beta reader for the next one. His loyalty is boundless.

My daughter Jordan again provided the beautiful cover and is even working with me on illustrating a future book project. It has been amazing to work together, and I have her to thank for help with book trailers and social media and... well, so many things.

To my daughter Ashdyn, thank you for your support of all

my writing projects, and for listening to all my book ideas. And for just being your awesome self.

Thank you again to those who provided feedback in many forms. To Andrea Beck, Jolene Zetterman, Mary Dek, and Megan Kalil who generously gave their time to review multiple drafts. To beta readers Heidi Lierz and Laura Putnam, thank you for your valuable feedback on the story, I hope to be getting your insights on all my future projects.

To the Shady Book Club and the ladies of the Bluewater Book Club, thank you again for your support and encouragement of this book, and my first as well. I love that these amazing groups of women continue to gather and support one another. You all inspire me!

Thank you to my parents for their unwavering support in everything.

To those who provided advice in many forms, be it legal, police-procedural, or otherwise, thank you also, so much.

Thank you to Lydia Kang, fellow author and doctor, for your invaluable advice and encouragement. You were right, this *is* like having two full-time jobs! Thankfully, I love them both, just as you do.

And once again, to the families in my pediatric practice, thank you for sharing your remarkable children with me, it means the world.

To my amazing editor and publisher Jessica Powers, who believed in Kaitlyn Kruse from the start and has been a constant support both in publishing and in the journey of becoming an author, thank you for your friendship and mentorship.

Thank you to the team at Flare Books, Kathy McInnis, Matt Powers, Lora Parker, and Henry Trotter for your support of the book in so many ways.

Finally, to all of you who found your way to these pages as readers, listeners or supporters, thank you.

Author
Karoline
Anderson

Karoline Anderson is a pediatrician with a love for books. Born in Vancouver, Canada, she currently lives with her family and cat Smoky on a lake in Nebraska. She runs whenever she can and has completed several triathlons and one marathon. This is the second book in the Kaitlyn Kruse series. Her debut novel *Killer Insight* was a finalist for Thriller of the Year in 2024.